MEDITERRAN

RÓISÍN CURRAN

Mediterranean Menopause

*Published in 2018 by Róisín Curran,
Dublin, Ireland
www.travelcounsellors.ie/roisincurran*

Copyright © Róisín Curran, 2018

*The right of Róisín Curran to be identified as the
author of this book has been asserted in accordance with
the Copyright, Designs and Patents Act, 1988*

*All rights reserved. No part of the publication may be reproduced or
transmitted in any form or by any means, electronic or mechanical,
including photocopy, recording, or any information storage and
retrieval system, without permission in writing from the publisher.*

*This book is sold subject to the condition that it shall not,
by way of trade or otherwise, be lent, re-sold, hired out or
otehrwise circulated without the publisher's prior consent in
any form of binding or cover other than that in which it is
published and without a similar condition including this
condition being imposed upon the subsequent purchaser.*

*ISBN (paperback) 978-1-9993526-0-8
ISBN (ebook) 978-1-9993526-1-5*

Printed by Amazon

For Patsy and Nuala

THE DAY BEFORE

AMELIA

Amelia was in the restaurant. It was her last service before the holiday and she was not in the mood for work but she and Paul had made a decision that one of them would always be there. The customers expected it and it was important to keep on top of the staff too. Paul had opened *Amelia's Restaurant* ten years previously and it had won a Michelin star within the first year, followed by a second four years later. It was an incredible achievement. The restaurant was always booked out for months in advance and, as a result, the couple were very well known around town. Amelia had responsibility for front of house at lunchtime and she was also patron of the Prema Foundation, a charity set up to fund research into premature birth, something which took up a lot of her time.

She couldn't focus on what she was doing; she was totally distracted by thoughts of the cruise and all the fun that lay ahead. She decided that she would leave early – that was one of the benefits of being the boss and they had enough staff to cover. She still had a long list of things to do before the day was over, including getting a pedicure and doing some food shopping for the house. On top of that, despite normally being the most organised person on the planet, she hadn't even packed yet.

Amelia cherished her friendship with Jess and Beth and she loved their annual holiday away together. She was thinking back to their thirtieth birthdays which they celebrated in San Francisco. Their budget hadn't been as large back then and they'd stayed with their friend, Susanna. After that, they started a pattern of celebrating their big birthdays by going somewhere a bit more special than the usual package trips Spain or Portugal. For their fortieth birthdays, they had really pushed the boat out. She smiled to herself as she remembered the antics of that trip and how they had lived it up in the best five-star hotels in Asia, leaving their husbands behind to mind the children.

They had a golden rule: 'Whatever happens away, stays away'. No secrets were ever shared with anyone else once they got home. When they were trying to think of an idea for their fiftieth celebrations, they knew that it would have to be extra special. Eventually, Jess suggested a cruise and now, here she was, hours away from the next adventure with her best friends.

***

She left the restaurant, walked towards her car and thought about what had happened the day before, still furious with him. It had been no different to most other days. At first. She'd parked her car down the side road, slipped out and walked towards the house. She had gone in the back door and he was waiting for her, as always. He cupped her face in his warm hands and pulled her to him, putting his mouth firmly on hers as she devoured him with sweeping strokes of her tongue. She smiled as she remembered how she had felt him pressing against her and how a rush of desire had cascaded through her body. He'd pushed her against the table, lifted her up and taken her hard and fast. She'd arched her back and cried out as waves of ecstasy pulsated through her; the feeling so intense she could hardly breathe. He held her in his arms for a minute, both of them caught up in the moment, and then he took her by the hand over to the sofa. She loved the illicitness of it.

It was then that he had confessed that he had booked a stateroom on the cruise. Her cruise. With her best friends. The very next day.

She started to think about it again. It was outrageous. How dare he? Did she know him at all? How could he have kept this secret from her up until the last minute?

One thing she did know was that she was going to have to end this affair; she couldn't risk losing Paul and the children – they were her world and she adored them, and it looked like Sam was getting too demanding of her. Most importantly, how was she going to tell Beth and Jess that he was going to be on the cruise?

She thought about how she felt about Sam. Was there more to their relationship than sex? They had never been away together before, and any time they dined out together it was in secret and far away from home. She pushed thoughts of Sam to one side. She had a lot to do if she was to get herself organised and leave everything neatly labelled in the freezer for Paul and Caroline. At least Charlie and Chantal were based in Dublin now, which made things easier but, to be fair to him, Paul was more capable than most husbands when it came to running a house.

JESS

Jess woke up exhausted. She had slept very badly again because she had been working the LAX flight the previous day. Although she had been flying long-haul for years, she still had difficulty with her body clock sometimes, and today was one of those days. Oh well, she was going on holidays where there would be plenty of time to catch up on sleep.

She thought about the girls, her beautiful twin daughters, Daniela and Emily. They were both still living at home but had gone to visit their father, James, who lived in Sydney. Jess hated it when they went out there; it was so far away and she always worried that they would decide to live with him, especially as they both worked in jobs that they could do in Australia. Daniela worked in Aer Lingus, like her mother, and was at senior cabin crew level. Emily was a nurse and worked in the Blackrock Clinic emergency department.

It had been very difficult when James had left, and Jess had found the role of being a single parent very challenging, but the girls had turned out well and the three of them were very close.

She thought about the cash and where she should put it. She had withdrawn the last of her savings from the Post Office on Tuesday and it had been an overwhelming experience. What, she wondered, was she going to do if she didn't win on the ship? €8,000 was all the cash she had left in the world. Well, she couldn't lose, it just wasn't a possibility. She couldn't afford to let it happen: end of story. She had been burying her head in the sand, refusing to open letters, cancelling her direct debits and hoping the bills would stop. But it was time to face the music; she knew she couldn't go on like this. She hadn't told anyone about her problems – not even her best friends – and the strain of bottling it all up was starting to get to her.

She had lost a lot of weight recently and had been taking time off work because of stress. She knew she was in trouble, but she tried to put it all out of her mind. She needed this holiday and was determined to enjoy it, no matter what.

Jess was really excited about the cruise with the girls but she couldn't help feeling a bit nostalgic and sad because she and James had booked a cruise that had to be cancelled when they separated. She asked herself most days if she would ever recover from her divorce. It had been four years now and it still hurt. Would she ever be strong enough to start dating again? Would she ever fall in love again?

Why was she thinking about James now? She hated the way she couldn't stop thoughts of him from coming into her head. Tomorrow she would be with her best friends and they would have a fantastic time together, as they always did. In fact, they always preferred their holidays together to holidays with anyone else. She thought back to how they had met all those years ago in Irish College. Why, after thirty-five years, could she still not wipe that awful time from her memory?

BETH

Beth was packing her suitcase, making lists and generally rushing around. She always left everything to the last minute. Ed needed to be collected from school and Bethany was flying in from London and needed to be picked up at 5pm. It was all hectic as usual. She was looking forward to seeing her adored daughter, Bethany, who was working in her father's company in London as communications manager. She was coming home to help Stephen with Ed; he was only fifteen and still needed to have his dinners cooked and to get lifts to school. Stephen worked long hours and would appreciate the extra support.

She was dying to see the girls but she was upset as she thought about Stephen and how they had argued the night before. She had been hoping that things would improve since they'd been to counselling. The counsellor seemed to think they were making progress but Beth had her doubts as they were both miserable. She had been making a real effort to initiate sex even though it was the last thing she felt like these days. She didn't know whether it was because of the menopause, or because she just didn't fancy Stephen anymore. Her hormones were all over the place and she had made a decision that when she came back from the holiday she would go to the doctor and demand to be put on HRT. Most of her friends swore by it.

She couldn't remember how the most recent row with Stephen had started. She had come in from work and he had started sniping at her about the holiday, saying things like, 'Isn't it well for some, skitting off on a cruise while the rest of us never get away'. She would never have begrudged him a holiday with his friends had he wanted to go, but he never did, so why could he not be happy for her? She couldn't help but wonder about how things would have been if Sonny's wife hadn't found out about her.

Day One

Port of Civitavecchia

AMELIA KNEW THAT PAUL was sad to see her go, but her mind was on the holiday now as she fastened her seat belt and waited for take-off. The fifty-minute flight from Galway to Dublin would give her a chance to wake up. She had just received a text from Jess to say that the passes for the business lounge were at the desk; all she had to do was pick them up. She was tired. Yesterday had been exhausting and she was still getting over Sam's revelation. Now that she thought of it, she had no idea how she was going to deal with the situation. Why did life have to be so complicated?

***

Jess hated the emptiness of the house when the girls weren't there so she was glad to be going away. She hopped in the taxi and was in Dublin Airport in fifteen minutes. Once she arrived at the airport, she dropped her luggage and went straight to the lounge, poured herself a glass of champagne and sat down to wait for her friends. She really needed this holiday but it had been a financial stretch and she had almost had to back out. She hoped that her plan would work.

***

Beth was running late. She didn't have time to put on her make-up, but she was one of these people with lovely sallow skin and she was pretty enough to get away with not wearing any. She knew that she should wake Stephen to let him know she was heading off, but it was 5am so she decided to leave without saying goodbye. She felt a bit guilty; how were they going to overcome their problems if she behaved like this?

Just as she was getting into the taxi, Stephen came to the front door and called her back. There was a sadness in his eyes as he asked her why she hadn't said goodbye. She made an excuse about not wanting to wake him, but they both knew she was lying.

She felt a bit sorry for him as the taxi drove down the road, but she forgot all about it when the car pulled up outside Terminal 2. She was fast-tracked through security and within minutes, she found herself standing outside the lounge.

***

'Will you look what the cat dragged in!' Jess said. She was standing at the desk in the lounge when Beth, and then Amelia, arrived, minutes apart. 'I would call that impeccable timing, my dears. Let's get the party started!'

They took a quick look at the monitor to check the gate number and then went over to the bar. They poured themselves a glass of champagne before settling down for a chat. Their friendship went back over thirty-five years and in that time they had each developed roles. Amelia was the organiser of their social calendar, Beth was the counsellor and Jess was in charge of booking their weekends away and holidays, but only after lots of discussion with the other two!

When they boarded the Aer Lingus aircraft, Beth and Amelia were thrilled with their surprise upgrade, which came courtesy of Jess. They enjoyed more complimentary champagne as they chatted and giggled their way to Rome. Even the captain gave them a special welcome on board.

Once the flight landed, the girls collected their luggage in the baggage claim area and went looking for their private transfer to the port. They searched madly for their names on the cards as they walked into the arrivals hall, but there was no sign of them. Jess was used to dealing with this kind of thing and went off to phone the car company. Amelia stayed with the luggage while Beth ran up and down in search of the driver.

After what seemed like forever, Jess got through to them. They told her to wait at the meeting point as the driver had been delayed. While they were waiting, they met a very loud American woman called Meredith, from Texas, who was also taking the transfer.

Somehow, they knew it would not be the last the saw of her.

***

The girls were taken directly to the ship by their driver where they joined the queue for check-in. It didn't take very long; the queue moved quite quickly and there were plenty of distractions along the way. They couldn't wait to get on board and have some lunch and a large glass of wine. Once the forms were filled in, they received their ship passes which were also their room keys and credit cards; cash was not used on board. They were each given a large glass of champagne and told that their stateroom was ready. They headed up to deck eight to their room where they were thrilled to discover that their luggage had already been delivered. They excitedly took a quick look inside the room and then decided to have some lunch.

They headed up to the Wayfarer buffet restaurant on the fourteenth deck. It was manically busy because it was the only restaurant open on the ship on embarkation day, and everyone had decided to dine at the same time. There were tables inside but they found a table outside where they had a great view of the Port of Civitavecchia. The buffet was excellent and offered food choices from all over the world. They settled for a delicious plate of salads and slices of pizza before returning to the table to order three large glasses of delicious New Zealand sauvignon blanc.

'I can't believe we are finally on the ship. Here's to an amazing cruise, girls!' Jess said as she raised her glass. They all laughed and toasted each other. 'Let's check out the room,' she added. 'We'll call over the waiter and get some more wine to take with us.'

***

They went down to their room, glasses of wine in hand, and opened the door. They were delighted with themselves to be on holiday with no children and no husbands for twelve whole days. But Amelia was nervous; she still hadn't told them about Sam and didn't know how they would react. Should she come clean now, or wait a while? She didn't know what to do and it was stressing her, but she decided to leave it. They were only finding their feet and she didn't want the cruise to get off to a bad start. She would do it when the time was right.

The room was a good size. There was a large balcony, two very luxurious single beds with plump, feather duvets and a sofa that was made up each night by Harriet, the stateroom butler.

'I can't believe how much storage space we have, especially considering we have brought all our glad rags. We need to ask Harriet for some more hangers,' Jess said as they took in their surroundings.

There was a newsletter on each bed which gave full details of the ship's timetable and all the activities for the day and where they were happening. The girls nicknamed it the 'bible'. Jess had been on many cruises because of her job and she loved the daily newsletter so she took her wine out onto the balcony and settled down to read it.

'The ship is departing at 5pm and there's a sail-away party on the poolside deck. What do you say to a cocktail, ladies? We can come back and get ready for dinner once we're out at sea.'

'Sounds perfect,' Amelia replied.

Both she and Beth felt that Jess knew the ropes and they were happy for her to take the lead, for the moment. They grabbed their ship passes and headed on up to deck fourteen to the poolside where the band was playing cover music from the 70s, 80s and 90s. They went over to the pool bar and ordered some cocktails. Then they found a good spot to make sure they could see everything as the *Santana* sailed out of Rome. The weather was a little dull but it was dry and still bright; according to the bible, the sun wasn't due to set until 6.51pm.

***

Over lunch, Jess had told them about the ridiculous cost of calls when the ship was out at sea so they decided to only use their phones while in port. They had told their families that they wouldn't be making or receiving calls while they were out at sea and gave them the ship's telephone number in case of emergencies. Another benefit of this was the total peace of being virtually uncontactable for much of the cruise: bliss!

Amelia was worried that Jess and Beth would wonder why she was bringing her phone with her out of the room but she couldn't stop thinking about Sam and was waiting to hear from him. She had her phone on silent in case he sent any texts, but she hadn't heard a word from him. She was confused and wished she could tell Jess and Beth about him, but she was afraid they would be disgusted with her. She had always been the 'good' girl out of the three of them.

She decided she was going to have to try and find him. She was still very annoyed with him, but he was here now and there was no point in fighting with him; she might as well enjoy their time together. She had made up her mind, though, that he was not going to interfere with her time with Beth and Jess. This, as far as she was concerned, was non-negotiable.

'I need to go and get a cardigan from the room,' she said. 'Does anyone need anything?'

'No, thanks, but don't be long or you'll miss it all,' Jess said jovially, referring to the sail-away party.

***

Amelia ran down to reception and asked for Sam's stateroom number but they wouldn't give it to her even though she pleaded with them. She decided to try phoning him on his mobile one more time. The phone rang instead of going to voicemail and Sam answered.

'At long last! What room are you in?' Amelia was surprised to find herself shaking, but she knew it was mainly due to her fear of being discovered.

'I'm in Room 6508. Will I see you soon?' His tone was wanting.

'I don't know Sam, you'll have to wait and see,' she teased.

***

There was no sign of Amelia and the *Santana* was well out at sea now. Jess and Beth wanted to go back to the room to get ready for pre-dinner drinks.

'She's been gone at least an hour now, Jess,' Beth said, 'Do you think she's lost or just meandering?'

'I don't know, but it's not like her. She never gets lost,' Jess replied. 'I think we should go back to the room. She'll realise when she comes back up that we have probably gone there. This ship is so bloody big we are going to have to make an arrangement about what to do or where to go if we get separated from each other.'

'I agree. I think the most logical thing is to go back to the room,' Beth said.

***

Sam opened the door and Amelia pushed him inside and slammed the door behind her. 'You naughty boy! I am so annoyed with you,' she said.

She couldn't believe how much she was aching for him with every inch of her being. Her feelings for him were stronger than she realised and she felt herself losing control. She had told herself the day before that she was going to make him suffer for what he had done, but now that she was here standing in front of him, it was different. They shared an intense physical awareness of each other and he pulled her towards him, his kiss urgently demanding a response.

She could feel the heat of his body and made no attempt to resist as he pushed her down on the bed, his hands swiftly undressing and exploring her. She had forgotten that she was supposed to be back with the girls, watching the ship sail away as she tugged at his trousers and felt him hard and calling her. He lifted her dress over her head and admired her beautiful round breasts as he gently caressed them, kissing her neck and breathing softly as he moved his tongue in her mouth.

She rose to meet him, sensations of erotic desire surging through her. She felt him inside her, thrusting as they moved in harmony. Her back tingled; the orgasm was moving from the base of her spine and racing through her body – waves of the most divine pleasure. Then they collapsed in each other's arms.

She looked at her watch and realised that she had missed the sail-away party. She chastised herself as she thought about how she had only been on the ship a few hours and was already putting Sam before her friends.

***

'I am so sorry. I got carried away looking in the shops and exploring the ship and didn't realise the time and then, when I went back up, you were gone,' Amelia said after she arrived back in the room. She felt a strange warmth inside her and thought that she must have a look of guilt on her face.

'Oh, don't worry about it. We were just saying that we need to have an arrangement in place in case any of us gets lost or separated, and you've just worked it out all by yourself,' Beth said ,as she put the final touches to her make-up. 'Jess is just out of the shower so when she's ready we'll head down to the grand foyer for pre-dinner drinks. You can follow us down.'

'Okay. I'll get myself together as quickly as I can. I've already wasted enough time,' Amelia replied.

***

Jess and Beth went downstairs. They had missed the 'Dancing with the Stars' competition in the foyer but the house band was playing and they found a nice spot and sat down, making sure they had a chair for Amelia. The waiter came over and they ordered two Hendricks gin and tonics and started to really relax.

'There was something funny about Amelia when she came back to the room this evening, Jess, I can't put my finger on it,' Beth said.

'I agree, she seemed a bit flustered or something. I think her story was a little flimsy, to be honest. She's been acting a little strange recently; she's just not herself. On the one hand, she seems very happy but, on the other, she seems quite stressed out.'

'Maybe it's the pressure of running a business and all the work she does for the charity,' Beth replied. 'She seems to be getting more and more involved in that. Things really should be easier now that Charlie and Chantal are living in Dublin and she only has Caroline at home. Do you think everything is okay between herself and Paul?'

'It's been a while since I've been down to Galway and it's hard to have a proper chat on the phone, but they've always had a good marriage, so it must be something else. I'm sure she'll tell us in her own time.'

***

'Hey gorgeous, you look fantastic!' Jess said as she saw Amelia coming towards them.

Amelia, who was tall and slender with thick, curly blonde hair and beautiful aquamarine-blue eyes, looked beautiful in a pale pink silk dress. She had a natural beauty which was enhanced by her kind and gentle nature. People couldn't help but notice her when she walked past.

'Thank you, Jess, you both look amazing too. Now, what is the plan? Am I having a drink here or are we heading off to the next bar?'

'Well, I thought we could go to the Morello Bar for another drink because DJ Coco is playing there, and then we can head down for dinner.'

They left the foyer and went up to the Morello Bar. It was packed because the barmen behind the stunning ice bar were doing one of their tricks with the spirit bottles, and people were crowded around, trying to catch a glimpse. The girls barely managed to find a seat and took ages deciding which Martini to order from the exotic menu.

'Well, hello there, my Irish friends. How are you getting on?'

It was Meredith, the American girl they had met on the transfer bus. Meredith was a tall, shapely woman with large breasts and pale skin. It definitely looked as if she'd had work done. She had shoulder-length, poker-straight auburn hair and green eyes with a look of devilment in them, but what was most attractive about her was her beautiful smile and infectious laugh.

She hadn't told the girls much about herself on the transfer, only that she was from Texas, had been married three times, and had come on the cruise to get over her most recent divorce.

'Hi Meredith, how are you getting on? We are having a quick drink before dinner, you're welcome to join us,' Beth said.

'I have a couple of things to do before dinner but would you like to meet up after dinner for a drink?' she replied.

'Absolutely, we'll see you here. Enjoy your dinner.'

When the girls finished their drinks they headed towards Orchid, the ship's main dining room. They were met by the Claudia, the maître d', who showed them to the table which would be theirs for the duration of the cruise.

Orchid took their breath away. It could cater for three thousand covers and was visually stunning, with a magnificent sweeping staircase separating the two floors, and exquisite chandeliers running the length and breadth of the room. Each table was assigned a head waiter, assistant waiter and sommelier who remained the same throughout the cruise so that a camaraderie could develop between the guests and crew.

The girls were seated and given the menus – an à la carte and table d'hôte. Claudia explained that the there was a lot of flexibility and if they had any special requests they need only ask. They settled down to read the menus and, within minutes, the team arrived at their table and introduced themselves. Solomon was the head waiter, Jojo the assistant waiter, and Antonio was the sommelier.

It was immediately evident that Solomon had more than a passing interest in Beth, but that was nothing new to Jess and Amelia. Anytime they went away with her, it was always the same, she had men eating out of the palm of her hand. Beth seemed to have a radiance about her that men couldn't resist. It wasn't that she was stunningly gorgeous, but she was very attractive and extremely sexy.

'I'm having the shrimp followed by the gazpacho and then the ravioli,' Jess piped up.

'I'm not quite sure what to have. Should I go for the shrimp or the spring roll? I'm going to have the arugula salad and the salmon after,' Beth said.

'Well, you know me, it's the shrimp followed by French onion soup and the beef,' Amelia replied.

'For someone who owns a Michelin two-star restaurant, you are surprisingly predictable, Amelia. I can never get over how conservative you are when we dine out!' Jess said laughing. Beth nodded in agreement.

'That's probably because I get tired of constantly trying out new dishes in the restaurant. I know what I like,' Amelia said firmly, smiling.

The three of them really enjoyed good food and fine dining and they tried to get together every few months, often in Galway to sample Paul's latest creations in *Restaurant Amelia*; they were very proud of their friend's success.

Antonio arrived to take the drinks order, followed by Solomon who took the food order. The girls began to settle in nicely.

***

'I want to see the casino. Is anyone coming or do you want to head to the bar and I'll catch you up?' Jess asked as they were leaving Orchid.

Beth and Amelia read each other's minds. 'We'll head to the Morello Bar to meet Meredith and we'll keep you a seat. We don't want her to think we are not turning up. Do you mind going on your own?'

Jess didn't mind one bit. She preferred going on her own but she didn't want the girls to know that. Amelia and Beth knew that she liked to play a bit of blackjack and to have a flutter in a casino, but they had no idea that she had a gambling addiction that was threatening to ruin her life.

***

Jess had grown up in Dundrum in Dublin. Her father, Lorcan, had a car dealership business and her mother, Jenny, worked in the business with him. Jess had three brothers and although she was a tomboy growing up, she had blossomed into a beautiful, glamorous young woman with rich, glowing auburn hair that hung gracefully over her shoulders. She'd had quite a strict upbringing and her parents were very focused on ensuring that their children got a good education and went to college, but Jess had always had her heart set on becoming an air hostess.

When she was nineteen, she had been delighted to be accepted for training by Aer Lingus. Over the years, she worked her way up the ladder until she eventually became purser, responsible for cabin crew and passengers on her flight. She worked hard in an often demanding and stressful environment, but she loved her job.

***

Jess arrived down on deck four and walked around the casino, trying to get her bearings. It was very busy and noisy and would have been very intimidating for a novice, but she was no novice.

She walked around for a bit and then found the blackjack table with the lowest stakes – $10. She had brought an allowance of $300 with her and she gave this to the croupier. As she looked at her chips, she felt a surge of excitement run through her. She looked at her watch and told herself that she would stay for half an hour and then leave with whatever she had on the table.

There were three players – all men – playing beside her. She had a very good run and quickly started to triple her stakes. She had been playing blackjack for years and was quite good at it when she played safely. It was when she took risks that things often went wrong. She decided to break herself in gently and not go too mad, but she didn't notice the time going by and after forty minutes she checked her watch and realised she had played for too long and needed to get back to her friends.

She cashed in with $900 and left, proud that she had walked away while she was so far ahead. Maybe she was on a roll? Maybe she would solve all her financial problems just as she had planned? Her luck might, finally, be in, she thought.

***

'Well, Missus, how did it go?' Beth asked. She and Jess were sitting with Meredith.

'I had a great bit of luck tonight. You'll be proud of me – I came away three times ahead. I just have to hope I can keep it up now. The adrenaline has really started to flow and it's gotten to me!'

She sat down beside Amelia while Beth continued talking to Meredith.

'I don't like the sound of that, Jess,' Amelia whispered to her. 'We've talked about this before and you know your limitations. I'm not going to lecture you, you're a big girl and we're on holidays, but I'm here for you if you need me. I can look after your money if you feel you can't control it yourself. You only have to ask.'

'Thanks, Amelia, but I can handle it,' Jess lied. She had no intention of admitting her weakness to her friend. She didn't want her to think she was a hopeless, gambling idiot.

The jazz quartet was really good and everyone was getting into holiday mood. Meredith and the girls had started to become friends and things were falling into place. It was going to be a wonderful trip. After the band finished, there was no more activity in the main areas of the ship so the remaining late-night revellers headed up to Panorama Nightclub for an after-party with DJ Coco. Beth and Jess were always the night owls whenever the three of them went away together and they had no intention of going to bed, but Amelia was fading and made her excuses. Little did they know that she had plans to go and visit Sam.

***

In Panorama Nightclub there was a small dance floor with a large bar and floor-to-ceiling windows. There was a minimal level of disco lighting which was a little disappointing if you were looking for the wow factor, but it was a nightclub on a ship and was used during the day as a lounge bar as it had superb views of the ocean. The music was predominantly from the 70s, 80s and 90s. The girls had deliberately chosen the *Santana* because its style and vibe suited their age group.

Beth and Jess noticed that there were a lot of people dancing who looked like professional dancers, which was a little puzzling.

'Do you think they are paying staff to dance, Jess?'

'It's a little bit strange,' Jess replied. 'Maybe they use them to encourage people onto the floor but there are too many of them. We'll have to get to the bottom of it but, to be honest, I'm a bit tired, it's been a very long day. Would you mind if I headed up to bed?'

'Brilliant idea, I'm exhausted myself but we're going to get a terrible slagging from Amelia!'

'Don't worry, she won't be awake!'

***

Amelia had gone back to the room and called Sam. She told him that she could come down and see him but that she couldn't stay for long.

Sam was waiting for her; he reached out and drew her into the room, leaning against the door for a moment. He gave her a smile that sent her pulse racing. She looked at him intensely.

'What are you doing to me? This is crazy. I am a married woman on holidays with my friends.'

'Sssh!' he said as he placed his mouth over hers and kissed her seductively. She felt a warm glow flow through her, but she knew she couldn't stay.

'I have to go back, Sam, I have a strange feeling that the girls are tired and won't stay out too long tonight. We had a very early start this morning.'

He withdrew reluctantly. 'Okay, I guess I'll have to wait until tomorrow. Sweet dreams, my love.'

***

Jess opened the door and, just as they had expected, Amelia looked like she was asleep so they got undressed quietly and went to bed.

BACK AT HOME

After Paul arrived home from the airport, he went into his office to check his emails. He hated saying goodbye to Amelia but he had always taken her to the airport and that would never change. It was only 5.30am and his inbox was already chock-a-block. He looked through his emails to see if anything was urgent but there was nothing that couldn't wait so he went into the kitchen to make some coffee.

He sat down at the breakfast counter and started to think about Amelia and how he always missed her when they were apart. He thought about how good his life was and how he should be happy – he had a beautiful wife, three gorgeous, healthy children and a successful business, so why was he messing around with Marla? It was dangerous, and he was risking losing everything.

He thought about the first time he had kissed her in the restaurant when everyone had gone home. It had been a long service and he was tired but there had been a spark between them from the moment he had interviewed her. She was totally different to Amelia in looks; she was petite and had dark brown, come-to-bed eyes and an infectious smile. He had known there and then that he had to hire her. It had taken only two weeks; he had tried to fight it but the urge was too strong, and she was flirting with him constantly despite the fact that he was her boss and she was new to the job. She had a self-confidence that was almost brazen, but when they finally got together the sex was amazing.

He should never have taken her on; he knew that now but it was too late, the damage was done and he was hooked. He remembered how close they had come to being caught on several occasions; he was playing with fire and had to make some decisions. It was make-or-break time and if he wasn't careful, he could lose his business, as well as his family.

Paul set off for the gym and made a mental note to have his decision made by the time Amelia came home.

***

Stephen was in a sombre mood when Bethany walked into the kitchen. Part of him wished that Beth hadn't asked her daughter to come and help him with Ed, but he knew that she was just being her usual thoughtful self. Anyway, he needed her there to give him time to arrange everything.

Everyone loved Beth; she was gentle and kind and always went out of her way to help everyone and her daughter was just like her. Bethany got on very well with Stephen and had been delighted when he and her mom had decided to marry as she always worried that Beth would never get over Sonny. Beth had told her about their love story when she was old enough to understand. When Bethany was twenty-one, Sonny had thrown a big party for her in Dublin. He had always remained in her life after he split with her mother.

Stephen was feeling very sorry for himself, he hadn't had a holiday since he and Beth had been in Barcelona the previous year. He hated it when she went away with the girls but he knew that he had to pull himself together. He wanted to make his wife happy again; she deserved it and he was determined to make it happen.

Bethany had just taken Ed to school so he had an hour to himself before he had to leave for Cork. He had a plan and, if it worked, he was convinced that it would fix everything between him and Beth.

DAY TWO

MESSINA (SICILY), ITALY

AMELIA WOKE UP. THE other two were still asleep so she went out onto the balcony to see what was going on. The sun was shining and they were still moving but she could see a town in the distance. She went back in and grabbed the bible then came back out and settled down to read it.

According to the daily newsletter, they were due to arrive in Messina at 10am but it looked as if they were ahead of schedule. She continued reading, looking up every few minutes to see what was going on. She stood up to watch the ship come into port. It was quite an amazing operation and Amelia was in awe of the crew as they ran around with ropes while the ship manoeuvred her way into position along the wall.

She sat down again and thought about Sam. Her mind drifted back to the night she had met him at the Prema Foundation ball. They had been sitting beside each other and had laughed and flirted all evening. The chemistry between them was instant and at the end of the night Sam slipped his number into her bag and whispered in her ear to call him.

When Amelia got home, she felt a strange sensation running

through her body and butterflies in her stomach. She was confused; why was she feeling like this? She was a married woman, for goodness sake. She put it down to alcohol, threw the piece of paper in the bin and went to bed. The next day when she saw the torn-up paper in the bin, she began to feel guilty. But she reprimanded herself for feeling bad and told herself that she had done nothing wrong.

Two weeks later, she was in Brown Thomas buying make-up when she ran into Sam. He asked her to go for coffee and she agreed. After making small talk for a while, he told her that he hadn't been able to get her out of his head and asked her if she felt the same way. Amelia told him that it was madness, that she was a happily married woman. But he was persistent and pushed her for an answer to his question. She tried to deny it, but he could see that she was lying and that she felt the same way. He told her that he would be there at the same time the following week if she wanted to meet him; if she didn't turn up he would leave her alone and never speak of it again.

Amelia went home but she wasn't able to get Sam out of her head. She had a tingling in her stomach that she hadn't felt since she was a teenager. She couldn't concentrate on anything; she knew it was ridiculous but she couldn't do anything about it. The following week, even though she knew it was wrong, she went to meet Sam. They sat down and talked for a while then Sam gave her his address. They lived in a small city and were both very well known so they needed to be very careful. They arranged that Amelia would drive to his house after they left the store. And so the affair began.

***

'How long have you been up?' Beth asked as she stepped onto the balcony.

'Oh, about an hour, maybe less. I have been watching us coming into port and it's been fascinating. I really don't know how they do it; it must be very frightening having responsibility for so many guests and crew, as well as a ship of this magnitude. No wonder they pay them well.'

'How do you know they pay them well?'

'I read it somewhere. Anyway, they have great perks even if they aren't paid well.'

'I see you've been doing Jess's job with the bible. We were too tired to read it last night. Did you get a chance to see if there is anything interesting on today?'

'I haven't really read it, to be honest, just skimmed over it because I was distracted by what was going on,' Amelia lied, not admitting that it was her thoughts of Sam that had distracted her from reading it.

'Why don't we get Jess up, get dressed and go to breakfast? We can bring it with us and plan our day then,' Beth said.

When they went back inside, Jess was coming out of the bathroom dressed in her sundress.

'Good morning, you two. I heard you outside so I took the liberty of grabbing the bathroom while the coast was clear. What's the weather like?' She was asking the most important question of the day as far as they were all concerned; weather was always a topic of conversation for Irish people.

Before they could answer, Jess flung open the curtains and made her way out onto the balcony.

'We thought we might head up to the Wayfarer for breakfast. We can make a plan while we are eating,' Amelia said.

***

Jess found a table on the terrace overlooking the port. Messina was not particularly attractive and they were underwhelmed by it, but they had not picked the cruise because of Messina; they had chosen it because of the Greek and Turkish offerings.

'I need to get new sunglasses before I lose my mind. I can't understand how I could have been so stupid as to leave mine at home. Do either of you need to get anything in particular? Messina doesn't look like it's going to be a mecca for shopping,' Jess said.

'No, I'm saving myself for the bags in Kusadasi!' Amelia said, laughing.

'Alright then, let's take a wander up through the town and have a look and hopefully we'll find some sunglasses. Then we can come back at our leisure to have some lunch. What do you think?' Jess asked.

'Yes, sounds good. Oh, life is tough, ladies,' Beth said with a laugh.

'Okay, let me have a good look at the bible while you two get some breakfast,' Jess said. 'I'll order the fresh orange juice while I'm at it.'

Beth and Amelia went off to the buffet and Jess started reading through the newsletter. The most important thing to note was the departure time as nobody wanted to be left behind. They had heard some very frightening stories of people shouting at the ship as it pulled away, leaving them on the quayside.

The show that night was clashing with the Rugby World Cup – England v Australia – and as Amelia was a huge fan of rugby they would have to watch it with her, Jess thought. Both she and Beth loved the Ireland matches but didn't really care about the other ones. However, they were on the cruise together and there had to be give and take. Anyway, it wasn't exactly a punishment to watch other countries playing rugby, not when they were on holiday sipping cocktails.

***

Back in the room, the girls got ready to set off. They took their ship passes, phones and money and put on some sun cream before heading down to deck three where they signed out and went ashore.

Jess had the bible with her and proceeded to tell them all about Messina. They wandered up through the streets and, as they had expected, there was nothing much to see. They did find a shop selling sunglasses and Jess bought a lovely pair that were very good value. They spent another couple of hours walking around, looking inside the odd shop here and there, but there wasn't much that interested them so they decided to head back to the ship, a bit disappointed that their morning had not been more exciting. They were tired so they were happy at the thought of an afternoon of relaxation on board.

***

When they got back to the room, they lay down on the beds and chatted for a while before deciding to go up to the grill beside the pool for lunch.

Amelia couldn't stop her thoughts from wandering. She was wondering what Sam was doing and where he was. She was going to have to find a solution to this situation before it drove her mad.

'A penny for them?' Beth said.

'Oh, I was wondering how they are all getting on at home,' Amelia said. She had seen a missed call from Paul and knew she should ring him back, but she wasn't in the mood. She wondered if she really loved him and how she could have such strong feelings for two men at the same time.

***

Amelia had grown up in a very affluent, loving environment and had had a wonderful, happy upbringing in Galway. Her father was an eminent cardiologist and her mother a midwife who had decided to stay at home to look after her children. She had a privileged upbringing and her parents had doted on herself and her sister, Sally. They spent as much time as they could with them, encouraging them in every way, taking them swimming and horse riding and to drama and music classes. They had spent all their holidays in their summer house in Westport in County Mayo.

Amelia had always known that she wanted to return to live in Galway when she got married because she was very close to her family. However, she felt that going to college in Dublin would give her a chance to gain a bit of independence and broaden her horizons.

She met Paul at a party in Dublin while they were in college. They were both from Galway and knew each other to see, but had never had a conversation before meeting in Dublin. Paul was studying hotel management with the aim of having his own restaurant one day, and Amelia was in University College Dublin doing communications and marketing. They fell in love and shortly afterwards moved into a small apartment in Rathgar where they loved entertaining their friends and trying out new dishes that Paul created.

When Paul graduated he started working in Michelin-star restaurant and Amelia worked in two of the major PR companies in the capital. They intended returning to Galway where Paul wanted to open a restaurant.

Paul proposed on their second anniversary and they decided to get married the following year in Galway, agreeing to wait a few years before having children. However, six months later, Amelia discovered that she was pregnant. Their carefully laid-out plans had to be changed and they got married straight away. After the baby was born, Amelia set up her own consultancy business, selling it a few years later so that she could work with Paul and they could concentrate on building up *Amelia's Restaurant*, with the aim of winning a Michelin star.

***

They went up to the restaurant and ordered their wine at the bar before sitting down under an umbrella to work out what to have for lunch.

'What would you like to do for the afternoon?' Jess asked. 'There is volleyball in the pool at 3pm and wine tasting in the Cave Bar at 4.30pm. Or would you just like to chill out?'

'I am going to find a sunbed by the pool and read my book. Anyone who wants is welcome to join me,' Beth said.

'I'll join you and you might even get me into the pool!' Jess replied.

'I'm going to go to the room to read my book on the balcony. I quite fancy a bit of peace and quiet,' Amelia said.

She was thinking about going to Sam's room but she hadn't told him so she didn't know if he would be around. They really needed to have some sort of plan for communicating worked out for spontaneous moments like this. She felt a bit guilty making secret plans, but that's what happened when people had affairs.

They finished their wine and returned to the room to change before Jess and Beth headed to the pool.

***

Amelia dialled Sam's room but there was no answer, so she switched on her phone and sent him a text.

The girls have gone to the pool for a while and I am in my room. Would you like me to pop by?

She went out onto the balcony and, after what seemed like an age but was in fact only five minutes, the phone beeped.

Just been to the gym, on my way back to the room now. Give me ten minutes.

Amelia smiled. She went to her drawer and pulled out her best bikini; a beautiful turquoise halter neck by Seafolly that Paul had bought her in Brown Thomas. She put on her white fluffy bathrobe over it and fixed her hair. She hadn't washed it that morning because she planned to wash it before she went to dinner, but her hair was lovely and thick and it always looked well. She had light make-up on which she touched up – she didn't want to look as if she'd made too much of an effort!

***

A few minutes after she knocked on the door, Sam opened it.

'I'm going to have to get you a key, darling,' he said.

'I think that might be a bit of a problem. What are you going to say? That you have a fancy woman calling secretly at different times of the day and night!'

He dragged her hard towards him, pulled open her robe and gasped as he looked at her. Loose tendrils of blonde hair softened her face, her seductive curves encouraging him to explore. He moved his fingers softly, sliding them underneath her bikini top and teasing her nipples. She pulled at the strings and it fell to the floor. He took off her robe and nimbly removed the bottom of the bikini. She looked at him; his handsome face was alive with a passionate longing for her. They both stood naked, admiring each other for a moment before he pressed his lips to hers, kissing her longingly. She quivered at the sweet tenderness of his kiss, her body aching for more.

He gently eased her down on the bed, his tongue caressing her swollen nipples and his hands moving down to her thighs. He could feel her wetness and moved his fingers down, playing until he could hear her gasp. He moved back over her, breathing heavily as his kissed her neck and then he entered her. Her body moved in harmony with him and she moaned as he thrust harder and harder. She couldn't stop herself from crying out. Blood pounded in her brain and the intensity of her orgasm surprised her.

They lay together for a while and then dozed off. When Amelia woke up and looked at her watch it was 5.30pm. She clambered to put her clothes on and fix herself up, getting slightly stressed at the thought of what excuse she was going to give the girls. She ran out of the room, barely kissing Sam.

He understood her panic. He had fallen in love with her the first moment he saw her and even though he knew she was married, he couldn't stop himself from wanting her. Being in the same industry was a big help in getting to see her and he met her plenty of times at functions but he couldn't believe his luck when he was seated beside her that night at the ball. He knew that this was his big chance to woo her. It was fate; he was sure of it. They were meant to be together and Amelia would soon realise it too. He was sorry about her husband and children but, when two people belong together, it can't be ignored. Paul would understand eventually. He would have no choice.

***

When Amelia arrived back at the room, there was no sign of Jess and Beth. She was just about to breathe a sigh of relief when the door opened and they came in carrying three glasses of wine and a plate of sushi.

'Where did you get to this time, Doris?' Jess asked in an accusing voice.

'Doris?'

'Yes, Disappearing Doris!'

Amelia had to think quickly.

'I decided to try and find the two of you so I went up to the pool but you weren't there. I looked all over the place and then came back down around by the shops, which were closed. I had forgotten that they only open when we are at sea. Then I went back up again to have another look. I must have missed you.'

Whatever way she said it, Jess and Beth believed her, but she knew she wasn't going to get away with it for very much longer. She was going to have to be more careful unless she came clean. She hated lying to them.

'Let's sit on the balcony, work out our evening and then get ready for dinner,' Jess suggested. 'The rugby is on at 9pm so maybe we should eat a little earlier if you want to see it, Amelia.'

'I don't mind. We can have dinner at the usual time and I'll catch the second half. It's not the Ireland match so I am not going to disrupt our evening.'

'Okay, let's finish getting dolled up and head down for drinks and take it from there.'

Jess tended to be a bit bossy sometimes but Beth and Amelia were happy enough at the moment. Once they had gotten the feel of the ship, they could start making more of the decisions.

***

Jess opened the safe. She took out $500 and her winning chips from the previous night and put them in her bag. She didn't want the girls to know how much she had with her so she kept it in a secret compartment in her wallet. She really needed her luck to keep going; she had to start winning big money if she was to get out of her debt problems.

She had always liked to gamble, but knew it was in her blood to become addicted so she tried her best to stay away from it. Jess had been to many casinos when they were on stopovers for work and the only thing that had been her salvation was her fear of the high stakes.

One day, when she was working the LAX-Dublin flight, she met a businessman who took a shine to her and gave her his business card. It turned out that he owned a private members club in Dublin. As this was a private club in a small city, she kept telling herself that it wasn't serious gambling. After many weeks of mulling it over, she decided one evening that she would take a look and headed into St Stephen's Green. She rang the doorbell of the club. The door opened and she was greeted by a very well-dressed maître d' who knew her name. He invited her in, closed the door and escorted her downstairs to a beautiful Georgian salon. The room was decorated with soft furnishings and low lighting and it had a lovely walnut bar. He offered her a glass of champagne, took her coat and led her to the tables.

So began a major problem which started to take over her life. Initially, she went once a month, but now she was going twice a week. She had never told anyone her secret, least of all her two best friends. Her gambling had become all-consuming and was starting to terrify her. She couldn't stop and knew that she was in serious trouble.

***

They went downstairs to the grand foyer and settled down with three glasses of sauvignon blanc and a bottle of Evian; they always tried to drink as much water as they could to avoid a hangover. Talk turned to Beth and Stephen and their relationship.

'How are things between you two?' Jess asked.

'Things have been bad for a while,' Beth replied. 'I don't know if it's him or me, but we always seem to be fighting or arguing.'

'Oh, Beth, it must be so stressful. What about sex – is that still okay?' Amelia asked. There was no subject off limits between the three of them.

'I've been making a huge effort but I really could take it or leave it, to be honest. I just find I'm not in the mood but I don't know why because, as you both know, I love sex. I keep wondering if it's the menopause, but then I find that I just don't feel attracted to him. We always had such a good physical relationship but now it feels like a chore. I shouldn't feel like this and feel guilty, but I can't help it. It's not just the sex, though, we are not getting on at all, and the atmosphere is awful, which is not good for anyone, least of all poor Ed.

'Do you think it's something to do with Sonny? You two never really had any closure,' Jess said gently.

Beth had met Sonny when she'd moved to London to escape from her manipulative, controlling first husband. Although he was almost twice her age, they had fallen in love and Beth had never been happier in her life. He was very wealthy and treated her like a princess. But Sonny was married; he didn't love his wife but he would not leave her. When his wife found out, Sonny left Beth and broke her heart.

'I don't know, Jess, I keep asking myself that. What I do know is that I have never felt that kind of love for any other man.'

'Have you heard from him at all?' Amelia asked.

'We keep in touch about Bethany, especially now that she is working for him, but sometimes I think it would be easier if I never had to talk to him at all. She looks so like him; every time I look at her, I see him. You know that his wife died six months ago?'

'No, Beth, I didn't but I think that could have some bearing on things. Could it be that maybe you are feeling that there is a chance for the two of you now that she is not in the way?' Jess took Beth's hand as she spoke.

'Maybe you're right, Jess, I think there might be an element of truth in what you're saying, but it can't happen. It's not fair on Stephen.'

'Hold on a second, Beth, this is not about Stephen – it's about you and what is best for you,' Jess said, almost argumentatively.

'Let's leave it for the moment. I'm dragging the mood down and I have a lot of thinking to do.' Jess looked at her friend. She couldn't help but feel a bit sad.

The klaxon sounded and the captain informed them that they were setting sail for Mykonos.

'I'm so excited about Mykonos. It looked so beautiful in your photos, Jess.' Amelia said, referring to the holiday that Jess had taken five years previously.

'I know, Amelia, it was so romantic. James and I had a fabulous time; little did I know it was going to be our last holiday together.'

'I don't mean to sound flippant, pet, but Mykonos is worthy of some fresh, positive memories now. Don't you think?' Amelia said as she winked at Jess and smiled.

***

Jess had met James at work. He was a trainee pilot who had joined Aer Lingus a year after her. He was Irish-Australian and, like most Australians, he had a hunger to travel. When he met Jess, James fell for her instantly. He was attracted to her personality and her sense of fun; he thought she was beautiful but he could also see that she was warm and loyal and devoted to her friends. It truly was a case of love at first sight for both of them. After a whirlwind romance, and without the blessing of her parents, Jess and James eloped and married in Las Vegas.

James was very romantic, always sending flowers and surprising Jess with little presents, and whisking her away to secret, sexy hideaways. They both had a high sex drive and their relationship was hot and steamy. They always made an effort to make things interesting and to please each other. They once joined the mile-high club but that was not too difficult when you worked in the industry!

Jess sometimes felt insecure about James because he was very good-looking and she would often notice passengers and crew admiring him in a way that they shouldn't, but he always reassured her that he only had eyes for her. Sadly, it wasn't long before her dreams were shattered and she discovered James had been having an affair and was having a child with another woman.

***

Although it was only their second day, the girls were already getting into a routine and when the band finished up in the foyer, they moved to the Morello Bar. The age group of those present was mixed, but it was mostly people around the same age as them. There were not too many oldies and absolutely no children. They were really starting to relax now and were looking forward to dinner.

Solomon spent a lot of time flirting with Beth and she encouraged him. Amelia and Jess told her it was not a good idea so she promised she would make an effort to stop. But they knew they were wasting their time; she was incapable of staying away from any man that gave her attention – it was like a drug to her.

They didn't linger in the restaurant because the rugby was on in a private room where a big screen had been set up for the matches. Once there, they found a good spot and ordered a drink.

***

Jess told them she was going to go to the casino for a while. She had decided to play roulette because the odds were better and she needed to start making serious money, but it was very much a game of chance rather than skill. She went to a table when the minimum bet was $5 and cashed in the dollars she had brought with her from the room. She placed the new chips beside her winnings from the previous night and felt a warm feeling of anticipation growing inside her.

There were three men beside her and they were playing quite aggressively, putting chips down all over the place, to the point that Jess wondered how the croupier knew which belonged to whom. She waited a few minutes, hoping they would calm down a little or else go away, but there was no sign of either happening so she started by putting $10 on red and $5 on zero. She decided that her strategy was going to be to put something on zero every time and to stick with one colour for a while. She never played numbers as she felt the odds weren't worth it unless luck was really on your side. She was trying to concentrate on her own situation, but the men kept distracting her and, before she knew it, she was down to $200.

Jess felt vulnerable but didn't want to leave the table empty-handed so she played on, this time switching to black. The tension she felt every time the wheel spun was making her feel sick. It was red again and again and again. How was this happening? Ten minutes later, her chips were gone so she thanked the croupier and left the table. She wanted to go upstairs there and then to get some more money. She found herself walking towards the lift, but something stopped her; she knew she was treading on thin ice so she went to find her friends. She felt very low and scared that she had lost her winning streak.

***

'How did you get on, Jess?' Amelia asked.

Jess didn't want to admit that she had lost, but she knew she would have to tell them; nobody wins all the time.

'I had a bad night, girls, but it's okay – there's always tomorrow,' she answered, as calmly and confidently as she could manage.

'Just as well you are giving yourself a daily budget. You will enjoy yourself more that way,' Beth told her.

Jess gave a false smile. If only they knew, she thought. She tried to do the sums quickly in her head; she had plenty left, but she would have to be more careful – these were her life savings and she had already blown too much.

***

The girls decided they would all go to the Panorama Lounge together because it was Abba night. When they got there, the place was rocking; the dance floor was full with all the dancers from the previous night and many more besides. Amelia and Beth couldn't wait to get on the floor where they started dancing their feet off. There were two girls dancing nearby in a very seductive manner. Beth noticed that they were moving in their direction; one of them took her hand while the other took Amelia's. Before they knew what was happening, they were being spun around the floor.

Dana and Alana were American. They told Beth and Amelia that they were dancers who were on a dancing trip with their club. That explained all the dancers, Beth thought; it was all starting to make sense. There were dancers from different clubs all over the US and South America on board the ship. They had classes every day with an instructor and there were lots of dance competitions organised to take place during the cruise.

Jess, who had gone to the bar, saw them all chatting and joined them on the floor. Soon they were all dancing away and the three girls were learning how to dance properly.

***

Amelia wanted to get away to see Sam; he was all she could think about so she told the girls that she was going to bed. They were so engrossed in the dancing that they didn't mind at all. She went to her room first to fix her hair and make-up and change her underwear; she wanted to put on her really sexy lingerie for Sam. She took out the black and pink Agent Provocateur lingerie with the suspender belt and stockings and put them on. Then she put on a black dress and high heels, fluffed up her hair, touched up her make-up, sprayed on some Agent Provocateur perfume and headed out the door.

She knocked three times before the door opened. When it did, Sam stood there, naked.

'I've been thinking about you all day; get yourself in here now,' he said in a slightly aggressive tone.

Amelia was a bit startled but she put it to the back of her mind as she felt herself getting wet. He grasped her a little roughly and lifted her dress over her head. He looked her over.

'You sexy woman, you're gorgeous,' he said as his eyes drilled through her body, unleashing feelings of arousal like she had never felt in her life. He went over to the bed and lay down on his back. 'Come over here, come down on me, darling.'

Amelia straddled him and moved her fingers up and down his face. She kissed him and took him in her mouth. She licked and used her hands to bring him pleasure before moving herself on top of him. They moved together and she could feel him inside her, thrusting as she gasped with delight. Afterwards, they lay in each other's arms, exhausted but relaxed.

'I'm going to have to go again, darling,' Amelia said. 'I'm pushing my luck with the girls and this time I am in serious danger of getting caught.' Doing her best not to spoil the moment, Amelia explained to Sam that their evening had to come to an early end.

'Do you not think you could tell them at this stage? They are your best friends and you say that you tell each other everything. What is the worst that can happen?'

'I know, darling, but I feel that they will be hurt that you are on the cruise that is supposed to be just for the three of us. I can't explain it; you'll just have to trust me.'

***

Beth and Jess were having the time of their lives with the dancers. They had no intention of going to bed until everything shut down on the ship. Beth started dancing with a guy called Kale who was swinging her around the floor. She had lost interest in dancing with Jess who was well used to this from previous holidays and didn't mind. She found herself joining in with the other dancers who were all very welcoming. When the music ended, the two girls decided to head back to the room and see if, by chance, Amelia was still awake. They were high on energy now and in no mood to go to bed.

They opened the door and saw that Amelia was asleep, so they crept out again. 'Let's see if we can find somewhere to get something to eat, I'm absolutely starving,' Beth whispered.

They took off their shoes and skipped down the corridor like schoolgirls. The only place they thought might be open was the Wayfarer so they went up to the fourteenth deck but when they got there it was closed for cleaning. They were told the only food on offer for the next two hours was room service. Disappointed, they knew they had no option but to go to bed.

DAY THREE

AT SEA (EN ROUTE TO MYKONOS)

AMELIA WOKE UP AND looked at her watch. She felt very tired. Then she remembered that it was an at-sea day so she turned over and went back to sleep. Keeping Sam a secret was taking its toll and she didn't feel very well.

When she woke up again sometime later, she got up; she was not very good at staying in bed once she was awake. She went out onto the balcony but it was a bit cold because they were moving so she went back in and put on her robe before going out again with the bible. It looked like there was a lot going on that day. The evening events included a formal dinner which would give them an excuse to dress up even more than usual. She noticed that Bellisima was open for lunch, as was Orchid, so they could have a leisurely, girly afternoon with plenty of delicious food and wine.

Amelia couldn't believe how many activities were on offer as she struggled to sift through them. She noted a cookery demonstration at 11am, a wine tasting at 12.30pm, an ultimate guide to shopping at noon, and a seminar on facial massage at 11am. The list went on and on and she knew they were going to have trouble choosing.

'What's the weather like?' Jess said as she popped her head around the door.

'I'm trying to work out what to do with our day, Jess; they have so much on it is unbelievable. I have to say, I am very impressed. I can see how people get hooked on cruises. To answer your question, it's a gorgeous day, but a bit chilly because we're moving.' Amelia was in good spirits, but she was still wondering when she should tell her friends about Sam.

'I feel a bit rough, to be honest,' Jess said. 'I'll have to stop mixing the drinks but a Bloody Mary should sort me out! I noticed that a few of the restaurants are open for lunch.' Jess liked to vary which restaurants they went to, and she felt the menus were a bit samey in Orchid. 'I'd like to try Bellisima if you two are happy with that,' she said. 'What's the story with activities? I never got a chance to go through the bible last night as we didn't get back until after 1.30am.'

'Well, there is so much on today we are going to have a very tough time choosing. We all love cooking and wine and both of those are on this morning, so we should try to squeeze the two of them in. I haven't got as far as the afternoon yet, but we probably won't be fit for much after lunch anyway. We had better get your woman up, otherwise it will be lunchtime and we haven't even had breakfast yet!'

They booked a table in Bellisima for the final lunch sitting at 1.30pm. They decided to do the cookery demo and the wine tasting in the morning and then chill out in the afternoon.

***

The cookery demonstration was on in the theatre on deck three and they took a seat towards the front so that they could get a good view. Marcus, the cruise director, introduced Tito, the executive chef, and his two assistant chefs and then the entertainment began. The subject was foie gras and Beth and Jess were thrilled; they always called it their death-row starter!

Tito began by showing them a large, whole goose liver – protected by cling film – and the passing it around the audience so they could have a good look. They had never seen one in its entirety before and it was very impressive. He went on to show them how to prepare it, to pan fry it, and how to make a foie gras parfait. He also showed them how to make the chutney to serve with it.

The girls loved the demonstration. It was such a treat and Marcus told them that there would be two hands-on cookery classes during the cruise, one with a Mexican theme and the other with a Greek theme. They put their names down for both; they could always change their minds but they were afraid all the places would be gone if they didn't book.

'Come on, girls, get your act together – time for the wine tasting!' Amelia said. She was in her element.

'This is where you can really show off, darling,' Beth said playfully. 'There isn't much you don't know about wine.'

'On the contrary, Beth, I am a novice, not a sommelier. It just seems like I know a lot because you see me in action in the restaurant.'

***

They went up to the Cave Wine Bar, which was just beside the Morello Bar, where they ran into Meredith. She seemed delighted to see them and they chatted away as they settled down in front of the carefully laid tables. There were a number of other guests present, including a very handsome English guy named Rick, who sat down beside Jess. Before the tasting started, they were all told to introduce themselves and say where they were from. Jess noticed that Rick seemed to be on his own; well, he was on his own at the tasting anyway.

The theme was Italian wines and they all confessed to knowing nothing about Italian wine except that they liked drinking it! There were four reds and four whites to taste and there were notes and glasses beautifully laid out on the tables in front of them. All the wines were of different vintages, but none were older than 2006. The ship's head sommelier, Seve, introduced himself and George, one of the barmen who was helping him, as well as a couple of waitresses who were serving light canapés.

The girls decided to play their own game amongst the four of them and give the wines marks out of ten to see which ones came out on top and if they agreed with each other. Jess looked at Rick. He seemed a bit lonely so she asked him if he would like to join in their little game. They sat back and the tasting began.

Whites:
- Pinot Grigio
- Soave
- Orvieto
- Gavi

Reds:
- Montepulciano
- Chianti Classico
- Barbera
- Barolo

Seve, who was Spanish, had a great personality and they found themselves laughing even though wine is quite a serious topic. They each scored the wines as they went along and there was quite a difference in how things turned out. Interestingly, the Irish girls all went for the soave, whereas Meredith liked the Gavi, and the Pinot Grigio was not popular at all. Rick agreed with Meredith, but did say that Italian wines were not his area of expertise. The overall winner in the reds was the Barolo, which was the outright winner for everyone. The general consensus at the end of the tasting was that they had all had a lot of fun and now had a bit more knowledge of Italian wine than they'd had an hour earlier.

Rick had been quite vocal throughout the tasting.

'You seem to know quite a lot about wine, Rick,' Jess said, smiling. 'I noticed you said to Seve that Italian wines are not your area of expertise. What wines do you know about?'

'I am a wine merchant and I import from France and Spain. I have to spend my time sampling so many wines from those countries that I need to keep my mind focused on them; after all, they are my bread and butter. I am on the ship because I supply the French and Spanish wine and the champagne for the *Santana* and her sister ships. Part of the contract is that I have to spend time with Seve and also do some product knowledge training with his team. I have to travel on each of the ships at least once a year for training so it's not the worst job in the world.'

'Wow, how fascinating!' Jess remarked.

'I would love to chat to you some more, Jess,' Rick said. 'Would you have a drink with me later?'

'Well, I'm with my friends on the cruise but why don't you join us after dinner in the Morello Bar?'

'Yes, that sounds wonderful. I'll look forward to it,' he answered.

***

Beth and Amelia had gone on ahead. They were a bit late for the last sitting for lunch and Jess ran to catch up with them back in their room. The speciality restaurants were quite formal and the girls were only looking for an excuse to put on their finery. Once they were ready, they made their way to deck five and arrived at Bellisima where they were greeted by Jacob who showed them to a magnificent table by the window. The restaurant was beautiful and the tables were set formally with linen tablecloths, silver cutlery and Riedel glassware that glistened in the light. This was clearly going to be an afternoon to remember.

'Well, madam, what's the story with the gorgeous Rick?' Amelia was dying to hear what had gone on after they had left Jess at the wine tasting.

'Oh, nothing really,' Jess replied, though she couldn't wipe the smile from her face.

'I am not going to fall for that, Missy! Did he ask you out?' Amelia persisted.

'Yes, well, sort of. He asked me to go for a drink with him so I asked him to join us in the Morello Bar after dinner.'

'You could have said you would meet him on your own, you know, we wouldn't have minded,' Amelia responded.

'Oh God, I've just realised that we are going to the grand foyer later because The Flutes are playing. What am I going to do?' Jess looked quite upset.

'Oh, don't worry. Can't you run upstairs and find him? Relax, you silly girl!' Amelia was taken aback by how upset Jess seemed to be by something so trivial. Maybe she really liked this guy or maybe it was that she hadn't been on a date for years.

Jess felt herself blush. She realised that she sounded like a schoolgirl but Amelia was right, she needed to relax about Rick; she would frighten him off if she wasn't careful.

They all laughed as they settled back and looked out the window. 'The sea looks so vast and scary, I wouldn't fancy falling in there. I wouldn't say you'd have much chance of being found,' Amelia said as she looked out on the ocean.

'But there's something very peaceful about the water,' Jess replied. 'I've always felt a sense of calmness whenever I'm near the sea, or even a river. Whenever I feel very stressed or worried, I head out to Howth for a long walk. Sometimes, if I have a lot of time, I hop on the DART and take a trip all along the coast out to Dún

Laoghaire. It is genuinely a huge help, though that probably sounds ridiculous!'

'No, it doesn't, Jess. I know what you mean. I am always willing to pay extra for a sea view when I'm on holidays. Right this minute I feel like I am in paradise and I never want it to end,' Beth said with a smile on her face.

'Okay, enough pondering. Let's get on with the serious stuff now: I saw you with Kale last night, Beth, and you looked like you are heading into dangerous waters, no pun intended!' Amelia said laughing. 'What a bloody awful name he has – you'll have to give him a nickname!'

'I don't know what you mean, my darling friend, you are reading far too much into things. We were merely dancing and, as for his name, I agree one hundred per cent!'

'Beth, there is dancing and there is dancing! I am just saying, be careful. Remember, we know you well and men fall for you very easily, even when you are not intending for it to happen. Am I right in saying that he is married? He is wearing a ring.'

'Yes, I think so, Amelia. I don't know much about him really, but I am married myself so I am going to be a good girl. I promise!'

'I hate to say it,' Jess stated, 'but I don't know if you are capable of being a good girl, darling, however well intentioned you may be.'

'Well, thanks for that, ladies, nice to know what you think of me.'

'Ah, now, Beth, don't be like that. You know we are on your side. We just want to protect you from getting hurt again. You need stability in your life.'

'We'll change the subject now,' Amelia said, kicking Jess under the table as a signal to let matters lie. She noticed that Jess was staring into space, looking very forlorn. 'Are you okay, Jess?'

'It's the anniversary and no matter how hard I try, I can't forget,' she replied, looking sadly at her friends.

Nothing more needed to be said. They looked at each other and reached out their hands to Jess, holding hers in theirs. After a minute had passed, they released hands.

'Thank God I have the two of you,' Jess said.

'Do you want to go back to the room and talk about things?' Amelia asked gently.

'Thanks, Amelia, but not right now.' Jess knew she didn't need to apologise for bringing down the mood.

The three friends were united by the events that had taken place all those years ago in Irish College and it was clear that the pain still lingered for poor Jess.

The waiter arrived with the dessert menus at just the right moment. Jess ordered crêpes suzette and soon they were back on track enjoying themselves. They had a great lunch and got nicely drunk; the food was delicious and they flirted with the waiters before heading back to their room for a siesta.

***

Amelia had forgotten about Sam but when she looked at her phone she saw a text from him.

Any chance we could get together?

She had set her phone up so that the texts didn't show on her screen, just in case the other two saw them. She went out onto the balcony and sent him a text saying that she would make some sort of excuse and come over in half an hour.

Jess and Beth had fallen asleep and Amelia left the room as quietly as she could. She decided that she would only get away with an hour and had taken her book and pool bag with her in case the girls asked her where she had been. This time she would have the perfect excuse; she would tell them she had gone to the pool.

***

When Sam opened the door she went in and sat down on the chair beside the balcony door. He sat on the sofa opposite her.

'We only have an hour, darling, so we need to enjoy every single second,' Amelia said. 'I had a dream about us making love on the balcony. It's the perfect time while we are at sea,' she continued in a bold, inviting voice.

Sam handed her the glass of wine and told her to wait a moment. He went onto the balcony and moved the recliner and table so that they couldn't be seen from the other staterooms, then he brought out a pillow and a duvet before coming back in. He took her hand and led her outside. He lay down and indicated to her to straddle him. Amelia felt a sense of carnal longing race through her; she loved the fact that there was a slight risk of someone seeing them.

Sam was awestruck by her beauty; he never tired of seeing her but she looked stunning today. Although Amelia had a lot of self-confidence, Sam felt she wasn't aware of how beautiful she was and this made him love her all the more. He moved his fingers around her breasts, gently massaging her and kissing her neck while she arched her back and tilted her head back. She could feel him hard between her thighs, her wetness gliding her to and fro. She turned around, still straddling him and he kissed her back as she slid down his legs, massaging him with feather-light touches.

After a few minutes, she moved deftly back around and took him in her mouth. She could feel every inch of him throbbing and felt a sense of power as she sucked and gripped him, moving him up and down. Just as he was reaching his peak, she moved back up and took him inside. He thrust deeper and deeper until they were both swept away by the intoxicating power of their orgasm. She opened her eyes and looked at him, shocked by the depths of feelings she had for him. This was no longer just an affair; she had fallen in love with Sam.

'I can't stay and fall asleep, Sam, don't let it happen, please. What time is it?'

He looked at his watch. '5.15pm, darling, we have a little bit longer.'

'I think I'll go now, just in case. I'll see you later, darling. By the way, how you've been spending your time or where you've been going for dinner?'

'I know I've to be extremely careful so I've spent a lot of time in the room. I deliberately booked a Jade stateroom because there is a restaurant that is for the exclusive use of Jade-class guests which means that I don't have to live on room service. I've also been in the gym but, obviously, I haven't gone near the bars in the evenings.'

'I wish I could do something about that, darling, but, at the moment, there is no way around things. We'll just have to carry on the way we are. At least we get to see each other more than we do at home. I'll see you later tonight, around 11.30pm or so.'

***

Amelia went to the Wayfarer and ordered three glasses of wine before returning to her room. She put the glasses down and put her key in the door. Jess heard her and opened it.

'Well, hello Doris, where did you get to this time?'

Amelia came in with her pool bag over her shoulder and the glasses in her hands.

'Off gallivanting again, were we?' Jess said with a smile.

'You two were asleep and I thought I would head up to the pool for a while, that's all,' she replied quietly.

Amelia felt as if the guilt she was feeling was written all over her face. She wanted so much to share everything with her friends but she felt that they would be disgusted with her and she couldn't bear the thought of their disapproval.

'Well, I've had a lovely nap and now I am going to have a shower and figure out what to wear tonight,' Beth said as she went into the bathroom.

Amelia and Jess went over to the wardrobe to pick out their own dresses for the evening. Amelia decided on a stunning figure-hugging, red maxi Amanda Wakeley dress with a slit up to the knees. She was very tall so everything looked fantastic on her, but in this dress she looked like a supermodel. Jess was also slim and glamorous, but she didn't have the money to buy designer clothes so she tended to buy high street. That said, she had very good taste and she chose to wear a gorgeous, pale pink Ted Baker dress with matching wrap, bag and shoes.

Beth decided on a beautiful dress she had bought when she was on holidays with Stephen. It was a striking emerald-green silk halter neck with an empire line and flowing skirt that reached just below the knee. It was absolutely gorgeous. When they were all made up and ready to go, they took a few photos and headed downstairs to get the evening started, feeling very confident in their finery.

***

'Don't forget that Ireland are playing Italy in fifteen minutes so we need to head down to the room we were in the other night. They said they were only showing it on the television but I went down to reception when I was out and about earlier and asked them if they would put it on the big screen.'

'Certainly looks like you've worked your PR magic, Amelia. All those years working hard in Dublin weren't wasted after all!' Jess laughed.

They settled down to watch the match, enjoying a few drinks and looking out for some fellow countrymen. Amelia thought about Sam; she knew he would be watching the match in his room because he loved rugby and now supported the Irish team – she wouldn't have had it any other way! Ireland won the match and the girls were on a high so celebrations were in order.

MEDITERRANEAN MENOPAUSE

They were dining in Orchid again and sat at their usual table. They ordered three glasses of champagne and perused the menu while Solomon came over and took the order, flirting madly with Beth, who reciprocated graciously.

'You are very naughty, Beth. It's not fair to be giving the poor lad false hope,' Amelia said.

'I'm sure he's well aware it's going nowhere, guys. I mean, how would he seriously expect anything to happen between us when he never even gets any time off?' Beth replied indignantly.

'Yes, but all the same, it's not a good idea, and besides, you already have your hands full with a certain dancer.'

'If you are referring to Kale, that is ridiculous. He is merely teaching me how to dance.'

Beth had no interest in Solomon, it was purely an ego boost but she was playing with fire with regard to Kale. She knew that she should pull back with him before things got out of hand, but the problem was that she was having too much fun and was enjoying the attention.

'Teaching you how to dance? You are priceless, Beth. If you really believe that, well then, fair play to you. But, somehow, I think you know that you are heading out to sea in very treacherous waters. Don't say I didn't warn you,' Jess said in an effort to be helpful, but sounding as if she was scolding her friend. 'I'm sorry if I sound like I'm having a go. I'm just trying to help, but I'm going to shut up now and leave you alone.'

They continued enjoying their meal and Claudia, the maître d', came over to see how they were. She was English and in her late twenties and had done very well to get to this level at such a young age. She had a great personality and the girls had already become quite friendly with her. They loved to hear about life below deck and she was happy to fill them in on the details.

Claudia had a small cabin, which she shared with her Mauritian fiancé. She had her own cleaner whom she paid $50 a month to change her linen and clean her cabin daily. As a manager, she enjoyed certain privileges that the lower-level staff didn't, such as dining in the restaurants. She told the girls that there was a staff nightclub and bar below deck, as well as a huge canteen. When they were on contract, all staff worked two shifts, seven days a week. The contracts were different lengths, depending on the job, but most were either six – or nine-month contracts. It's a very tough life and not for everyone, but she enjoyed it.

***

After dinner, they headed to the grand foyer where The Flutes were playing. They saw all their new dancer friends on the floor, moving to the music. Kale came over to them.

'Good evening ladies, how was your dinner?'

'Fantastic, we've done nothing but eat and drink all day, including attending a fantastic wine tasting so we certainly need to dance off a bit of it or we are going to go home two stone heavier!' Beth joked.

'Where is your other friend – Jess, isn't it?'

'She's gone upstairs to meet someone. She should be back in a few minutes.'

Kale didn't want to separate the girls while there were only two of them so he went back to the dance floor. 'When Jess comes back I'll take each of you out on the floor and you can show off your talent!' he joked.

A few minutes later, Jess returned alone. Kale came over to Beth and pulled her onto the floor. She looked at Amelia and smiled.

'I won't be long, I promise,' she said. Beth had been so absorbed in watching Kale that she hadn't noticed that Jess had come back on her own.

'Jess, where is Rick?' Amelia asked.

'I looked around the bar and he was nowhere to be seen so I decided to wait five minutes and then come back down.'

'Maybe he thought you weren't coming. I'm sure there is a very good explanation for all this. Do you know his room number or his surname?'

'No, it doesn't matter. If he wanted to meet me he would have been there.'

Jess was quite surprised at how disappointed she felt; why was she feeling this way about someone she had just met?

They sat enjoying the music and watching everyone dance. Kale occasionally came over to ask one of them out on the floor but he mostly danced with Beth. When the music finished they moved up to the Panorama Lounge and, shortly afterwards, Jess said she was going to go to the casino for a little while.

***

She couldn't wait to get to the roulette table. She needed to win back some of the money she had lost and to forget about the disappointment she was feeling over Rick. She had brought $500 with her and hoped her winning streak would return. She gathered herself together, headed to the $10 table and sat down. She exchanged her cash for chips and the game began. The adrenaline was pumping through her; it was intoxicating and she adored the sensation. She started off well. The players around her were losing and she was playing red and zero and winning, but then her luck changed. Fifteen minutes later, all her money was gone. Again.

***

Amelia knew that Beth was lost in Kale's spell so she left the Panorama Lounge and decided to pay a visit to Sam. She went upstairs to the room and pulled out more of her sexy lingerie; this time a Myla confection in a gorgeous duck-egg blue with a matching suspender belt and seamed French stockings. Sam loved it when she wore stockings and she felt really sexy in them. She had a matching robe for this set but she had left it at home, fearing that it would be too sexy for a girls' holiday. She fixed her make-up and was just coming out of the bathroom when Jess came in the door – she had come back to get some more money from the safe.

'Jesus, Amelia! What the fuck is going on?' Jess exclaimed. She was not normally someone who swore. 'Why are you dressed like that? Where are you going?'

Amelia was so shocked to see her friend that she almost couldn't breathe.

'I … I don't know, Jess, I can't explain.'

'Well, you had better try, because I have never seen you in anything like this before and there is obviously an explanation. Are you meeting someone?'

Amelia broke down in tears, pulled on her bathrobe and sat down on the bed.

'Oh, Jess, I'm sorry. I wanted to tell you but I couldn't. I was too embarrassed.' She was stuttering.

'Go on, I can't wait to hear this,' Jess said callously.

'I have been having an affair with a guy called Sam and he is here on the ship.'

'Oh my God, are you serious? I can't believe it! What do you mean he's here on the ship? You are so happy with Paul. I don't believe it; you're messing. Tell me it's not true!'

Amelia went on to explain how she had met Sam and how she had never meant to fall for him and didn't know what to do because she was now in love with him. She also explained how he had booked a room on the ship without her knowledge.

'Are you really annoyed, Jess?'

'No, but I am shocked and surprised. To be fair, Amelia, this is totally out of character for you. The only thing I am annoyed about is that you didn't feel you could confide in me or Beth. I am struggling to believe this; you were always our little goody two-shoes.' Jess was completely stunned by Amelia's revelations and it would take a while for them to sink in.

'I don't know what I'm going to do, Jess. I'm falling in deeper and deeper and I have so much to lose, but you'll understand when you meet him, he is divine.'

'I don't mean to sound cruel, Amelia, but at this moment in time I am not interested in meeting him. I need to absorb it all and we need to talk about things first. You have to remember that, even though you are my best friend, I love Paul too and I can't bear the thought of him being hurt. We need to find Beth.'

Amelia tried to fix her make-up and cover up her tear-swollen eyes with concealer. 'Can I go to Sam for a few minutes? I'll come straight back.' Amelia felt she had let Jess and Beth down; she should have trusted her friends and told them her secret.

'Yes, you go. I will try and find Beth. I'll see you back here shortly,' Jess said in an unintentionally snappy tone.

***

Sam opened the door and was surprised to see a very forlorn-looking Amelia standing in front of him. She pushed past him and sat down on the bed.

'It's out. Our secret is out. Jess knows.' Her voice was quivering and her body was shaking.

'Okay, love, try and take a deep breath. You say Jess knows about us. What happened?'

'I was getting ready to come and see you and I came out of the bathroom and she was standing at the safe getting out more money because she had run out of chips in the casino.'

'Surely you're not that surprised, sweetheart? I mean, it was probably inevitable they would find out no matter how hard we tried to conceal it.'

'I am surprised, actually, Sam, and you could sound a little more contrite about it all.'

I'm only saying that I am not shocked, that's all. How was she about it? Was she understanding and supportive?'

'Well, no – I don't know really. The thing is, she loves Paul and it's all been a huge shock but, ultimately, I know she will support me; she just needs time to digest it all. She quite rightly wanted to know why I hadn't trusted her enough to tell her in the first place.'

Sam put his arms around her and held her tightly. He knew that he had a tough battle on his hands fighting for the woman he loved.

***

Jess looked everywhere for Beth but she was nowhere to be seen. She started in the Panorama Lounge and then walked the decks, around by the pools and down the stairs to each of the bars, most of which had finished up for the night. It was a very large ship but surprisingly small in the main areas once people had gone to bed, so it was not difficult to see that she was not around.

She returned to their room and discovered that Amelia was not back. She didn't know Sam's room number so she scribbled a note saying that she was going to the casino. She threw it on the bed and left the room.

She was furious with both of them; the least Amelia could have done was come back to the room, she thought.

***

Beth had been dancing with Kale and hadn't noticed when Amelia had left.

'Remember I said that I am very friendly with Angelo, the hotel director?' Kale said. 'Well, he upgraded my stateroom to a suite when I came on the cruise.'

'What are you saying, Kale? That you have a beautiful room and you would like me to see it? Or are you hoping to seduce me?' Beth said flirtatiously.

'I am mad about you, Beth. I can't get you out of my head. Do you not feel the connection between us?'

'I do, Kale, but I am married and there is a lot at stake. I don't know how you can say you are falling in love with me when you barely know me. I have been hurt too many times in the past and need to take care of my heart."

He took her hand and pressed the lift button for deck nine.

***

Amelia went back to the room. She found the note but decided not to go down to the casino to look for Jess. Instead, she went to bed. For the first time since they had come on the cruise, she was not looking forward to the morning.

DAY FOUR

MYKONOS

BETH WOKE UP AND looked at Kale lying beside her. Her mind flashed back to last night. They were dancing and he had told her that he had this beautiful room and asked her if she would like to see it. The next thing she remembered was she was drinking champagne. After that it was all a bit of a blur.

She got out of bed, put on a robe and walked into the sitting room where there were three exquisite cream sofas forming three sides of a square in front of a fireplace, a huge flat-screen television, a large dining table for eight people, a bar with mirrors and crystal glasses on display along with different bottles of spirits. There was a baby grand piano in all its polished elegance but the best thing of all was the view. The curtains were open and there were floor-to-ceiling views of the sea and a beautiful village with whitewashed houses in the distance; it was breathtaking.

She walked around looking for the bathroom and found a stunning room with marble floors, double sinks, a raised Jacuzzi, a hydro shower and a separate toilet behind a glass partition. She had never seen anything like it before, even when she'd travelled with Sonny. This was in a different league and she couldn't believe you could have this kind of luxury on a ship. She went back to the window to watch as the ship came into the beautiful port.

She felt his arms around her. 'Enjoying the view?'

'I didn't realise how amazing it was last night. I don't remember much. Did we do anything?' she asked nervously, but seductively.

He kissed her neck, breathing into her ears and sending a shiver through her body. He gently opened the belt of the robe and pulled it so that it fell from her shoulders. He gasped at her beauty.

Choosing to ignore what she said, he replied, 'You are beautiful, Beth, I haven't stopped thinking about you since the moment we met'.

She turned around and moved her body so that her breasts were pressed against him and she could feel his hardness between her legs. His hands slid down; she was wet as he flicked her. They kissed urgently, their tongues hungry with desire and impatient for what lay ahead. She bent down, moving her hands with an experience that surprised him. He shouted out and lay down on the carpet, pulling her down on top of him.

He turned her over gently so that he was on top and she could feel his breath against her chest as he entered her; the sensation was heavenly as she lifted her legs, pulling him closer. They moved together. It was spicy and erotic and they knew there was no going back. Beth was playing with fire as usual.

She got up and took his hand; she pulled on her robe for privacy as they walked to the window to watch the ship. It was too late – they had docked.

***

Amelia woke up and saw that Jess was fast asleep. She had slept badly and had been tossing and turning all night. She was at her wits' end; she knew that she had upset Jess and, on top of that,

Beth still wasn't back. She went out onto the balcony. They had arrived in Mykonos and it was absolutely beautiful, with lots of whitewashed houses, endless small narrow streets, little cafes looking out on the water and, of course, the famous windmills. The ship had already docked and there was lots of activity going on so she went inside, poured herself a glass of water and went back out to watch the goings-on.

Jess had woken up. 'No sign of Beth yet, then?' she said in a very tired voice. She had been awake half the night thinking about Amelia's situation.

'No, but I think we both know that she hasn't fallen overboard. I can't believe that you couldn't find her last night but, more importantly, I can't believe that she wouldn't make any attempt to let us know that she is okay.'

'I suppose she was swept away by the moment and figured she is a big girl and doesn't need to answer to anyone for her actions, not even us.'

'I know, Jess, but I still think it's a little bit much. At least I have been coming back at night.'

'I don't think you have had much choice under the circumstances, do you?' Jess didn't mean to speak so sarcastically but she was still a bit peeved with Amelia.

'Alright, point taken. I'm sorry about last night, Jess. I really don't know what else to say. What do you think we should do about Beth? I worry about her sometimes. One of these days she is going to land herself in hot water.'

Amelia hadn't forgotten that they had not sorted out her own situation yet. They were so distracted by the disappearance of Beth that everything had been put on hold, but she was glad of the reprieve.

'Let's order room service and sit on the balcony drinking in this magnificent view while we wait for the prodigal daughter to return,' Jess said.

Half an hour later. the door opened and Beth arrived in. She noticed the girls were on the balcony and went straight out.

'Well, here she is!' Jess exclaimed. 'This had better be good. Presumably you were with Kale?'

Beth felt a bit uncomfortable. 'I know I have a lot of explaining to do but firstly I want to apologise for not telling you where I was and for causing you worry. As you already suspect, Kale and I were getting on better than we maybe we should have been and when we were dancing he told me that he was friendly with Angelo, the hotel director, and that he had been upgraded to a suite for the cruise. So, of course, he asked me if I would like to see it and curiosity got the better of me and …' Beth didn't need to say anything further.

'And the rest doesn't need much imagination,' Jess blurted out.

Beth tried to salvage some of her dignity. 'I told him that I was married and had been hurt many times before but, to be honest, I don't remember very much about last night. This morning, though, I will remember for a long time!' She was grinning from ear to ear. 'I think part of it is the physical chemistry – the sex was amazing!' Beth knew she could discuss this sort of things with Jess and Amelia.

'I'm not trying to be a wet blanket here but can you trust that he is not messing you around, Beth?' Jess asked. 'I don't mean to be cruel, but are you sure he is not using you. I mean, you hardly know him. Men don't get emotionally involved when they have sex the way women do. I don't want you to get hurt again. Is he married? Does he have children?'

She was quite firm with her friend. They were well used to her carry-on with men, but she didn't mean to bombard Beth with questions.

'I know, Jess, and I appreciate you being protective and concerned, but it's not one-sided. I'm enjoying being with him and I think it's what I need at the moment. I don't know much about him, but we are both consenting adults and the chemistry is definitely there, believe me,' Beth said dreamily.

'Okay, it seems that a lot happened overnight so there's nothing we can do about it but you are not going to be let off the hook just like that, Madam! We are your friends and have a duty to look after you so we will be discussing this a lot further,' Jess answered in a kind voice. 'There was another development while you were in the posh suite and I think we all need to have a long lunch after we've explored Mykonos.'

Jess brought everyone back to reality for a few moments. She felt that the conversation was getting a bit heavy and, besides, they needed to get their skates on if they were to see Mykonos. Amelia looked at her and smiled, grateful that she was holding off on telling Beth about Sam for a couple of hours so that they could enjoy Mykonos.

Beth would normally have wanted to know what Jess was referring to, but she was so distracted by what she had just told them that it didn't cross her mind.

***

They got themselves organised and took the sea shuttle to the waterfront in Mykonos. Once it landed, they hopped out and headed off to explore the town. They went through the cobbled streets, which they found a bit confusing, but they ended up at the windmills and once they had taken some photos, they found a café.

'It is the most stunning place I have ever been to,' Beth announced.

Amelia and Beth hadn't been to Mykonos before, and even though Jess had told them it was stunning, they couldn't believe the beauty of the place when they saw it in all its magnificence.

'I agree, Beth, it is beautiful. I have travelled far and wide and there are few places that surpass this,' Jess replied.

'Wait until you see Santorini. If you like Mykonos, you are going to fall madly in love with Santorini. My only hope is that it won't be too crowded, as that can detract from the experience a little.' Amelia said.

She had been to many of the Greek Islands with Paul and the kids when they'd gone island-hopping a few years previously.

'Okay, guys, I think we should head back to the ship and have some lunch. We have a lot to talk about and I think we've seen what we came for, unless anyone wants to do some shopping?'

'Is the shopping good here, Jess, or should we wait for some of the other ports?' Beth asked eagerly.

'Santorini has great shops; they are very touristy but good and, of course, we are going to Kusadasi tomorrow which is fantastic for shopping so I don't think we need to shop here.'

The girls knew that they had a lot to discuss and it was going to be a long lunch.

***

Once back on the ship, they headed up to the Wayfarer and helped themselves from the buffet before finding a table on the terrace. After they ordered wine, they sat back and the discussion started.

'You said something happened while I was gone last night, Jess?' Beth asked. She was curious but knew she was not off the hook herself.

'I think I'll let you take over here, Amelia.'

Her tone was sarcastic and Amelia felt a little uncomfortable.

'Last night, when you were dancing with Kale and Jess went to the casino, I went up to our room. Jess came back because she needed to get more money and she discovered me in my lingerie, getting ready to go out.' She hesitated for a moment and then continued. 'I have been having an affair at home with a man called Sam and he is on the ship.'

Amelia looked at Beth, who was in a state of shock. Amelia was the good girl out of the three of them, the one who never put a foot wrong.

'Say something, Beth, please!' Amelia pleaded.

Beth spoke as casually as she could manage.

'How did this happen? This is not you, Amelia. This is the sort of things that happens to me and nobody is very shocked when it does, but it is different with you. You adore Paul and you have such a good marriage – how did all this happen? I can't believe it; are you're both winding me up?'

Jess looked at Beth. 'It is not a wind-up, Beth,' she said. 'I know it's a shock. I reacted exactly as you have but none of us is perfect and these things happen, even to our saintly Amelia!'

Jess had had time to absorb things and was calm as she spoke, even though she was still astounded by the revelations.

Amelia broke down and sobbed. She felt sick and confused. Beth put her arms around her and told her that it would all be fine, that the three of them would work it out together, but, deep down, she was horrified, simply because it was Amelia.

Amelia went on to tell her how she had met Sam and how, against her better judgement, she had fallen in love with him. She told her that she was terrified that she was in love with two men and didn't know what to do.

'Amelia, I am afraid of saying the wrong thing now because I love you and have always looked up to you, but I am totally shocked. This really is so out of character for you, I can't believe that you are jeopardising your wonderful family like this. I am assuming Paul hasn't a clue?'

Beth was aware that she was treading on dangerous ground. She didn't want to hurt her friend, but she was horrified by what she'd heard.

Amelia looked over at her as the tears rolled down her face. 'No, he doesn't. I am so stupid, I don't know how I let this happen. I don't know what to do.'

They talked a bit more but they were going round in circles. They were emotionally drained so they decided to go and relax by the pool for a while in the hope that things would seem better in a few hours. Right now they needed a break from all the talk.

***

Later in the afternoon they came back to the room, feeling more relaxed.

'I think we should get a few glasses of vino and sit on the balcony. We need to work out a few things.' Jess spoke quietly but firmly. 'I'm going up to the Wayfarer. I'll be back in ten minutes and hopefully neither of you will have disappeared on me!'

Amelia and Beth went onto the balcony.

'This is really hard for Jess,' Amelia said. 'Between me and my mess, and you and Kale, we need to sort out what we are doing so as not to ruin the holiday for her. We came here as a threesome and now you and I have turned everything upside down. I think the priority should be spending time with each other, Beth. We booked the holiday so that we could be together. Sam booked himself without my knowledge so, as far as I'm concerned, he will have to take whatever time with me that he is given and Kale will have to do the same.'

'Okay, how are we going to work it?'

'The same way as when we came on the holiday. It's about the girls and if there is any time left over, that's fine. We need to have serious discussions about both situations and how we are going to resolve them. Neither of us can afford to lead double lives,' Amelia replied, making it all sound simple.

'I agree with what you're saying. I think it's vital that Jess feels we are putting our friendship first. Nothing should jeopardise the bond we have.'

'Do you think everything is okay with her? Last night when she discovered me she was returning to the room to get more money. Do you think she is gambling too much?'

'I think she is fine, Amelia. She knows she can talk to us if the gambling is getting out of hand and, anyway, she only brought $300 with her.'

'What about Rick – do you think that is a write-off? I'd love if she met someone special and he seems very charming.'

Just as Amelia was about to answer, Jess arrived back with the wine. Amelia and Beth told her what they had discussed and she was happy that the girls were going to make every effort to put their friendship first. She was still very concerned about Amelia; Beth's situation was not as serious as far as she was concerned.

They looked at the bible and planned their evening. They were going to have dinner in Orchid and go to a pool party afterwards. There was also a wine and cheese event before dinner in the Cave Wine Bar so they decided they would check that out too.

***

Meredith enjoyed her day in Mykonos but she'd felt lonely on her own. When Jean Claude had told her to come on this cruise from Rome, she had been quite surprised. They'd agreed at first that she would take a shorter, seven-night cruise out of Barcelona, but then the company had transferred him to captain the *Santana* so all their plans had to change.

She made a mental note to spend more time with the Irish girls; they seemed to be having a lot of fun together and didn't seem to mind her tagging along.

***

The grand foyer was full of the dancers and a 'Dancing with Stars' competition that was going to run over a few nights was under way. The couples were put together by the judges and it made for interesting viewing. Kale was taking part and that gave the girls a particular interest. They found themselves lovely comfy chairs very close to the dance floor. After round one, Kale and his dance partner were in first place but they dropped to second place in round two. It would be all to play for the following night!

The girls went to the wine and cheese tasting in the Cave Wine Bar where they met up with Meredith. Just as the tasting was about to begin, Rick walked in and came over to them.

'Any room for an errant, apologetic wine lover?' he asked.

The girls smiled and moved over a bit to make room for him just as the tasting began. It was a very interesting session, with different grape varieties, both red and white, being paired with cheeses. Some of the matches that they would never have considered surprised them, and they all made promises to host wine-tasting parties when they got home.

Rick approached Jess. 'I'm sorry, Jess, I was called away by the food and beverages manager last night and couldn't contact you. I know it seems like a lame excuse, but I am primarily supposed to be working while on the ship. I probably shouldn't have made an arrangement without taking your number in case I needed to let you know that something like this might happen.'

'It's fine, Rick, I didn't wait very long. I'm not in the habit of hanging around bars on my own and I'm here with my friends, so it really wasn't a problem,' Jess replied. She had been a bit upset but was determined not to let it show.

'Will you give me another chance?' I will take your mobile number and you can have all my details.'

'I think I can manage one more chance but that's it, so you better not mess it up this time!' Jess laughed. 'I am off to dinner now but we are going to the pool party later so maybe I will see you there?'

'Yes, that sounds good.' Rick was delighted that Jess had agreed to meet him; he was very keen on this pretty Irish girl.

***

Rick was a handsome man in a rugged way. He was fifty-two, about five foot seven, with dark features, bright blue eyes and a well-toned physique. When he had divorced his wife it had been very amicable and they had split the assets. He had bought a lovely three-bedroom penthouse apartment in Notting Hill so that there would be room for his two daughters to stay whenever they wanted. He was very close to his two girls and was very proud of them. Even though they were independent and leading their own lives, they were still the most important people in his life. For now.

***

The girls were a bit late coming to dinner because of the tasting but it didn't matter as their lovely team welcomed them with open arms. The drinks were delivered swiftly; the waiting staff had gotten to know them well by this stage!

'What is the story with Sam and Kale? Are you meeting them?' Jess asked. She looked at the girls, her coolness evident.

Beth answered first.

'I am not going to lie to you. I know Kale will be in the Panorama Lounge later because he is always wherever the dancing is.'

Amelia chimed in.

'I told Sam that nothing had changed in so far as he wouldn't be joining us in the bars or restaurants. I told him I will see him later on tonight at some point. I know that this has been a shock for both of you and that we need to talk about it, but I promise you I really had no idea that he had booked the cruise. There is no way I would have allowed that, so I am not going to let him intrude on our time together.'

Amelia meant what she said but she couldn't help wishing she could have some more time with Sam; the desire was killing her and all she could think about was sex.

***

They finished dinner and headed for the Morello Bar for a quick digestif. When they arrived up to the Solarium, the pool party was taking place in the indoor pool area. It was lit up with sophisticated lighting that changed from green to blue to pink at regular intervals. There was loud music and mermaids and other exotic creatures in the pool – all human but in fantastically real costumes. Waiters were walking around with champagne and there were acrobats in big balloon balls; it was all very different and entertaining.

There was a VIP area and Kale, who was well in with the powers that be, had put the girls' names on the VIP list. Cocktails and champagne were being handed around by ladies dressed in skimpy outfits with not a lot was left to the imagination. It was a wonderful evening and everyone was having a great time.

Beth was on the lookout out for Kale but he was not around so she figured she would see him later in the Panorama Lounge. Jess spotted Rick wandering around looking for her. She waved at him to come and join them. There was no problem getting him in as he was well known amongst the crew. She felt a strange feeling of happiness run through her; Rick seemed to be a decent guy and she wanted to get to know him a lot better.

There were a lot of the ship's officers at the party, mingling with the crowd in a somewhat formal manner. The girls ran into Meredith and were chatting to her about her recent visit to Ireland when a man approached their group and said: 'Hello there, my name is Angelo, the hotel director on the ship. I believe you are

Beth, Kale's friend?' Angelo was very charming in a wouldn't-trust-him-as-far-as-I'd-throw-him sort of way.

'Yes, that's right,' Beth replied. 'These are my friends, Jess and Amelia, and our friend, Meredith. It's very nice to meet you.'

Beth was taken aback that he knew who she was, but when she thought about it she realised that security on ships was very tight and it would have been his job to know these things, particularly when his friend was involved.

They stayed at the party and enjoyed themselves, mingling with the officers and drinking champagne; they were getting used to being treated like VIPs.

***

After the party ended, they all went up to the Panorama Lounge and, as expected, the floor was full of dancers, including Kale. As soon as they came in, he spotted them and winked at Beth, signalling that he would be over in a minute. They found a table and sat down, chatting away about the pool party and discussing Angelo, the handsome officer.

Jess and Rick started to chat were soon totally absorbed in each other. They discovered that they had a lot in common. Like Jess, Rick travelled a lot because of his job, had two daughters in their early twenties and was divorced. He told Jess that he had not had any serious relationship since his divorce. Whether or not that was true, she didn't know, but for the moment she was happy to take him at his word. They danced a couple of times and just as the moment felt right, he kissed her gently but in a way that left her wanting more. She could feel a butterfly sensation running through her body and wanted the feeling to last forever.

Beth was still on the dance floor with Kale so Amelia decided that nobody would notice if she went up to Sam. She didn't feel that she owed it to Meredith to stay with her. She hardly knew the girl and even though she was always the 'do anything for anyone type of person' she wasn't really in the mood to talk to her. She needed to talk to Sam.

When the music ended, Kale asked Beth if she would like to invite Jess and Rick back to the suite for a drink, remarking that they looked like they would appreciate continuing the evening!

They were delighted to accept and were completely stunned when they saw the suite. Beth had described it well but it was different to see it in reality. The suite had a butler but Kale dismissed him for the evening and served them drinks from the bar. He put some music on the Bose sound system and they settled down to enjoy the rest of the evening in style.

After about an hour, Jess reminded them that it was Kusadasi the next day and they would need to be ready for a lot of shopping so they decided to call it a night. Rick said he would walk her back to her room.

***

'I had a wonderful evening, Jess. I'll text you tomorrow and we can arrange to meet up, if that suits you. I really want spend time with you and get to know you. ' Rick cupped her face in his hands and kissed her gently. 'Sweet dreams.'

***

Jess felt as if her heart had skipped a beat. She couldn't remember when she'd last felt so happy. She opened the door and went inside; there was no sign of Amelia. A few minutes later, Beth arrived back.

'I thought you were staying with Kale?' Jess remarked.

'No, we came on this trip together and this is where I want to be.' Beth gave her friend a hug. 'What's the story with yourself and Rick?'

'I'll tell you tomorrow. I'm too tired now.'

BACK IN IRELAND

Paul had been sleeping really badly since Amelia had gone on the cruise. The reason for this was that the guilt was catching up with him. They had only spoken once since she'd left, but she had explained beforehand that they could only phone when they were in port because of the hefty satellite call charges and, to be fair, she had tried to ring him but he had missed a couple of calls.

She didn't deserve a husband like him; she was such a wonderful wife and he wondered why he was risking his marriage in this way. He made up his mind that he was going to end things with Marla. Then there would be no need for Amelia to find out about any of it. But it was easier in theory; the fact was that he was having an amazing time – Marla was insatiable and it was just as well he was fit because she was demanding every ounce of his energy.

When he went into the restaurant, it was full as usual. He couldn't believe how successful it had been since they had been awarded the first Michelin star. The second star seemed to attract a more international clientele and a longer waiting time for people to get a table, but he had set up a new online booking system which was working efficiently. They were always lucky enough to be full and had a long waiting list for cancellations. But he knew that he could not take all the credit; it was a joint effort and his beautiful wife had poured her heart and soul into the restaurant that bore her name.

Nobody at work knew about Marla and himself; Paul was sure about that. They were very careful and when they got together it was always in her apartment, but lately she had become a bit more demanding and had told him she was tired of being his 'dirty little secret'. Paul was worried that Marla was going to start becoming a problem for him and he needed to sort it out before she ruined everything. But he knew that he didn't want to give her up, not really.

***

Stephen's trip to Cork had gone very well and things were going to plan. As soon as Beth came home, he knew that it should all be ready. He thought about how long it had taken him to find the right location. He had been planning it for months as a surprise for her and couldn't wait to see the look on her face when she saw it. She had no idea of his plans, but he had been determined to make her dream come true.

When he had met Beth that day in the restaurant all those years before, he had fallen in love with her instantly. They had been on a blind date with mutual friends and he had thought the evening had gone brilliantly, but it had taken him a while to woo Beth; she had played very hard to get, however unintentional it was.

Stephen knew that her heart had been broken before she had met him, but she never told him much about her past. He often wondered if she truly loved him the way that he loved her – there wasn't a thing in the world he wouldn't do for her and he knew he just needed to show her and maybe that would make everything right between them.

Bethany told him that Beth had called a couple of times to check on Ed. She said she was having a great time but he hadn't heard from her himself since she had called to say she had arrived safely. He wasn't worried; it would all be different when she came home and saw what he had done for her.

DAY FIVE

KUSADASI

AMELIA WOKE UP IN Sam's bed and it was a wonderful feeling; she had never spent the night with him before and found herself wondering if she wanted to wake up with him every morning. The contemplation was overwhelming and she pushed it out of her mind.

She moved her body so that she was lying against him, her breasts flat against his back as she caressed him with her hands, moving her fingers gently all over him. She kissed his neck, breathing seductively into his ear and letting her hair tickle him as she moved. She felt a longing growing inside her and, just as she was about to slide herself on top of him, he turned around and looked at her lovingly. They kissed and moved together and after a few moments he plunged into her with a gentle force. He thrust hard and fast and she cried out, wanting more and more, until he finally collapsed into her arms in ecstasy.

'I love waking up and finding you here beside me, I wish it could be like this always,' Sam said. His kiss was tender.

Amelia knew she should say she wanted the same, but she couldn't; she suddenly felt really confused and strange. What was she doing? She was a happily married woman with a fabulous, sexy, successful husband who loved her, and here she was, lying in the arms of another man. She would have to stop. It wasn't right and she knew she shouldn't be here in bed with Sam. What about her friends? She had come on holiday with them and had spent the night away from them too.

It was all wrong, wrong. Tears started to roll down her cheeks. She had made an agreement with Beth only yesterday and had broken it already. She got out of the bed and pulled on her robe.

'Where are you going, darling?' Sam looked at her, puzzled by her movements.

'I can't do this, Sam, I'm sorry. I have to go back to the girls.'

Amelia was very upset. She rushed out the door without saying another word, leaving Sam alone trying to understand what had just happened. He had thought everything was going brilliantly; he could not fathom what had happened to her. He played it back in his mind, but nothing made any sense. He felt helpless and out of his depth.

***

Sam owned the trendiest restaurant in Galway. It served modern Mexican food and super-cool cocktails, and was so popular that it got away with having a 'no reservations' policy. He had grown up in New York but his parents were Irish and he had spent most of his summers in Ireland. Years earlier, he had decided that when he was older and ready to settle down, he would buy a home there. But it happened a lot sooner than he'd expected.

His parents owned a steakhouse in New York and he had grown up in the restaurant business but he was hungry for something of his own. After doing some market research, he knew that there was a particularly high density of young people living in Galway and that the city didn't have many mid-price restaurants, so he decided to open his first restaurant there. It was a brave move for a foreigner, but Sam was no amateur; he knew the area and he knew the trade. It wasn't long before the word spread, and *Sam's Place* and its owner became the talk of the town.

He seemed to have it all. He was good-looking, sexy and wealthy. He was the most eligible bachelor in Galway but nobody knew that he only had eyes for one woman and that she was already taken. Sam was forty, six foot tall and in very good shape. He had dark hair and hazel eyes and always dressed in high-end designer clothes. And he spoke with a New York accent, which added to the intrigue.

***

Amelia ran all the way back to the room. When she got to the door, she looked at her watch and saw that it was only 7.30am. She felt it was too early to disturb the girls because they liked to sleep on and they'd all had a very late night. Although she really needed to talk to them, she decided to go for a walk around the ship to be alone with her thoughts.

The *Santana* was amazing; you could walk for hours inside and out and never get bored, discovering new things you hadn't seen the day before. She went to the top deck and walked along the jogging track. She could see the shops and restaurants of Kusadasi in the distance and got excited at the thought of the shopping that lay ahead. It distracted her but she knew she needed to gather her thoughts so she decided to go inside and down to the library where she would be able to get some peace and quiet.

When she sat down, she had a strong feeling of anxiety in the pit of her stomach. She knew that she had to sort out this situation but she didn't know where to start. She had always thought that her life was pretty much perfect until she met Sam, but now she didn't know if she could live without him. One thing she knew for absolute certain was that she couldn't continue to lead a double life. She knew that Sam loved her, but the price she would pay to be with him would tear her apart; she would have to sacrifice her family and she didn't know if she could do that. Her head was thumping and she felt sick. Why, she wondered, had she let this happen?

She looked at her watch again; it was only 8am. She decided to go up to the Wayfarer, get a glass of juice and go and lie in the Solarium for a while.

When she looked at her watch again, it was 9.30am. She had dozed off on the sun lounger in the heavenly heat of the Solarium. She got up and headed down to the room. When she got to the door, she paused for a moment and then entered quietly. The two girls were still asleep, but Jess woke up when she heard her come in and called her over. She put her arms around her and gave her a big hug.

'I am so sorry for not coming back last night,' Amelia said as her eyes welled up. Jess was startled to see her friend so upset.

'You don't need to apologise to me. You are a grown woman and you can do what you like, sweetheart.' Jess was doing her best to comfort Amelia.

'I don't know what to do, Jess, I am so confused.'

Beth woke up. 'What's wrong, Amelia?' she asked gently.

'I'm so sorry, I'm ruining the holiday and I don't know how to fix it. I don't want this mess with Sam to spoil it all,' Amelia said, getting more and more distressed.

Beth and Jess looked at each other. Then Beth took over. 'Alright, let me just say that you are most certainly not ruining the holiday,' she said.

She settled Amelia and when she had calmed down, they changed the subject and talked about Kusadasi and their shopping lists; they had been planning this shopping trip for ages so they needed to get going.

***

'Kusadasi, here we come!' they all chimed together.

As they disembarked they saw that there were four other ships docked, so they knew the shops would be busy. They couldn't get there fast enough, each of them was worse than the other when it came to shopping. They had individual lists of presents and requests from home but they had one item in common on those lists – handbags.

A lot of the passengers had gone on excursions to Ephesus, but the girls preferred to do their own thing. The shore excursions were very expensive and you had to travel for hours in a coach, get up frightfully early and, most importantly of all, you lost a day of fantastic shopping! There was a tour guide handing out maps of the city so they took one, asked a few simple directions and headed off on their travels, excited at what lay ahead.

Almost every shop sold bags and many of them had people outside trying to lure potential customers in with promises of bargains. They went into every shop that caught their interest initially, but then realised that they would have to be more selective as there wasn't time to look in all of them. They were afraid to buy a bag in a shop in case they found better ones in the next shop; what a dilemma!

They stopped for a cold drink and to make a plan and do a spot of people-watching. There was a fantastic buzz about the place with hordes of people meandering through the streets and chatting to each other in different languages.

'Why don't we go down the street the guide recommended, the one that is off the beaten track and have a look at the shops there? If we don't see anything, we can go back to the second one we saw,' Jess suggested.

She was a bit of an expert at this which was not surprising given all the travelling she did. She and James had travelled extensively throughout Asia so she was well used to bargaining. But Jess didn't have much money. A lot of that was her own fault because of the gambling, but she also had a bit of an addiction to shoes and bags so, whenever she had the opportunity, she loved to go to a place with good shopping bargains and designer copies to stock up, even though it would never be the same as the real thing. She had quite a few genuine designer bags that James had bought her over the years, and she adored them. She had a special wardrobe in her bedroom just for her bags and shoes which would not have looked out of place in a celebrity's home.

The other two agreed with her and they wandered down a side street where they happened upon a large, glass-fronted shop with a gold sign above the door that read 'Jesika'. They knew it had to be a good omen, and they were not disappointed. Inside was a treasure trove of designer handbags, belts, sunglasses, suitcases and clothes and shoes. The girls were so excited they didn't know where to begin. Jess had a look at the quality and the prices and when she gave the thumbs-up, the shopping began!

'I can't believe we've been here for two hours,' Beth said, as she struggled to lift her bag of purchases. The other two were in the same boat.

'I can't ever remember having so much fun shopping – probably because my money has never gone so far!' Amelia said, laughing hysterically.

'This is one of the best designer copy shops I have ever come across and, believe me, I've seen hundreds. You can rest assured you've done brilliantly!' Jess said, thrilled for

Beth and Amelia and delighted with her own purchases too.

'I don't know how we are going to fit these in our luggage, Jess,' Amelia said, laughing.

'We'll worry about that later. Don't be fussing,' Beth cut in. She was always relaxed and casual about this sort of thing whereas Jess and Amelia were always extremely organised.

They had a few more bits and pieces to get before they headed back to the ship for a well-earned lunch.

'I'm starving. Does anyone feel like a burger?' Beth asked; she wasn't usually a 'burger' person and the other two were delighted to agree with her suggestion. 'Perfect, exactly what I want, all washed down with lots of delicious rosé.'

She was feeling the buzz of a successful shopping day and of the sex she would be having in a few hours' time.

'Amelia, do you want to talk about last night?' Beth asked tentatively.

'No, not really, though I know I have to sort this out and you are the only two people in the world that can help me do that. Oh God, I'm in such a mess, what have I done?'

They sat down and Beth put on her counselling hat. She was ready to try and sort out Amelia's problem.

***

Beth was slim, with beautiful sallow skin and dark-brown eyes that sparkled and shone. She was the eldest of three girls and had grown up in a small rural village in the south of Ireland. Her childhood had been a happy one until her mother tragically died of cancer when she was fifteen and her father, Dano, turned to the drink from the loneliness of losing his beloved wife.

Beth had been left to take on the responsibility of running the house and bringing up her two younger sisters, Jane and Anne. It had not been easy but she'd never complained because she had made a promise to herself that when she turned eighteen, her sisters would be able to look after themselves and she would be free to leave home and move to the big city to make a life for herself.

Dano didn't appreciate his wonderful daughter. Most of the time he just went out to the pub and left her alone but, a few times over the years, he hit her for no reason and she knew that she never wanted to marry a man like him.

When she had eventually left home and moved to Killarney, she found a job in a pub and this was where she met her first husband, David. They married within six months of meeting so they didn't really know each other properly. It was not long before Beth discovered that David was controlling and manipulative. She knew that she had to get away from him and decided to go to London. She didn't know anyone there but she was a survivor and knew that she would be okay. She worked in an Irish pub at night and did a secretarial course during the day. She finally found a job in a multinational company where she met Sonny, the father of her beloved daughter and the man who was responsible for breaking her heart.

***

'I have a system that we use in therapy sessions at work and we find it to be very successful,' Beth explained. 'It works on the basis of listing the pros and cons of both sides of an argument so that they are visually in front of you. You prioritise them and it should make things easier for you to assess the situation. If you want to discuss it afterwards, that's no problem, but if you don't, that's fine too. You should find the process helpful and it should give you answers that you can't see at the moment.'

Beth spent a few moments writing out the list of questions and answers and then gave it to Amelia who looked at the list with tears in her eyes.

'Thanks, Beth. You always know what to do. I hope the decision jumps out at me when I answer these questions, but, somehow, I don't think it's going to be that easy. Let's enjoy our lunch and I will go to the Solarium afterwards to work on the list.'

'And speaking of decisions, Beth, what are you going to do?' Jess asked.

'At the moment, I don't even want to think about it. I know it seems irresponsible and selfish but I am enjoying this holiday so much, and being with Kale is the icing on the cake. Stephen and I are not getting on and I don't know what's going to happen to us. We don't want the same things and I am not good at playing happy families.'

Jess looked at Amelia; she hadn't realised that things were as bad as this between Stephen and Beth and felt guilty at the thought that she hadn't been there for her friend.

'I'm not going to nag you, Beth, I want you to enjoy yourself and be happy but, like Amelia, you have decisions to make.'

'While I'm at the Solarium working on the list, what are you pair going to do?' Amelia asked. She was not looking forward to the task that lay ahead and was tempted not to bother with it and head up to Sam instead, but she knew she had to face the reality of the situation sooner rather than later.

'I'm going to take a wander around the ship and then go back to the room for a rest,' Jess said.

'I think I'll go and sit on the balcony with another glass of wine and read my book.' Beth was wondering if Kale was around; she would text him from the room.

***

Amelia found a sun lounger in front of the pool in the Solarium. It was quite busy which was unusual for a port day. What she loved about the Solarium was the peace and quiet and gorgeous warmth. The pool was heated; there was no music and no children were allowed. The atmosphere was one of utter relaxation, perfect for the task that lay ahead. She lay down with the back of the chair raised and began:

Paul

Do I love him?	Yes
Do I want to be with him all the time?	No
How is our physical relationship, do we have regular sex?	Yes
Is he good to me?	Yes
Does he love me more than anyone?	I think so
Will he be faithful to me always?	I think so
Can I see myself growing old with him?	Yes
Can I give Sam up?	Not sure

Sam

Do I love him?	Yes
Do I want to be with him all the time?	No
Are we sexually compatible?	Yes!
Is he good to me?	Yes
Does he love me more than anyone?	Yes
Will he be faithful to me always?	I think so
Can I see myself growing old with him?	Yes
Do I think he will mind not having a child?	I don't know
Will my children forgive me if I leave?	I don't know
Can I live without Paul?	I don't know
Can I live without my children?	No

Amelia couldn't believe how quickly she had answered the questions. She read over them a couple of times and realised that the only thing that really stood out was the children.

There was one question that she didn't have a definitive answer for and it was pretty crucial: would Sam want a child? After all, she already had three and he had none and she didn't want any more. Amelia knew her child-bearing days were over and she was very content to be enjoying the freedom that went with it. The last thing she wanted was to go back to changing nappies and doing school runs.

It appeared that Paul and Sam were pretty much on an equal footing. She couldn't believe it; if she hadn't filled out Beth's questionnaire, she would never have realised how strong her feelings for Sam were. Now she really was in trouble. She was a bit sad; in a strange way, she'd hoped that Paul would have come out ahead of Sam, but he had not and now she knew she had to choose between them. Would she be able to make her children understand if she chose Sam? The thought of it all made her feel physically sick again. She grabbed her bag, ran for the nearest bathroom and vomited. When she came out of the loo, she was visibly shaken and quite weak, so she went outside and sat down.

Amelia had always been a kind, good-natured person who would never hurt anyone, and that she was now considering tearing her family apart was so out of character for her that she felt as if she was in the wrong person's body. How was she going to do it? How could she break Paul's heart and turn her children's lives upside down? After a few minutes, she got up and wandered back to the room in a daze; she just couldn't think about it anymore.

***

Beth sent a text to Kale.
Are you around, do you have a couple of hours?
A minute later she got his reply.
At a dance session, will be finished in ten, see you in the suite in fifteen.
Beth smiled; she hadn't expected Kale to be free so it was the perfect addition to an already great day. She went back to the room, put on her bikini, fixed her hair and make-up and went out to the balcony for a few minutes.

Moments later, she walked down the stairs to deck nine, located at the front of the beautiful *Santana* and rang the bell. The door was opened by a butler dressed in full uniform. He invited her in and offered her a glass of champagne. After pouring it into a crystal flute, he disappeared.

Beth walked over to the window and looked out. There were people everywhere and the sun was splitting the rocks. She noticed that two of the ships had left already and, just as she was about to turn around, Kale came up behind her and kissed her intimately behind her ears, lifting her hair back as he whispered gently.

'My gorgeous, sexy, Irish girl! What a lovely surprise. Come and sit on the balcony. The view is truly spectacular.'

They sat for a while and talked. Beth told him about her day in Kusadasi while they drank more champagne. Then, when they couldn't wait any longer, he took her hand and led her through the arch into the bedroom, took off her robe and threw her gently on the magnificent oval bed which adorned with Egyptian cotton sheets and gold, silk drapes.

'Do you trust me, Beth?'

'What do you mean?'

'Do you think I would ever do anything to hurt you?'

'I don't really know you, Kale, but I feel in my heart that I can trust you and that you would never hurt me. Why are you asking me that?'

'I want to take you to a level of ecstasy you have never experienced. I want to make love to you so that you have the best orgasm of your life.'

Beth felt intoxicated by the rush of desire. She didn't know what lay ahead. She had never experienced an erotic, illicit situation like this before. She knew she should feel intimidated, or even a little bit apprehensive, but she didn't. There was silence and then she heard the sound of Led Zeppelin's 'Stairway to Heaven'. The scene was set.

He started at her toes with a feather, moving it up and down her body as he licked and caressed every inch of her. His teasing fingers made her wetter and wetter and he pulled away every time she moaned. She tried to pull him towards her but he kept teasing and stopped her anytime she tried to kiss him or touch him. She was aching now, and just when she thought she couldn't stand it any longer, he lifted her over the edge of the bed and turned her so she was hanging, face down on the bed; then he held her and entered her.

Her body quivered and she went into orbit. The feeling was sublime; she had never felt anything like it in her life.

When it subsided, she lifted herself back up onto the bed. She kissed him on his neck and shoulders and moved down his body gently, sensuously kissing him, touching his nipples and inside his thighs. She took him in her hands and licked up and down, rolling her tongue around before reaching the tip. She took it in her mouth little by little, flicking and swirling her tongue, teasing him as she went. She could feel him reaching his peak as he shouted out 'Yes, baby! Oh, yes!'

***

Jess went downstairs. She had a huge urge to visit the casino and she desperately needed to win. Rick had sent her a text her while they were in Kusadasi asking her if they could meet up later so she had only an hour or so to try her luck because she had made a hair appointment for 6pm. She had brought some cash with her so that she wouldn't have to go back to the room. She needed to be discreet so that the girls wouldn't find out but they had so much going on it was highly unlikely they would notice anyway.

She decided to stick with the roulette even though she loved blackjack but it was not lucrative enough and she really needed better odds. The problem with roulette was that it was about courage and risk and you had to be in the right frame of mind in order to hold your nerve.

The casino was on deck four, near the theatre. It was huge and opened onto the foyer so it could be seen as you walked past. Jess had been on other ships where the casinos were much smaller but she knew that it was a huge money-maker for ships and she wasn't surprised at how big the one on the *Santana* was. It had a bar at one end and shops lining the outside; it was opulent, just like the rest of the ship, and it smelled of money.

The slots were available all the time, but the tables only opened when the ship was at sea. Once it got busy, there was a croupier at each table and managers floating around supervising. There was a large section allocated to the slot machines; there must have been over a hundred of them and the main area was filled with poker, blackjack, roulette and craps tables.

When Jess saw all the tables closed she remembered the 'at sea' rule. Totally disheartened, she went over to the bar and ordered a gin and tonic. It didn't take her long to decide to have a little flutter on the slots. She had long felt the slots were a bit of a fix but the draw of the gamble was too much for her and she couldn't walk away. She looked around and was overwhelmed by the choice of machines. They all appeared to be the same, with flashing lights and multi-coloured symbols all begging her to choose them.

She sat down at a $1 fruit machine with three panels and a jackpot of $10,000, and tried to find the slot for the coins. She was quite surprised to see that the only way she could pay was by using her ship pass which she put in the slot without a moment's thought: this was dangerous with a capital D.

Jess played happily, winning small amounts here and there. When she looked at her watch, she saw that it was 6.05pm. She hadn't noticed the time flying by and hoped they'd kept her appointment in the hairdressers. She pressed the button to check her winnings and the balance on her card and couldn't believe her eyes when she saw that there was only $10 left from the $200 she had put in her 'virtual wallet'. What had she been thinking of playing on this stupid machine? At least if she had been using real money instead of her ship pass, she would have had a better idea of how much she was spending. It was a total scam and she was furious and disgusted with herself. How was she going to save herself from bankruptcy at this rate?

She ran down to the hair salon which was situated in the spa area next to the Solarium. It was truly luxurious with every pampering treatment imaginable available if you were willing to pay the madly inflated prices. Jess knew her blow-dry was expensive at $50 plus gratuity, but she didn't care; she hadn't been on any dates since her marriage had broken up. Candice did her nails while Nicki did her hair and she had a glorious time chatting to them about life at sea. Jess couldn't believe that they were working on nine-month contracts, seven days a week with no day off, but they all seemed to be so happy, like the other crew all over the ship. She figured that they must be well looked after, otherwise they wouldn't do it.

***

When she got back to the room, the other two were already dressed and ready.

'Your hair is gorgeous. I forgot you were meeting Rick. I was wondering where you were and thought you might have been in the casino,' Amelia said jokingly.

'I'm going to jump into my finery, put on my make-up and I'll follow you two down.'

Jess was taken aback by Amelia's remark about the casino and hoped it hadn't shown.

***

The girls went down to the foyer. The second heat of the 'Dancing with the Stars' was taking place and Kale and his dance partner were in it. The place was packed and they couldn't get a seat so they got their drinks and found a spot to stand. The competitors had to dance the waltz, the foxtrot and the cha-cha. Kale had told Beth that his best dance was the waltz and she was relieved that it was one of the dances tonight. The music was in full swing and, as the couples danced, Marcus – the cruise director – commentated while the judges walked around with notebooks. At the end of the three rounds, Marcus thanked the contestants and announced that the two finalists were Kale and Dana and Sid and Alana.

When Jess arrived they moved to the Morello Bar; they needed to plan the evening now that things had become a little more complicated. Beth and Amelia were delighted that Jess had met someone. They had been trying to encourage her to do online dating but she wasn't keen and they really wanted her to be happy again.

'What are your plans with Rick?' Amelia asked excitedly.

'I have no idea. I told him that I would let him know once we had made our plans for the evening.' She hadn't been out with anyone since she'd separated from James and she was really keen to meet up with Rick. 'I am so nervous. I feel like I've forgotten what to do with a man! What if he wants me to sleep with him?'

'You will be fine. Just be yourself and don't feel any pressure to do something that doesn't feel right. I think you will know yourself and you have the protection of three thousand passengers and the ship's security team if things get out of hand,' Beth said. She was confident that Rick would treat Jess with respect; she got a good vibe from him.

'I guarantee you that your body will be in control, and if things are right between the two of you, it will happen naturally. You will feel nothing except pure excitement, just like you did when you met James!' Amelia interrupted, giggling.

'Well, you should know!' Jess retorted jokingly although, underneath it all, she was worried for her friend.

Amelia thought about Sam and what had happened earlier that morning. She hadn't heard from him since and wasn't sure what to do.

'I need to talk to you two about Sam, but I don't want you to be mad with me. I had a bit of a problem with him this morning. We woke up together and it was a wonderful feeling but then I felt this wave of panic sweep across me. It was really strange. I didn't know what to do. All I knew was that I had to get out of there, so I left him without any explanation and ran out the door, and I haven't had any communication from him since. I don't know what to do now. The poor guy must be wondering what the hell is going on.' Amelia sounded flustered.

'I can understand exactly why it happened, Amelia. You have to understand that this is totally outside the norm for you. Firstly, you had never spent a night with Sam before you came on the ship, and, secondly, it was probably the reality of the seriousness of the situation after yesterday's outburst. You are a very genuine and kind person, and the very thought of making the decision that you are facing has obviously been playing on your mind. I think you should find Sam and tell him exactly how you are feeling. Why should you feel all the pain? Let him share the burden.'

Beth was handing out her expert advice again, but she didn't feel a bit sorry for Sam.

'I'm not trying to be harsh, Amelia, but unless you give Sam up, you are facing a very tough road so you need to be prepared and you need to be sure it's what you want. Your children and your family are probably going to turn against you, and maybe some of your friends too. You need to ask yourself if you are willing to pay the price.'

Amelia usually felt better after talking to Beth but this time she felt a sense of fear run through her body. The tears came rolling down her cheeks but she left her friends before they could comfort her because she knew that Beth was right and that she needed to talk to Sam.

***

Amelia knocked on Sam's door but there was no reply. She figured he must have gone to dinner so she went down to the private restaurant that was for the Jade-class passengers. She found him sitting alone at a table by the window. She realised how lonely it must have been for him over the past few days.

When he looked up and saw her, he smiled and beckoned her over. She walked nervously across the small dining room and sat down opposite him.

'I'm sorry about this morning,' she said, anguish evident in her eyes.

'I am still trying to understand what happened. What did I do, love?' He was clearly concerned.

'You didn't do anything, Sam. I was just totally overwhelmed by the situation and I felt panicked. I am in a very different situation to you; I have so much to lose because of our relationship, especially my children. I spent some time yesterday trying to work things out in my head because I am so confused. I need to have a long talk with you about everything but I can't do it now because I have to go to dinner with the girls. I'll try and come up to your room straight afterwards.'

'That sounds good. I'll see you later,' he said. They kissed and Amelia left.

***

The girls had a reservation in Bellissimo and they were really looking forward to it, having had a fabulous lunch there a few days earlier.

'How did it go with Sam?' Beth asked.

Amelia told her friends that she needed to talk to Sam and they agreed that Jess would go on her date and that Beth would meet Kale.

'It's getting harder and harder. I can't go on like this I'm going to tell him that I have made up my mind,' Amelia said, wondering if her stomach would ever start feeling normal again.

'And have you made up your mind?' Beth asked, curious to hear the answer.

Amelia looked at her sadly but didn't answer.

***

As they walked towards the Cave Wine Bar, they could see that Rick and Kale sitting opposite each other with a bottle of champagne on ice on their table. They were chatting and didn't notice the girls arrive. Jess could feel her nerves rising. Rick looked up and smiled, then he walked over, took her hand and kissed it.

'You look beautiful, Jess. That's a lovely dress.' Rick was clearly very keen on her and Beth and Amelia were grinning like Cheshire cats.

'Thank you, Rick, I bought it in New York especially for the cruise.'

'I took the liberty of ordering a bottle of my champagne. It is exclusive to the *Santana* and her sister ships and I would be very interested in your feedback, ladies.'

The girls loved a bit of glamour and style and were very taken with Rick; they could get very used to this treatment! He poured the champagne, explaining about the grape it came from and the story of the small family vineyard in Champagne, France, and their long history of wine making. It was a fascinating insight to the world of champagne and they enjoyed it immensely.

***

When the bottle was finished, Rick asked Jess if she would like to go for a walk. He put his arm around her shoulders to lead her out of the bar then he took it away and held her hand instead.

'I have to be a little bit discreet in the public areas, Jess, I am sure you can understand.'

'Of course. Where are we going?'

'I thought we could go to the Piano Bar. There is a fantastic pianist playing tonight called Andre and I think you will really enjoy it.'

'I don't know that bar. Is it only for officers?'

'Yes, it's a private bar for the captain and senior officers, but I can use it too. We can invite a small number of guests when there are music nights and tonight is a music night.'

Jess began to forget her nerves as she became excited at the thought of seeing the captain's Piano Bar. The bar was on deck nine, very close to the bridge and not far from Kale's suite. Rick explained that they would be going into a private part of the ship as he entered his code on the keypad but he assured her that she did not need a code to exit. He then led her down a corridor that looked identical to the one that her own room was on. When they reached the end, Jess could hear the soft sound of 'Ballade Pour Adeline'.

Rick opened the door and they went inside. The room was not dissimilar to the one Kale was using as his love nest but it had a different shape. It had a very opulent with a large crystal chandelier overhead and floor-to-ceiling windows. There was a grand piano at one end of the room where Andre was playing, and a beautiful rosewood bar with several stools at the other end of the room. In another area there was a large glass dining table with eight ornate chairs and three large, stylish but comfy looking sofas. All the walls were covered with beautiful, expensive looking paintings.

Jess felt a little intimidated, but Rick took her by the hand and led her over to the captain to be introduced. She then met a few more of the officers and was offered a glass of champagne before they sat down to enjoy the music.

When the music ended, Rick spoke:

'Jess, I don't want the night to end and I don't think you do either. Would you join me for a nightcap in my room?'

Jess didn't know what to do; she wanted to go but she felt it would make her look cheap. 'Rick, I have had a wonderful evening but I really don't think that is a very good idea,' she said.

'I think I know what's on your mind,' Rick replied, sensing her hesitation.

'I'm not in the habit of going to bedrooms with men that I barely know,' she added, somewhat indignant.

'I understand completely but I just want us to have a bit more time together in private and, anyway, the bars have all finished. I promise you, Jess, I won't do anything you don't want me to do.'

***

Rick took her by the hand and led her down the corridor to his room. He opened the door and stood back to let her go in ahead of him. The room was the same as hers but had a double bed instead of twin beds.

He went over to the table and opened a bottle of champagne; he always had one on ice in his room. He poured two glasses and came back over to Jess. He looked into her eyes; he could see she wanted him just as much as he wanted her but he knew he couldn't rush things or he would frighten her off.

He put the glasses on the table and took her in his arms, kissing her expertly and sending a rush of desire shooting through her. She responded and he took her by the hand over to the sofa where they sat down. Jess was feeling very turned on and quite tipsy. She knew she needed to take control of the situation before it got out of hand.

'I want you, Jess. Will you let me make love to you?'

'Maybe, Rick, but not tonight. We agreed to have a nightcap and take it slowly, remember?' She reminded him of what he already knew.

'You are beautiful and I am crazy about you, but I can wait if that is what I have to do. Let's sit on the balcony for a while and then I will take you back to your room.'

Jess felt relieved but desire was rushing through her and she knew that she wanted Rick to make love to her, but it was no harm to make him wait. At least now she knew that she wasn't afraid. The girls were right, as usual!

***

Once Jess and Rick had left, Beth and Amelia looked at each other. Both of them knew that they wanted to be with the guys so, rather than beat around the bush, Amelia made her excuses and left. Once she arrived at Sam's room, she hesitated for a moment, unsure of how she was going to approach things. After a minute or two, she knocked on the door. Sam opened it and, as always, gave her a passionate kiss and held her in his arms, showing her how happy he was to see her.

Amelia pulled away from him and went to sit down on the sofa.

'I am so confused, Sam, I really don't know what I'm going to do. Part of me is really angry with you because you have turned this holiday into a time of emotional turmoil and anxiety, and the other part of me is insanely happy to spend time with you. I am feeling sick from the pressure of it all. I feel tired and actually vomited yesterday, so I really need to sort it out. I want to be with you but if I leave Paul, my family and – most importantly – my children, will hate me. I don't know if I can bear it.'

Amelia had become quite stressed and fidgety. Sam had never seen her like this before.

'I am sorry that you are going through this, sweetheart. I just don't want a future without you in it. I know it is very selfish, but that's how I feel. They will come around in time. They all love you and want you to be happy. I will help you; you know we are in this together.'

'It's not that simple, Sam, I don't know how I would tell Paul and the kids. How do you tell your husband and children that you are leaving them? I need to go back to the room to the girls, my head is swimming and I am not feeling well. This was supposed to be a holiday with my friends and now I find my life has been turned upside down. You'll have to be patient with me.'

She got up and kissed him before heading back to her room.

***

Beth and Kale left the Cave Wine Bar shortly after Jess. While they were dancing, Beth noticed Meredith arriving and waving over at them so, at the end of the song, they sat down and joined her. They talked about their successful shopping day in Kusadasi and Beth told her all about the bags they'd bought and how she had no idea how they were going to fit them all in their suitcases.

'How was your day, Meredith?' Kale asked.

'Oh, I just had a quick look around Kusadasi and came back on board to relax and have a massage. I don't feel like doing very much at the moment,' she replied.

'I hope you don't mind me asking but was your marriage break-up very recent?' Beth asked.

'We split about a month ago and I really needed to go on a break somewhere but none of my friends were free to come with me so I decided to go alone and a cruise seemed to be the perfect choice. I figured I would meet a few people on board to chat to,' Meredith replied without giving away very much. She knew she needed to keep to the same story so if she kept it brief it would be easier to remember.

'I don't mean to be rude, Meredith, but don't you think you should have gotten it right by now – this is your third marriage, after all.'

Beth was being uncharacteristically sharp-tongued and unsympathetic but she had been drinking all day and, for some reason, she didn't like the woman.

'Yes, I probably should,' Meredith replied snappishly, 'but if you knew the reasons, maybe you would understand a bit better and not make assumptions.'

Kale decided to intervene and whisked Beth away to dance; both women had already said too much for one night.

When the music ended, Beth went down to Kale's suite. She knew she was going to have a good time but she would have to make sure she went back to her own room tonight as she'd promised Jess and Amelia that she would.

DAY SIX

RHODES

Amelia looked around when she woke up. She was happy that all three of them were in the room together, just the way it should be. She went out onto the balcony and was delighted to see that they were portside and docked against the pier in Rhodes. She noticed a high, medieval wall that looked like it was hiding the town behind it. She was really looking forward to visiting Rhodes and wanted to make the most of the day. The situation with Sam was going to have to wait until later; she needed a break from it.

She hadn't slept very well. She had been worrying about the fact that she had been feeling nauseous in the mornings for the past couple of weeks. Could she be pregnant? Surely not! She was in menopause now and hadn't had a period for six months. But if she was pregnant, it would certainly explain why she had been feeling so unwell. She made up her mind to do a test later in the day because she needed to know once and for all.

She read the bible and noticed that a 'Who Wants to be a Millionaire' show was on at 7pm. There was another hands-on cookery demonstration at 5pm; that would be a definite. She thought it might be an idea to do a hop-on hop-off tour in Rhodes as they had most of their shopping done, so the pressure of getting the presents was over and she knew Rhodes was full of history.

Jess and Beth woke up and joined her on the balcony.

'I was just thinking that this is what it's all about – the three of us being together,' Amelia blurted out remorsefully.

'I know, and here we are, so let's not say another word,' Jess said, hugging her.

'We are portside today which is brill, especially here because it's a particularly lovely view,' Amelia told her friends.

'How long have you been up?' Beth asked her.

'I woke at 8am and I've been having a lovely time reading the bible and watching the action. It's a really historic place and I'm dying to get off and have a look around. What would you think about taking a hop-on hop-off bus?'

'Perfect. We certainly need a bit of culture after all that shopping in Kusadasi. It might be nice to have lunch here, too, it looks so quaint,' Beth answered.

***

They disembarked and headed for the bus stop. There was already a long queue forming when they saw Meredith who called out to them; she was nearly at the top so, very cheekily, they joined her, not looking behind them at the glares they were getting.

'Thanks, you're a star!' Jess whispered in Meredith's ear, delighted they hadn't had to join the long queue.

'No problem at all, Jess. Maybe we could all get together after the ride for a drink or some lunch locally?'

Meredith had a strong Texan accent and the girls had warmed to her from the moment they'd met, even though Beth was having second thoughts.

'That's a great idea. In the meantime, enjoy the bus,' Amelia said.

Even with the breeze of the moving bus, it was very hot but they stuck with it and put their earphones on. They had made a decision to stay on board and listen to the guide rather than get on and off as the queues were too long at the stops and they didn't want to waste the day. They enjoyed the tour which took in all the main sights, and they were given a chance to take plenty of photos along the way.

When they finally got off the bus, they met up with Meredith and decided to head towards the main square where, they had been told, there were lots of local restaurants.

'This is such a pretty place, I am totally loving it which is funny because I would never have thought of coming here for a holiday,' Beth said.

'That's the lovely thing about a cruise. You get a taster of different places and can decide if you want to come back for a longer stay,' Jess said. She always considered herself the expert on everything to do with travel even though she wasn't a show-off.

'I know, but all I am saying is that it was unexpected. We were all prepared for Santorini being amazing, and we knew Mykonos would be beautiful, but I don't recall anyone saying that Rhodes would be special.' Beth felt she needed to justify her previous remark.

'Let's pick a restaurant, guys, I'm starving and thirsty,' Meredith said. She was getting a little tetchy which amused the girls since they hardly knew her. 'How about this one here? It has a lovely view.' She was pointing to a rooftop restaurant to the left of the square and up a narrow staircase.

'Great, decision made. Let's go,' Amelia said as she and the girls followed Meredith up the stairs.

Within minutes they were sitting looking out on the square watching the world go by.

Perfect.

***

The restaurant offered a combination of Greek and Italian cuisine and they ordered a meze of different dips and starters between them and a pizza each. The prices were very reasonable, especially the wine which arrived in a hand-painted carafe. The view was wonderful and they were in their element.

They spent a bit of time getting to know more about each other. Beth had forgotten about the previous night's conversation with Meredith and had said nothing to the other two. Meredith acted like she had forgotten about it too. The girls found out that the Texan was fifty-three years old, recently divorced for the third time, and had two grown-up children. She was managing director of her own cosmetic surgery company, and her keen interest in wine had come from her first husband who'd owned a chain of wine stores in Texas. She had come on the cruise at the last minute to destress from her third divorce.

They lingered over lunch and when Amelia looked at her watch she saw that it was 5pm. 'Oh my God! The ship is leaving at 6pm and we have to be on board by 5.30pm. I can't believe we've been here for four hours. Let's get the bill and hurry back.'

She hated being late for anything and her stress levels were rising. She was also thinking about the pregnancy test she had bought and she was anxious to slip away to do it.

***

They arrived to the ship just in time; the crew pretended to be cross and wagged their fingers at them, but the girls knew very well that the ship would most definitely have left without them and that they were very lucky they had noticed the time.

They suggested that Meredith join them for dinner and she was delighted. It seemed they had developed a new friendship and, for a change, it didn't involve a man! They had missed the cooking class but decided they would aim for the 'Who wants to be a Millionaire' show at 7pm.

As she was getting ready for the evening, Jess heard her phone beep.

Hi Jess, are you free this evening after dinner?

Jess turned to the others and told them what Rick's text said.

'Tell him you will meet him in the Cave Wine Bar at 10.15pm. We have to encourage this romance,' Beth said, delighted for her friend.

I can meet you at 10.15p., I'm having dinner with the girls first. Will that work for you?

Yes, that suits me perfectly. I have to be around for service anyway. See you then. Rick xx

'Things seem to going well, Jess. How do you feel about him?' Amelia asked.

Jess blushed, suddenly embarrassed.

'Don't ask me that! You know it's early days and I'm shy about it all.' She changed the subject immediately. She didn't want to tell them too much just yet. 'What do you think of Meredith?' she asked, to distract them from her and Rick.

'She is so much fun; maybe she will take our minds off our problems for a while,' Amelia answered. She couldn't help but feel that she had cast a bit of a shadow over the trip and was feeling guilty.

'There is no doubt about it, Amelia, she might even be able to offer some advice about what to do about you two and your tricky situations,' Jess said in jest.

'I'm not sure she's best placed to be doling out advice given her relationship history. She has just divorced for the third time, has she not?' Beth commented. She was not sure if she wanted to involve her too much in their holiday.

'Well, I think it would be interesting to hear what she has to say. Maybe she's been in a similar situation. One thing I do know is that dinner will be a bit different tonight,' Jess said, quite pleased at the thought that Meredith might be able to offer a different perspective on things.

***

They headed down to the theatre where 'Who wants to be a Millionaire' was on. It was quite full so they only managed to get seats at the back. Marcus was in full swing; he loved his job as cruise director and particularly loved the shows that involved audience participation. The set was exactly as it appears on the TV show, with the ship's guests as the live audience. They were doing it the original way where there was a panel of people with buzzers for 'fastest finger first'. The contestants would be chosen from the winners of those rounds.

It turned out to be a lot of fun. The winning contestant got as far as $125,000 and won a free cruise. It was such a success that Marcus said he would organise another one, this time with couples. Anyone interested was invited to put their names down for inclusion in a draw for contestants. Without thinking too much about it, the girls decided they would put their names down before heading off to the Cave Wine Bar. Meredith met them there, as arranged, and they had a drink before heading to dinner.

***

In the restaurant, Solomon and the team gave the group of women a huge welcome. The menu was perused and decisions made and then they sat back and relaxed in each other's company. They chatted for a while about their day in Rhodes and how it had been an unexpected delight and then Jess, who was never one to beat around the bush, turned to Amelia.

'Amelia, I think you should tell Meredith about yourself and Sam and see if she can give you any direction, a fresh approach maybe?'

Amelia looked at her friend, a little embarrassed but not at all surprised; after all, they had said in the room that they were going to tell Meredith about Sam and Kale despite Beth's misgivings.

'Meredith, I will give you the short version or else we will be here until the ship docks tomorrow morning,' Amelia said.

She explained about herself and Sam and how she had now come to a crossroads where she had to make a choice. She told her about the list of questions Beth had given her to try and help her sort out the situation, and how Sam had come out marginally on top but she didn't tell any of them about her pregnancy worries. She knew she needed to do the test; aside from anything else, she was drinking a lot of alcohol and would have to stop if the test proved positive.

Meredith didn't seem at all fazed by what Amelia said.

'You seem quite distracted, Amelia, I think you are very stressed by the situation and you need to get it resolved as quickly as possible. Like you, I married my childhood sweetheart and always thought we would live happily ever after, but he cheated on me and I couldn't get over it. My second husband was younger than me by ten years and he was very handsome but it didn't last. We were together for ten years and then I realised we didn't have anything in common. When I married my third husband a year after divorcing the second one, I really thought I had finally found my soulmate but he turned out to be bisexual and I came home one day to find him in bed with a man. That only happened very recently so it is still quite raw.'

Meredith couldn't believe how well she was able to concoct such a story.

'Jesus, Meredith, you've really been through it. How did you cope?'

Beth was fascinated by Meredith's story but she wondered if it was a little exaggerated. For some reason, she didn't trust her.

'I guess I went from one man to the next without taking proper time to recover from each break-up and so I found myself on the rebound all the time. From as far back as I can remember, I've always had boyfriends. I hate being on my own and I've gone from one relationship to the next without really knowing whether they were truly right for me. I have decided now that I am going to make some changes. I am fifty-three and three times divorced so I have to re-evaluate the situation and take stock.'

She made a mental note to remember what she had told them, maybe even make notes; she couldn't afford to forget any details.

'Well, I think we all need to do that, Meredith, especially me!' Beth said. 'I am on my second marriage but the true love of my life was a married man and he is the father of one of my children.'

Beth told Meredith about David, Sonny and Stephen. The conversation was getting a bit too deep and Jess began to wonder if perhaps they shouldn't be telling this woman so much; she was a stranger, after all.

'I will give you this one piece of advice. Think every decision through very carefully before you make it; you can't reverse damage once it has been done,' Meredith said.

At that point, they looked around and saw that they were amongst the last tables still in the restaurant. They didn't want to hold Solomon and the team back, so they moved out to the Morello Bar where The Flutes were playing.

Amelia was conscious that she hadn't done the pregnancy test yet because she hadn't had five minutes to herself all day.

'I want to fix my make-up and I forgot to bring it with me so I'm going to run upstairs for a few minutes. Does anyone need anything from the room?'

'Yes, can you bring down my wrap?' Jess asked, 'I don't know if I'll be going outside with Rick.'

Amelia nodded and went upstairs, her stomach churning in anticipation.

***

She had hidden the test in her suitcase under the bed so she pulled it out and went into the bathroom knowing that she had a few minutes of agony ahead while she waited.

***

'There is something else going on with Amelia,' Beth said. 'I know she is stressed over Sam but there is something else and I can't put my finger on it.'

She was directing the comments at Jess but Meredith overheard her.

'I don't know if I'm speaking out of turn here, ladies, but would there be any chance that Amelia could be pregnant?'

Beth and Jess looked at each other, both completely speechless. Meredith continued.

'When a woman is pregnant, she has a certain aura about her and it is not always noticeable if you know them well, but I am rarely wrong when I see it and I am pretty sure Amelia is pregnant.'

'What do you mean, Meredith? How can you tell? I mean, she isn't even showing a bump.'

Beth was horrified and concerned for her friend and she didn't appreciate this intrusion from Meredith.

'It's difficult to explain, Beth, it's just a presence and a way about her. As I said, if you know the person, you probably won't see it.'

'Oh my God, we're all fifty, Meredith! This is not funny and I hope you are wrong. Amelia will have a heart attack. None of us want any more children at this stage in our lives. Do you think she is pregnant and she's not telling us?' Jess said, looking at Beth.

'Of course not. How would she keep something like that to herself? That is enough to send anyone our age over the edge, Jess. Think about it. And besides, she is still drinking alcohol which she wouldn't do if she knew she was pregnant.

'I know, but she did manage to keep Sam a secret,' Jess said in a panicky voice.

At that moment, Rick came over and Jess stood up. He kissed her on both cheeks.

'Are you ready to go or do you want to have a drink here first?' he asked.

'I've just ordered one so why don't we have one here and then head on?'

Jess didn't know if Rick had made plans for them, but she had been totally thrown by Meredith's comments and wanted to wait for Amelia to return.

'Absolutely, suits me fine.' He called the waiter and ordered a Martini.

***

Amelia looked at the two lines and the tears rolled down her face. Her mind started to race as she tried to count the days back to her last period. The problem was that she was perimenopausal so she had been missing periods and had only had two in the past year. She had heard stories about women getting pregnant during the menopause but never in a million years did she think it would happen to her. Her heart was pumping and she felt sick. What was she going to do? She couldn't have a baby, not at her age. She tried to gather herself. How far gone was she? She couldn't bear to think about it.

She sat on the bed, feeling dizzy; everything was such a mess. She remembered how she had gotten pregnant before she was married and how much it had affected things. Now, here she was again, with an unplanned pregnancy, only this time it was a lot more serious. She reprimanded herself; had she not learnt anything? It suddenly dawned on her that she didn't even know if the baby was Paul's or Sam's. She started to cry. She cried and cried until she remembered where she was.

She wanted to stay in the room and never face the world again but she knew they would all be wondering where she was so she hurriedly fixed herself up and reluctantly went back downstairs.

***

She saw them all sitting together and noticed that Rick had arrived too.

'You look a bit weary, Amelia, are you okay?' Jess asked.

Amelia hoped she would be able to hold her composure but the shock was just too much. She needed to talk to her friends but she didn't want Meredith or Rick to be there. She was fighting back the tears.

'I need to talk to the two of you for a minute in private. I'm sorry, Meredith and Rick, please excuse us, we'll be back in a few minutes.'

Amelia was so distraught with her situation that it hadn't occurred to her that Jess was on a date. Jess didn't know what was going on. She shrugged her shoulders at Rick and said she would be back shortly.

***

They all went up to the room. Beth and Jess were worried as to why Amelia was in such a state of distress. Once they were safely inside the door, she blurted it out.

I'm pregnant! I can't believe it, what am I going to do?' she said, becoming hysterical.

Thanks to Meredith, Beth and Jess had been somewhat prepared and weren't too shocked by her announcement, but it didn't take away from the fact that it was a nightmare and they had absolutely no idea what she was going to do, or what they should say to her.

'Amelia, calm down, love. Sit down.' Beth had coped with hundreds of difficult situations in her time but this was one of the hardest because it was happening to her best friend and she was starting to feel a little out of her depth. But she didn't get a chance to say anything else, as Amelia started to tell her story.

'I haven't been feeling well for most of the trip and I thought it was the anxiety of having Sam on board, but then alarm bells started to ring when I vomited for no apparent reason. I thought that there could be a remote possibility that I might be pregnant.

I bought a test, not really thinking that it would be positive; it was really just to make myself feel better by ruling it out. What am I going to do?' She looked at her friends, terrified.

'Look, pet, it's not the end of the world. I know you are in shock and scared and upset but when you've had a bit of time to digest it, we can talk it through. The most important thing for the moment is that we make sure you and the baby are well, so, first thing tomorrow morning, you are going down to the medical centre.'

Beth tried her best to reassure her friend even though she was terrified for her; the implications of the situation didn't bear thinking about.

Amelia wasn't listening.

'How am I going to know if it's Sam or Paul's? My periods have been completely erratic over the past year? It's such a disaster. I'm too old. What if there is something wrong with the baby? I won't be able to cope. I don't want another child.'

She was getting herself into a complete state now, and was barely able to breathe.

'Maybe the doctor will be able to give you a due date, which will be of some help. If not, you may have to wait for DNA tests, which I think they can do while you are pregnant.' Jess was hoping Amelia would be able to at the very least find out who the father was.

'I am such a fool, a complete idiot. Why was I not more careful?' Amelia was starting to calm down, comforted by having Beth and Jess with her.

The phone rang and Jess answered; it was Sam. Amelia shook her head to say that she wouldn't take the call.

'Amelia is not well, Sam, and has gone to bed. She vomited during dinner. I will leave a note for her that you called and get her to call you back when she wakes up.'

She could hear the disappointment in his voice but, right now, her priority was Amelia, and to say she didn't care how Sam felt was putting it mildly.

Beth had received a text from Kale which she hadn't answered but her phone beeped again. Amelia told her to reply to it, guessing that it was Kale.

'I'm going to tell him that I'm staying here with you. There is no way I'm going anywhere tonight,' she said.

'No, Beth, we left Rick and Meredith in the bar and you should be meeting Kale too. We have to go back down.'

Amelia suddenly realised that Jess had left Rick in the bar and she felt really guilty. 'Why don't you two go back down and I'll come down in a little while when I've tidied myself up. There is no point in us all being miserable. Jess, I want you to go on your date, I've caused enough trouble already.'

***

By the time Beth and Jess arrived in the Morello Bar, Kale had turned up and was sitting happily, chatting to Meredith and Rick.

'Amelia had a bit of a family crisis but she's okay and will be back down shortly. Sorry about the disappearing act,' Beth said, trying to make light of the situation.

'Once she's alright, that's all that matters,' Meredith said.

She didn't like not knowing what was going on and would find out if it was the last thing she did!

Jess was delighted that Rick had waited for her, and as soon as they finished their drinks he led her by the hand out of the bar. She felt a bit guilty leaving the girls but she knew they wanted her to spend time with Rick.

Meredith started to quiz Beth about Amelia.

'Is Amelia okay, Beth? I don't mean to pry but she seemed very distressed.'

'As I said, Meredith, Amelia had a family problem and needed our advice. She has asked for our discretion, which is what she will get.' Beth didn't intentionally snap at her, but Meredith got the message.

Beth was taken aback by Meredith's nosiness; she had already explained the situation and didn't appreciate being prodded for further information. One thing that really irritated her was people not respecting other people's privacy. She was starting to get a bad vibe from Meredith; there was something strange about this woman and she was becoming a bit too intrusive in their lives. She decided to go dancing upstairs with Kale. She didn't care what Meredith did; it was not her problem and she just hoped the woman wouldn't follow them.

***

Rick led Jess down to the casino. She was puzzled and thought that maybe he was bringing her through it as a shortcut to somewhere else.

'You mentioned that you love casinos but your friends don't like them and so you have to go on your own.' Rick was holding her hand as he spoke. 'I thought it might be nice for us to have a harmless bit of fun here together with low stakes. What do you think?'

Jess was surprised. This was totally unexpected but at the same time she thought it was very romantic. When she went to the casino on her own, she always felt guilty, as if she shouldn't be there and here she was now, on a date in a casino! She wasn't sure that the girls would approve, but she really didn't care. Right this minute, such was her happiness she felt as if the butterflies were going to fly up through her body and out of her mouth.

'What is your idea of low stakes?' Jess was curious.

'$5 bets. I have $500 for us to play with so how's about we have some fun with that and see what happens?'

'I can't let you put up all the money,' Jess said, impressed by

Rick's generosity and secretly relieved that she didn't have to use her own cash. It was lovely to be spoiled by a man again.

'Why not? After all, it's my idea and I invited you. I just have one question now, my dear Jess, what would you like to play?'

'Well, I love blackjack and roulette, so maybe we could play a bit of both?'

'Let's get started!'

They walked around looking for a $5 table for blackjack and found one at the end of the casino. It was full so they observed for a few hands until two people left and they took their places.

Rick handed over $200 and the croupier gave him the equivalent in chips which he split with Jess. And so they began. They played well and enjoyed themselves immensely, eventually leaving the table with a combined $460 – a profit of $260. They turned down the offer of a drink at the table and instead went to the bar to do a post-mortem.

'My dad always told me to leave the table when I was ahead and I am proud of us for doing that,' Rick said. 'I played blackjack with him on a cruise a few years ago and he had the luck of the Irish and won $2,000 from an original stake of $100. He left the table immediately; I think it was to try and be a good example to me.'

He leaned over and kissed her gently.

'I really enjoyed that, Jess, I know it's not a good thing to like gambling, but if we keep it under control, we can have a bit of fun.'

'Are we going to play some roulette? We seem to be on a roll,' Jess said.

She was having the time of her life and didn't want the night to end.

'I think that is a very good idea, bring it on,' Rick said as he got off the stool.

He took her by the hand and led her towards the roulette table where they found two seats even though the table was very busy. They each had their chips and their own methods of playing. Jess like to play on a colour along with zero and Rick liked to play with numbers, which meant that they were probably going to have quite different result from each other this time around. Rick asked Jess when her birthday was and when her two girls' birthdays were. He bet on them, along with his own birthday and those of his two daughters.

Jess started off well but then everything started to go wrong and, before she knew it, she was down to her last $20 which she decided to risk on black. The ball landed on zero. It was all gone; all the money Rick had lent her and the cash she'd won on blackjack.

On the other hand, Rick was doing very well. He was now up at $1,500 profit and still hadn't used all his original $230 stake from the blackjack. Jess was a bit embarrassed but sat beside him, encouraging him now that she had nothing left to play with. Rick wanted to leave the table but the draw was too strong and every time he said that he was going to cash in, she turned to him and said 'Just one more'. He didn't need much persuading. After an hour, Jess told him that he would have to stop. He had won $3,500 and if he stayed any longer it would just be sheer greed.

***

As Rick led her out of the casino, there was a silent understanding between them about where they were going. He unlocked the door and she went inside, her heart beating so fast she thought it would burst.

'That was one of the best nights I can ever remember,' Jess said as she looked into his eyes; she was falling for Rick and it was too late to stop things. Even though she had lost in the casino, she had met a man who made her feel alive again.

'It's just effortless with us. That's what makes it feel so right,' he replied as he kissed her tenderly until she thought she would melt.

Then he led her over to the bed. 'You are truly beautiful, Jess, and I want you in my life.'

Jess thought she would lose her desire if he didn't get on with it. She had waited for him and had played hard to get for long enough. It had been so long since she had been with James that she was slightly nervous that she wouldn't be any good and that he would be disappointed, but she soon forgot all such thoughts.

Rick started caressing her body while kissing her neck. He breathed heavily as he licked her ears and played with her hair. He could feel she was starting to relax as she moved her arms up and down his back. She was groaning as he started to explore her, his fingers flicking her and pushing her to a point where she was digging her fingers into his back and urging him to enter her. He moved up and she opened her legs, lifting them as he found his entrance and they had sex as if they had been together for years.

Jess lay in his arms afterwards and felt a sense of happiness that overwhelmed her. It was more than the sex; she felt truly cherished for the first time in a very long time, and she didn't want it to end.

***

Beth and Kale had gone dancing and Beth felt she was improving no end. When she'd first danced with him she hadn't had a clue, but he had been patient and had taught her different moves. She was a fast learner and was loving her time with him.

'I think we should call it a night. I am worried about Amelia and don't want to be gone too long,' Beth said. 'I hope you understand.' She was really concerned about her friend and had no idea what she was going to do.

'Yes, of course I understand. I'll text you in the morning and we can arrange something for tomorrow evening,' Kale replied.

***

When Beth arrived back at the room, Amelia was asleep and there was no sign of Jess. She went to bed, figuring that Jess would be back before morning.

DAY SEVEN

SANTORINI

Amelia hadn't had much sleep all night but she didn't want to disturb the others so she had stayed in bed. In the early morning, she got up and went out onto the balcony. Her mind was in turmoil and she was still in shock. They must have anchored because they weren't moving and she looked at Santorini in the distance. She remembered that it was a tendered port and Jess had told them disembarking and heading onto the Island of Santorini was going to be quite hard work because, besides the tenders, the only way up to the town was via cable car, by donkey, or on foot, and that all took time, especially on the way down. They were going to need to have a fairly early start so she gave the girls a call.

'Beth, Jess! We're in Santorini.'

The girls got up and came out to the balcony.

'How are you feeling today?' Beth asked.

'I had a terrible night. I feel horrendous and my head is swimming with the confusion and worry of it all.'

'Okay, I'm going to ring the medical centre now before we do another thing,'

Beth made an appointment for 8.45am then she ordered some coffee and croissants to be delivered to the room before going back outside.

'Okay, that's done. We can come with you if you want.'

'I think I'll go on my own, if that's okay.'

'We'll be waiting and then we can get the tender into Santorini if you're feeling up to it,' Beth said gently.

'Of course I'll be up to it – I'm not missing Santorini. Thanks, Beth,' Amelia responded.

***

Amelia went down to the medical centre where she was met by a nurse who brought her into a room that looked like a small version of the accident and emergency department in a hospital. It had three cubicles with curtains and hospital beds and lots of medical equipment. The nurse introduced herself as Kulap. She brought Amelia over to one of the cubicles and told her to make herself comfortable on the bed, saying that the doctor would be along in a moment.

Amelia felt very tense. She had only ever been in hospital when she was having her children and she didn't like the environment. The doctor appeared just as she was gathering her thoughts.

'Hello Ms Brady, I am Doctor Sakim and I will be taking care of you. Can you tell me what the problem is?

'Yes, Doctor, thank you for seeing me. I have discovered that I am unexpectedly pregnant but my problem is that I am perimenopausal and I have no idea how far gone I am. Can you do an ultrasound and tell me? I also need to know if it is possible to do DNA testing in advance of the birth because there are two possible fathers.'

Amelia felt embarrassed but she knew that it was a small price to pay for her peace of mind. Dr Sakim showed no signs of shock at what he had just heard.

'I can do an ultrasound now and we can get a pretty accurate estimate of your due date but I cannot do the paternity test here. You will be able to have it done when you get home. It's fairly straightforward and there are a number of different options available. The thing I am concerned about now is checking the health of yourself and your baby.'

Amelia was rigid with tension as Dr Sakim and Nurse Kulap proceeded to do the ultrasound.

'You need to try and relax, Ms Brady, your blood pressure is very high which is not good for the baby.'

Amelia couldn't take her eyes off the screen, or Dr Sakim, as she searched for clues in his expression that would give her an insight into her situation.

'You are five months pregnant, Ms Brady.'

'What? I can't be! I'm not even showing a bump.'

'The baby is lying in towards your back rather than to the front, but the good news is that she is healthy and everything looks as it should.'

'She?'

'Yes, oh, I'm sorry, Ms Brady, did you not want to know?'

'No, that's okay, Doctor, I'm in such a state of shock that it really doesn't matter either way.'

'We need to get your blood pressure down so I'm going to have to keep you here and monitor you until I am satisfied that you are stable again. Is there anyone I can call for you?'

'Yes, can you call my room and ask my friends to come down, please? I need to tell them to go ahead into Santorini without me.'

Amelia felt totally and utterly miserable. She was stunned that she was five months pregnant, fifty years old and didn't even know who the father was. Surely it was time for her to cop on to herself and make some decisions. How could she bring another child into the world when she was so irresponsible?

***

Beth and Jess came straight down once they had received the call. When they saw Amelia in the cubicle, the reality of the situation began to hit home. She looked really stressed and upset.

'I'm five months pregnant, due at the beginning of February and it's a girl. They can't do a paternity test here but it can be done while I'm still pregnant, which is something, I suppose. Although what good it's going to do me, I really don't know anymore.'

'What about yourself and the baby? Did he tell you how you're both doing?' Jess asked. She was really worried about her friend and felt totally helpless.

'Yes, he told me the baby is fine, but my blood pressure is very high and he won't let me go back to our room until it comes down so I want you two to go into Santorini without me.'

'Oh God, Amelia, that's probably the stress of it all. Try not to worry, we need to get you well and out of here.' Beth was quite worried about Amelia; she knew high blood pressure in pregnancy was very dangerous.

'I brought your book and your phone. We'll check in with you in a little while.' Jess was doing her cabin crew thing, taking care of Amelia like she would her first-class passengers.

'I wish I was going with you. It was the place I most wanted to see on the whole cruise,' Amelia said.

She felt really sorry for herself when the girls left. She lay in the bed trying to work out what she was going to do. She hadn't called Sam back since the night before and she knew that he would be really worried about her. She decided to send him a text to let him know that she was in the medical centre. There was no reason to hide this from him, especially when there was a chance he could be the father.

I am sorry about last night, please don't be alarmed but I need you to come to the medical centre now.

***

Beth and Jess took the tender where they ran into Meredith. They were pleased to have her company after what had happened to Amelia, but Beth was on her guard; she was still not sure about Miss Meredith.

'How is Amelia? Why is she not with you?' Meredith appeared genuinely concerned, but the truth was that she was very curious about what was going on.

'She went to the medical centre this morning and they told her that her blood pressure is sky high and won't let her leave until it comes down. She doesn't have great health.'

Beth wasn't prepared to tell Amelia's secret without her permission.

'Are you sure she isn't pregnant?'

Meredith seemed to be directing the question at Beth, who was quite annoyed now. She didn't like the American woman's pushiness.

'Amelia is still really confused and upset and this is probably what is causing her raised blood pressure. I think you will need to talk to her yourself about anything else, Meredith,' Beth answered in an almost rude manner.

'Is she any closer to making a decision about Paul and Sam?' Meredith clearly had no idea when to stop asking questions.

'I think she is leaning towards Sam, even though she still loves Paul,' Jess started to explain but Beth glared at her so she stopped.

'I think we've discussed Amelia enough. She is perfectly capable of filling you in on all of it herself when she recovers,' Beth said firmly. She was very irritated at this point and couldn't work out why Meredith made her so uneasy.

They walked towards the cable car and began to queue. Luckily it wasn't busy and they were only waiting ten minutes. Beth tried to gather herself on the way up so that she wouldn't let her feelings towards Meredith spoil the rest of the day.

***

Sam got a terrible fright when he read Amelia's text and went straight down to the medical centre. When she saw him, Amelia burst into tears. He put his arms around her, taken aback when he saw that she had a monitor switched on beside her.

'What is wrong, Amelia? What has happened?' he asked.

'I don't know how to tell you,' she responded. She looked exhausted and was in a terrible state.

'It can't be that bad, sweetheart. There is nothing that you can't tell me.'

'I'm pregnant!' She blurted it out without another thought.

Sam looked at her in disbelief. She was fifty years old – how could she be pregnant? They didn't use protection because she said that she was in the menopause. Surely it was dangerous to have a baby at her age? Why was she hooked up to a monitor?

As she looked at him, searching for signs of acceptance, Sam took her hand and squeezed it. He leaned down and whispered in her ear.

'I love you, it's going to be fine.'

The doctor came over and spoke to Amelia.

'Ms Brady, your blood pressure has come down slightly but still not enough for me to be happy to let you go. Have you had difficulties with any of your other pregnancies?'

'Yes, my last baby was eight weeks premature and very sick, I nearly lost her.'

'That puts you in a high-risk category and I would imagine your doctor will recommend bed rest for the remainder of your pregnancy. In the meantime, I will keep you closely monitored here. I am aware that you are on holiday and don't want to spend your time in the medical centre so I will let you go as soon as I can. The best thing you can do for the moment is to try and relax; you are very stressed.'

'Why don't you try and get some rest, love, and I'll come back in an hour unless you want me to sit with you?' Sam suggested.

'No, darling, you go and see Santorini. There is no point in the two of us missing out. I will try and sleep for a while. I'm very tired because I didn't sleep all night.'

Amelia felt better now that she had told Sam and he had said he loved her; maybe everything would be alright, after all.

'If you are sure, I will go, but I won't be gone long. Hopefully the doctor will let you go soon.'

Sam felt confused. He was very worried about Amelia and he didn't know what to think about the baby. It would take time to sink in.

***

As the girls walked around Santorini's narrow little streets, they were overwhelmed by the beauty of the place. They kept stopping to take photos anytime the sea was in view. They took photos of the magnificent *Santana* in all her glory, as she sat, tendered out in the beautiful blue green waters. The shops were interesting and they each bought some designer jewellery that had been handmade locally.

It was scorching hot and they soon needed to take a break from the heat. They decided it was time for some light refreshments and set about looking for a place to have lunch, the view being the number one consideration. Having looked at endless menus they eventually decided on a pretty Greek restaurant with tables on the cliffside overlooking the sea; the location was magnificent, a true paradise. The menu was totally Greek and they ordered a meze of dishes to share with a bottle of rosé. Then they settled down to enjoy the view.

Just as they were taking their first sip of wine, Jess, who was looking towards the door, thought she saw Sam looking at the menu outside their restaurant. Neither of the girls had met him; they had been a bit annoyed with him and had shown no interest, but Amelia had shown them his photo so they knew exactly what he looked like. Jess got up and called his name as she ran up the steps. Sam looked at her; he had also seen photos of the girls and knew who she was.

'Sam! Would you like to join us? We have just sat down,' Jess said.

She hadn't thought about whether the other two wanted Sam in their company but it was all about Amelia now and there was no time for recriminations.

'Oh, hi Jess, yes, that would be lovely. I'm getting rather tired of my own company.'

Sam had been lost in his thoughts and was startled when Jess had called his name. He sat down beside Meredith who introduced herself, as did Beth. They made a toast to cruising and the beauty of Santorini.

'Have you been to see Amelia, Sam?' Beth asked.

'Yes, of course. She is resting and insisted that I see Santorini. The doctor seems to be very concerned about her blood pressure and feels this is a high-risk pregnancy because of Caroline being so premature and, of course, Amelia's age. He told us that she will probably have to be on bed rest for the remainder of her pregnancy. She won't find that easy.'

Meredith looked at Beth but said nothing; she had been right about the pregnancy. She thought about how protective Beth was of Amelia and considered it pathetic but she knew that, if she was honest with herself, she was actually jealous of their closeness. She didn't have any friends with whom she had that kind of bond.

Beth was annoyed with Sam for talking about Amelia so openly. She felt he should have been more careful with Meredith there, but she knew that there was no point in worrying about keeping it a secret anymore.

'How do you feel about it all, Sam?' Jess was curious.

She asked the question that was on everyone's mind, but she was forgetting that Meredith was there and that they barely knew her.

'I haven't had time to process it properly, but my initial thoughts are worry about Amelia's age and the risks attached for both herself and the baby. On the other hand, I am not yet a father myself so it would be very welcome,' he said, despite the fact that he hadn't really had time to digest it all properly.

Jess and Beth smiled at Sam. Both were relieved that he felt happy at the thought of becoming a father. At the same time, they couldn't help noticing that he was assuming the baby was his, and it seemed that he had not been told otherwise.

'I think it has all been a shock for everyone but once Amelia is okay, that is all that really matters,' Meredith said. 'I am a real believer in karma; things happen for a reason and everything will work itself out. You guys need to chill out for a bit now and drink in this view.'

She spoke in a kind voice and brought them all back to the point where they could talk about something else.

***

After lunch, Sam took the cable car down and went back to the ship as he didn't want to leave Amelia alone any longer. He went straight to the medical centre and when he arrived he was delighted to see that the monitor had been removed and she was getting ready to go. Doctor Sakim told him that her blood pressure had come down but that she was to take it easy and avoid stress and had to visit her doctor as soon as she got home.

'I met the girls in Santorini. That's why I was so long,' Sam said to Amelia. 'Jess recognised me as I was passing the restaurant they were in and asked me to join them. You must have shown them a photo of me.'

'Of course I did. I wanted them to see why I haven't been able to resist you!' Amelia responded; she seemed to have cheered up a little. 'Anyway, it was good you weren't here because I slept and

I needed the sleep. How were they towards you?' She was curious about Jess and Beth and how they felt about Sam.

'They were really nice. Meredith was there and they couldn't have been friendlier.'

'Thank goodness. I've been really worried about how to handle the situation. Let's go back to the room now.'

***

The girls decided it was time to head back to the ship so they paid the bill and made their way up towards the cable car. However, when they got as far as the shops they noticed a seemingly endless queue. It was so long that they knew there was no point in joining it; if they did they would miss the ship's departure. They had heard that there were three other ships in Santorini that day, so the pressure on the cable car was immense. Their only other choice was to walk down the five hundred and eighty-eight steps or else go by donkey, and they had been advised not to take the donkeys. There was nothing else for it but to walk back down to the port.

The route was lovely, wrapping itself around the cliff, but it was not easy to negotiate because it was uneven and full of stones; it was also full of the excrement from the donkeys which had to be avoided as they made their way up and down the narrow path. It was a hot day and none of them had a hat or proper footwear, which only added to the challenge. They decided to take it slowly and concentrate, staying together at all costs. They were a little unnerved because they'd heard about a woman who had been trampled to death by a donkey the previous week. Despite the challenge, they made it down to the port in an hour.

They were tired and had sore feet but they were looking forward to getting back to the ship and checking on Amelia. Once back on board, they went straight to the medical centre where they discovered that she had been discharged. They went up to their room only to find that she wasn't there either.

'I think we need to call Sam's room; it's the only other place I can think that she would be,' Jess said.

'Just one problem – we don't know his room number,' Beth answered.

'I'll text her now and let her know we're here, I think she has her phone with her.'

Just then the phone in the room rang; it was Amelia.

'Hi Beth, how was Santorini?'

'It was great. I'll tell you about it when I see you. More importantly, how are you doing? What did the doctor say?'

'I'm feeling much better but I am so sorry for putting a dampener on things and causing so much stress. I bet you never imagined I would be the one causing all the trouble!' Amelia said.

'You are not to say another word about it! How could you have known this was going to happen? This is what friendship is all about – being there for each other.'

'That means so much, thanks, Beth. I am going to rest here with Sam for an hour or so and then I'll come back to the room.'

'Grand, mind yourself, love,' Beth replied.

***

Sam sat on the bed beside Amelia and took her hand in his.

'I don't want you to worry. We will get through this together, darling.'

'I wish I could believe you. I can't help thinking that my world is going to come crashing down around me. Right at this moment, I am terrified. Can I ask you a question, Sam?' Amelia looked at him with a nervous expression on her face.

'Of course, sweetheart.'

'How do you feel about the idea of becoming a father? It's not going to be easy with all the baggage I have. It all seems so crazy, I can't believe I am sitting here asking you this. Please be honest, Sam.'

As she finished speaking, her phone rang. She saw that it was Paul and ignored it. When it finished ringing, she switched it off. She was suddenly overcome by a wave of nausea and ran to the bathroom.

***

The girls went out onto the balcony with a glass of wine each. They were both bursting to talk about Amelia and her situation.

'What do you think, Beth? What is she going to do? I am so worried for her. Thank God it's not me, I don't know what I would do,' Jess said.

'If it were me, the first thing I would want to know is who the father of the baby is because that would make a big difference as to how I would handle things, but I'm not sure if that is a priority for Amelia. Do you think that Sam knows that the baby might not be his?'

'I doubt that he does. I mean, it would be very hard for him to put up with the situation if he thought that she was sleeping with Paul at the same time as him, so I think he probably assumes that she has no physical relationship with Paul. I would say she doesn't find it easy to keep two men happy either, I can't imagine it.'

Jess was thinking how she had enjoyed the previous night with Rick but how she couldn't even contemplate juggling two men.

'I think we should leave her alone with regard to decision-making unless she looks for advice; her head will be in turmoil for the next while. I think, in the end, she will probably choose the father of the baby and whether that is the right decision or not, only time will tell. In the meantime, we will just have to be there for her.' Beth was being very philosophical but she knew she was right.

'I agree. Now all we need to do is sort you out!' Jess said with a laugh.

'And what about you, Jess? Are you happy? Beth winked at her friend.

'Why do you think I've been walking around like a lovesick schoolgirl? I'm just a bit nervous of getting hurt.'

'You have to put that out of your mind. You'll never fall in love if you build a fortress around yourself.'

Jess knew that Beth was right. She was going to have to try and take her advice but she wondered if she could ever truly trust a man after what had happened to her at such a young age.

'I was just thinking that the sail-away party is starting at 6pm and we've booked the Sunset Grill so that we will get the best views. I'll ring Sam and tell him to remind Amelia. Do you think we should ask him to join us after everything that has happened?'

'No, not for dinner, Beth, but I think it would be a nice idea to ask him to join us afterwards. Things are serious now and there is no point in us holding a grudge against him and making things harder for Amelia. On the other hand, I think we need time together on our own more than ever so we should stick to just the three of us having dinner together.'

'What are you doing with Rick later?'

'There's a really good show on at 10pm tonight. I know we haven't been to any so far but this one has been recommended by other cruisers on *Cruise Critic* and I'd like to see it. It is based on the Freddie Mercury story and I love Queen. Rick said he can reserve a table for all of us in the VIP area.'

'I'd love that,' Beth said enthusiastically. 'Ask him to reserve it for all six of us. I'll check with Kale and then we can ask Amelia.'

Hi Rick, the girls would love to come to the show. Can you reserve the table and we'll see you there at 9.55pm. Jess

Fantastic, when you come into the theatre, turn left and head down towards the stage, you will see the VIP area. I can't wait. R xxx

***

Amelia arrived back to the room looking a bit better than she had earlier but she was still quite pale. Going to the sail-away party was the last thing she felt like doing, but she knew that she had to push herself for the sake of her friends; she just wished she could get the pregnancy out of her head for five minutes.

'I'm going to get ready as fast as I can,' she said. 'You both look fab.'

'How are you feeling?' Beth asked.

'I'm a bit tired and I suppose I am still in shock but I'll be okay. I just wish I knew who the father was because not knowing is driving me insane. Hopefully when I find out, it will take a bit of the pressure off, although I am totally petrified."

'Is Sam being supportive?'

'Yes, but he gave a very bizarre answer to a question I asked him earlier.'

'What do you mean?'

'We'll be late for the party, I'll tell you later.'

'Before I forget,' Jess said, 'Rick has invited us to the Queen show in the theatre tonight. He has reserved a table for the six of us.'

'Do you mean I can take Sam out of hiding?' Amelia asked, smiling.

'Yes, I think, in fairness to him, he's served his time! We forgot to tell you that we had lunch with him in Santorini,' Beth answered.

'Yes, he told me. And what did you think?' Amelia was hoping they liked Sam.

'He's lovely, Amelia. We didn't have long with him but he seems very sincere and he is very handsome!' Beth replied with a grin.

***

When they were all dressed up and ready to go, they headed up to the top deck where there was a band playing and waiters walking around serving cocktails and champagne. The scene was stunning as the ship left Santorini and the sun started to set in the distance. All the phones were out as everyone tried to capture the moment, knowing in their hearts that it would be impossible to truly capture the magnificence of the scene on camera.

'It's simply breathtaking. I've waited for this moment since we booked the cruise,' Beth said.

'I know; at least I didn't miss this. Was Santorini amazing?' Amelia asked.

'Yes, it was beautiful but hard work. You wouldn't have been able for it in your condition. We had to walk down five hundred and eighty-eight steps on the way back,' Jess said before going on to tell Amelia all about their day.

The maître d' announced that dinner was ready and they were called into the restaurant once the sun had set and Santorini had disappeared out of view. All the tables had been put together in long rows, seating about twenty at each. Big platters were placed at intervals along the tables. There was a large barbecue with fires blazing and lots of chefs scurrying around. The executive chef introduced himself and explained that everything would be barbecued and served up in platters as soon as it was ready, starting with the flatbread and dips which came with an array of different toppings, and followed by a selection of salads and dressings. After that, there were meat platters consisting of steak, veal, chicken and lamb and then a fish course of salmon, scallops, langoustines and lobster.

It was a truly delicious meal and great fun. The girls met lots of people from all over the world and were sitting beside a really good fun gang of Welsh people who they arranged to meet later on in the Morello Bar. By this stage, however, Amelia was feeling very tired. It had taken all she had to keep herself in good spirits so as not to bring down the mood of the evening. She was not drinking anymore and it was a different evening when everyone else was getting more and more inebriated while she was staying sober.

'Would you mind if I went upstairs for a lie down for half an hour? I'm really not feeling great,' she said.

'Are you okay, love?' Jess asked. 'Do you want to go back down to the doctor?'

'No, I don't want to see the doctor, I just want to lie down. It's been a long day.' Amelia felt guilty abandoning her friends but she knew they understood; this whole ordeal was a mess and there was no other way of looking at it.

'Shall I call Sam for you?' Beth asked.

'No, it's okay. I'll call him when I get to the room. We'll be back down for the show.'

'I haven't been down to the casino for a while and I'm desperate to play some roulette so I hope you don't mind if I head down there,' Jess said with a look of animated anticipation.

'That's fine with me, Jess, you've been very well behaved so you deserve it,' Beth stated. 'Meredith and I can go and meet up with the Welsh people until it's time for the show.'

She didn't begrudge her friend a flutter; she felt that Jess couldn't do too much damage in such a short space of time and, besides, she hadn't had much of a chance to play since they arrived, or so Beth thought.

***

Jess settled Amelia into bed and then the latter phoned Sam. He said that he was on his way over. Jess had her bag beside her at the safe; she didn't want Amelia to see how much she was putting into it.

'How is the casino going, Jess? We haven't had any time to talk about it what with everything that's been going on.'

'Oh, it's fine, Amelia, I haven't had much of a chance to go down. It's good that we have Meredith now because she can keep Beth entertained and I can go and enjoy myself playing roulette,' she said, beaming with delight.

'Just promise me you'll be careful, Jess. I really am worried about you. At least you can't do too much damage with the limited funds you brought and with only an hour before the show.'

Jess felt sick; she was sure that her friend knew she was lying. She knew that Amelia would be even more shocked if she knew that Rick liked a flutter too.

'I promise, Amelia, now stop worrying about me and concentrate on relaxing and keeping your blood pressure down. Sam is here.'

She let him and headed down to the casino.

***

The place was buzzing. She walked around for a few minutes to get her bearings and found the two roulette tables, one with a minimum bet of $5 and the other with a minimum bet of $10. She noticed that the $1 table wasn't operational – she guessed that they only offered that during the quieter periods to encourage business. She sat down at the $5 table and took out $200. She looked around while the croupier was exchanging her money for chips. To her right were two ladies who appeared to be friends. They were very well dressed and had platinum ship passes prominently displayed on the table. To her right were three men who seemed to be playing individually.

Jess took her time and watched the first round. It would have all been very daunting had she not been familiar with the way things worked. The croupier had a security manager standing behind her. Jess wasn't sure whether that was for the customers' benefit or to make sure that the croupier wasn't cheating, but it was certainly intimidating. There was also a big screen above the roulette wheel which showed the ball spinning, where it landed and the results for the previous spins.

She started to settle in. She had made a plan; she was going to play black and zero. She started off well, playing slowly and winning steadily. Black was coming up all the time and then zero came up; she was thrilled. It came up again in the following spin and she was in ecstasy. The croupier paid out and she was up to $1,500 from a $200 start. She knew she was nearing the end of the holiday and needed to make a lot more money than that so she decided to keep playing.

The men beside her were crowding the numbers on the board; she found this very irritating but it made her wonder if she should change her strategy a little? But why change a winning formula? The men were polite but quite serious in their demeanour while the wealthy ladies to her right were very unfriendly. They were dripping in expensive jewellery and she reckoned they put the ship passes in full view just to show off. She tried to make conversation with them but they weren't interested.

She got back to the business at hand and tried to focus on the screen to study the previous ten spins. Eight out of ten of them had been black; two in a row had been zero (very unusual) and none had been red. Before she'd started playing, there had been a long list of red results. The question was, should she keep going with black, or change to red? She had changed to red the other evening to her detriment, so she decided to stick with black for the moment and to up her stake considerably.

She put $200 on zero and $200 on black and took a deep breath. She knew the zero was a crazy bet, seen as it had been called twice in the past ten spins, but she had a gut feeling that it was going to come up again. If it did, she would win $7,000! It was worth the gamble. Just this once.

The wheel started spinning and the ball was flying around. Jess couldn't look. She suddenly felt a hand on her shoulder and jumped with fright. It was Rick.

'My beautiful Jess, what are you doing in the casino all alone?'

She was speechless. She turned to look at Rick in the middle of what was the biggest bet of her gambling career. Everyone at the table was looking at her as the croupier raked all the chips off the board and placed a marker on the zero. Jess realised that she had won but she also knew that Rick had seen her make this ludicrous bet.

***

Sam walked over to Amelia and sat down beside her.

'How are you feeling, darling?'

'I am wiped out, Sam, I don't know if it's just physical at this stage, or if the whole shock is manifesting itself physically as well.'

'You need to try and relax or your blood pressure will go up again. I will look after you, I promise. Would you like me to stay and chat for a while or do you want to sleep?'

'You go downstairs and relax with the others, you'll find Beth and Meredith in the Morello Bar. I really need to try and rest for half an hour before the show. If I take it easy tonight hopefully I'll be better for Athens tomorrow, although the thought of climbing the Acropolis fills me with dread.'

Sam left her to sleep. He was quite worried about her and wasn't too happy about going downstairs but he didn't want to upset her by fussing.

***

He found Beth and Meredith chatting to the Welsh people Amelia had mentioned earlier; they were the centre of attraction and laughing loudly as they held court.

'Mind if I join you ladies and gents?' he asked as he pulled over a chair.

'Hi Sam, great to see you,' Meredith said as she stood up and gave him a hug.. 'How is Amelia?'

'She wanted to rest and insisted that I come down and join you, but I am very concerned about her.'

Beth and Meredith were aware that the Welsh people were listening and they didn't want to discuss Amelia in front of them.

'I know. Sam,' Beth said. 'Try not to worry, it's been a long day and she'll be fine in the morning.'

Sam felt like he was being fobbed off by Beth but then he realised that they were in company and guessed that she was being discreet; he smiled at her to signal his understanding.

***

Jess pulled the chips towards her and turned to face Rick. She didn't know whether to feel embarrassed or proud, but she was leaning towards the former.

'Rick, I thought we were meeting you in the theatre,' she said, a bit flustered by her win.

'I finished work early so I thought I would take a wander. I didn't expect to find you here,' Rick said, shocked to find Jess alone in the casino making such large bets.

'I don't make a habit of hanging around casinos on my own. What must you think of me?'

Jess was surprised at the words as they came out of her mouth. After all, she was an independent woman who could do what she liked, so why was she apologising? The croupier handed her the chips in large denominations so that they weren't obtrusive and she put them in her bag.

Rick took her by the hand. 'I think it's show time,' he said.

***

Beth and Meredith were enjoying the conversation with their newfound friends, though Beth was wondering why she hadn't heard from Kale. It had been a long day and her mind had been occupied with Amelia and the trip into Santorini, but she thought he would have made contact. She had sent him a text in the morning but she hadn't heard back from him so she sent him another text a bit later, telling him about the theatre show, and he still hadn't replied. Just as she was about to get up and go down to the theatre, he arrived.

'Are you still talking to me?' Kale spoke softly.

'Why did you not answer my text?'

Kale sat down beside her and took her hand in his. 'I know you have been having a tough time with Amelia's situation and I wanted to leave you in peace.'

'That is ridiculous, Kale, I can't understand why you wouldn't have sent me back some sort of reply. Anyway, we are going to the show now. Are you coming?' Beth was upset but she didn't have time to talk to him about it, not now.

***

Rick had arranged for a lovely table with a fantastic view of the stage and, of course, the champagne was on ice. Staff bustled around them, taking drinks orders and serving olives and nuts. The cruise ships were famous for their shows and the girls hadn't been to any of them so far so it was lovely to finally get to experience the extravaganza, especially in VIP style.

The theatre was just like a theatre you would see in any city or town. It had lovely comfortable velvet seating but the really impressive thing about the show was the presentation; it was hard to believe that they could produce something so professional on a ship in the middle of the ocean. They all felt like they were in London's West End and they had a fantastic evening.

When the show ended, Rick invited everyone to the senior officers' bar for drinks but Amelia said that she was tired so she and Sam went up to the room instead. Beth and Kale said they were going dancing.

'It looks like it's just you and me,' Rick said, looking at Jess.

***

Beth and Kale went up to the Sky Lounge and straight onto the dance floor. She loved it when they danced and she was really starting to learn the moves. She hoped she would get a chance to continue dancing when she got home. After a little while, she whispered in his ear that she wanted to sit down and get a drink.

'The past two days have been a rollercoaster for Amelia and we have been spending our time supporting her so I haven't had time to think about you and me. When I came on the cruise it was supposed to be a relaxing holiday with the girls to celebrate our friendship and our birthdays, but it has turned into a very emotional and complex trip for all three of us. I never allowed for meeting you. I have a husband and two children and I thought I was happy, but now everything has changed. I don't know what's going on between us. We don't know each other very well and we are both married. I am not completely sure of your feelings for me and I don't really know what is going on in your life because, for some reason, we have never discussed it. We live in different countries and it is all very complicated. I am not the sort of woman who goes around picking up men on holidays and, to be honest, Kale, I am very confused. Where is this going? Are we just having a bit of fun?'

As if she had said nothing, he pulled her towards him and looked into her eyes. He could see the worry but he could also see that she had a longing for him and he kissed her lovingly.

'I want to make love to you, Beth,' he whispered in her ear as he held her firmly in his arms.

'No, Kale, have you not been listening to me, I need to think things through. Do you have anything to say?'

Beth wanted Kale just as much as he craved her, but she was beginning to think that he was messing her around and she felt that he owed her some sort of information about himself.

'I'm going for a walk,' Beth said, getting up and leaving. She needed to clear her head.

***

Jess allowed Rick to take her hand and lead her towards the lift. He brought her to a room she hadn't seen before. When he opened the door, she couldn't believe her eyes. The lighting was set really low and the ceiling looked like a starlit sky. There were flowers everywhere and there was music playing. The terrace doors were open, revealing a beautifully laid table with a white linen cloth and candelabra. A waiter in an immaculate, crisp uniform was standing by the table with a bottle of champagne while another held out the chair, inviting her to sit down. The music was soft and gentle in the background and as she walked out onto the terrace, she felt a tingling of excitement rush through her body.

'I know it is late and you have already eaten, my beautiful Jess, but I thought we could use some little tasties to have with my champagne.'

'This is beautiful. The setting is so romantic – are you trying to seduce me?' Jess was amused by the efforts he had gone to but was loving it all and, besides, she was on a high after her win in the casino earlier so she deserved to celebrate, however naughty it was! 'This is fantastic. I love it! I am having the most wonderful evening. How am I ever going to go home after this?'

'This is only the beginning, Jess. We have it all ahead of us. Did you have a good day? I was up to my eyes here and never got to leave the ship.'

'Yes, we went into Santorini and then we had a lot of other things to do, so the time flew,' Jess replied.

She didn't see the point in telling Rick about Amelia; she wanted a break from it and would tell him another time.

'I had to do some training with the staff and I had a meeting with the captain and food and beverages director so I couldn't visit Santorini which is one of my favourite ports.'

The waiter poured the champagne and Rick made a toast.

'You are a very special lady. Would you think I was crazy if I told you that I am falling in love with you?'

Jess looked at him and smiled. She didn't think he was crazy because she felt the same way but she didn't answer him. Instead, she leaned over and kissed him gently as she looked tenderly into his eyes. A few minutes later, the waiter arrived again, this time carrying a platter of oysters which came with a delicious shallot and vinegar dressing. Before Rick could say a word, Jess asked if they were Irish oysters.

'They don't serve anything else on the *Santana*, my darling.'

She was impressed; she hadn't known that the oysters on the ship were Irish and she was very proud. Another course arrived; this time a small plate with canapés of pan-fried foie gras with a drizzle of rhubarb relish.

'That is my absolute favourite thing – my death-row starter!' Jess was in ecstasy now, and developing an appetite despite having a full stomach. 'I can't keep going like this. I hope you haven't got too many more surprises!'

The waiter arrived with a mini-cheese board and Jess shook her finger at Rick.

'That's it, no more!' she said.

She was feeling a bit lightheaded; she always got drunk easily on champagne and she'd had quite a bit to drink earlier in the evening. The waiters took the plates and disappeared.

Rick looked into her eyes. 'Come with me,' he said as he stood up and took her by the hand and walked her over to the bed which was beautifully turned down.

Jess was feeling very aroused; she couldn't believe how strong her desire was. 'I'm not sure, Rickl, maybe I should go to bed. It's very late.'

'Sssh! Lie down beside me, I want to make love to you.'

He kissed her, their tongues moving around hungrily as he expertly caressed her body, relaxing her so that she started to remove her clothes herself. Soon they were lying naked, their bodies touching. She looked at him, smiling. Nothing could have prepared Jess for him even though they had already had sex. He was a very experienced lover but she had not been expecting him to be so generous and considerate, putting her needs and desires before his own. She lay in his arms as he swept his fingers through her hair, sending waves of ecstasy through her.

'I feel happier than I have felt in a very long time. I hope you are not playing with my heart, Rick.' She spoke gently.

'My sexy, beautiful Jess. I know we have only just met, but I give you my word, you are already very special to me and I won't hurt you.'

As they lay there, Jess felt like she never wanted the moment to end.

'Can I ask you something, Jess? I was worried when I saw you betting such a large amount earlier. Do you have a gambling problem?' Rick asked as he looked directly into her eyes.

Jess was startled and suddenly felt vulnerable.

'No, of course not. It's just the temptation of the cruise. We don't have casinos in Ireland,' she said meekly as she pulled away from him.

BACK IN IRELAND

Paul was finding it difficult to keep focused on the restaurant; his mind was on Marla and how quickly he could get service finished to be with her. He knew that this was crazy – he was not running a burger joint, *Amelia's* was the best restaurant in Galway and the second best in Ireland, and he couldn't afford to behave like this or his customers would suffer and his staff would start asking questions. Amelia was away and one of them needed to be there to make sure that things were running smoothly and professionally.

He thought about his wife; he had her itinerary on the noticeboard in the kitchen. The girls were going to Santorini today and he was envious. He loved Greece and remembered the wonderful holidays they'd had there over the years. He felt a wave of guilt wash over him. He needed to talk to her, to hear her voice. Perhaps that would help him to see things more clearly.

He picked up the phone and dialled her number. It was 4pm and she would probably be back in the room but there was no reply. He tried again and it went to voicemail. Paul was totally disheartened. He rang the restaurant to make sure everyone had turned up for work before heading to Marla's. He knew that she would cheer him up.

***

Stephen and Bethany were talking about his plans. He explained everything to her and she couldn't believe how much he loved her mother. Then the phone rang; it was Beth ringing on Facetime from Santorini to show them the stunning views. Bethany was bursting to tell her about Stephen's surprise. It was so hard to keep it a secret, especially because they told each other practically everything, but she didn't say a word.

DAY EIGHT

ATHENS

AMELIA WAS NOT THE first to wake in the morning. She looked around and saw that Beth's bed was empty. It had clearly been slept in, so she went out onto the balcony to see if she was there.

'You're up early, Beth, are you okay?'

'I'm fine. I just didn't sleep very well. How are you feeling this morning, love?'

'Sam stayed with me and we talked for a while. Then he left and I fell asleep and slept right through. My body is clearly telling me that it needs rest.'

'Did you discuss things with Sam? Does he know that he may not be the father?'

'God, no, Beth. Maybe I am a coward, but I just feel that it might not be necessary. If the baby is his, then there will have been no need to tell him, and if she isn't, well, then it may be over. So, either way, I don't think now is the time to tell him. Unfortunately, that means that I will have to carry the burden on my own until I do the paternity test.'

'You're not on your own, but I know what you mean. Has he been asking you if you are going to leave Paul?'

'He mentioned it briefly last night, but I told him that I was too tired to discuss it and that we could talk about it another time. I really can't ignore things any longer. I think the baby has made my decision easier in a way because I don't think Paul or Sam will want to knowingly raise another man's child, and I don't think I could ask them to do that either.'

'I think you are probably right. Do you have a gut instinct on whose it is?'

'I feel different than I did with my other pregnancies, which is making me think it might be Sam's but, then again, maybe that is because I am an older mother, or it's my imagination running away with me. I don't know, Beth, I just hope the baby is healthy. It is very late in life to be having a child. I have heard of menopause babies and I have to wonder why I was not more careful.'

'You shouldn't be so hard on yourself. Fate intervened in things and forced your hand.'

'What's happening with yourself and Kale? I get a sense that all is not well.'

Beth told Amelia what had happened the night before, about how he hadn't contacted her all day and how she had told him that she needed to think things through and had walked out on him.

'I really don't know what to do. I can't seem to get my relationships right. I spoke to Stephen yesterday and he seemed in great form, but I can't for the life of me figure out why. When I left, we were hardly speaking and now look at the way I am behaving – imagine if he could see me! I came on this cruise with you two and the last thing on my mind was meeting a man, but now that I have met Kale, I don't think I will ever be happy with Stephen. It's not about Kale and whether or not we have a future; it's the fact that I can get involved with another man. If I was happy with Stephen, I wouldn't be looking at anyone else. What is wrong with me?'

'I don't know, but you have to remember that you had a very tough childhood, Beth, and you had to grow up way too quickly.

You married the first man you met when you left home, and when that didn't work out, you kept on going, searching for love and security. All you have ever wanted is to be cherished and taken care of, and I think if Sonny hadn't been married you would still be together. He adored you. You have been happy with Stephen, but I think you are looking for another Sonny – an older man who will spoil you and protect you, and I can fully understand that.'

Amelia was trying to be gentle; there was a lot more she wanted to say but she didn't want to hurt her friend.

'Yes, I can see exactly what you're saying, but if that is true then I need to stop this thing with Kale. He is not like Sonny and there are so many complications attached to our relationship.'

'Well, you certainly pick them. This has to be one of your better challenges, Beth. I don't know how you do it, but men can't stay away from you. Do you really think you and Kale have a chance? Do you want it to go somewhere?'

'I don't know, Amelia. Don't think I'm getting carried away when I say this, but I'm not prepared to leave Ireland; my friends are too important to me and, anyway, I don't think Stephen would allow me to take Ed out of the country.'

Amelia was horrified by what Beth was saying. Surely she knew that she was running way ahead of herself? She decided that she would have to say something more forceful before her friend made a fool of herself.

'Do you really think things are at that stage so soon? I suggest you text him and meet before you spend any more time trying to figure out what you are going to do. You are married, you have a good life and you need to think carefully about things before you make any rash decisions. He needs to give you some clear answers. You can't plan a life together when you know so little about him. You have only just met, after all.'

Beth's mind was in a tizzy and she felt a bit sick; she wasn't really listening to her friend but she decided that she would text Kale.

Good morning, Kale, can you meet me at 8.30am by the Solarium? It's important. Beth

Jess could hear the chatter coming from the balcony and went out to join the others. 'Good morning guys, did you see us coming into port?'

'No, they always arrive at the crack of bloody dawn which is very annoying,' Amelia replied. She would have preferred if they left it just one hour later to dock to be a little more civilised.

'You two look like you've been having a serious conversation. Have I missed anything?'

'Not really. We were just talking about the pregnancy again and then Beth was telling me about Kale,' Amelia said. 'It's nothing that we haven't talked about already. I just need to decide where I'm going with it, that's all. I am still pinching myself in the hope that it's all a dream and I will wake up and everything will be back to normal,' Beth said.

Ignoring Beth, Jess said, 'I'm a bit confused by something. I was in the casino before the show last night and Rick found me there.'

'That was down to us, Jess, he came to the Morello Bar looking for you and I told him where you were. I hope that was okay? I guess it's a bit late now if it's not,' Beth replied with a sigh.

'It's fine, Beth, I had a huge win last night. Admittedly, I was a naughty girl and took a very risky bet but it paid off and I am now $10,000 richer than when we came.'

Beth and Amelia were gobsmacked. They had no understanding of gambling and how it could get hold of a person.

'I don't believe it, Jess, that's incredible! How could you have won so much from such a small stake? How much did you have to bet to win that much? I assume you are going to leave it at that and take it home with you?' Beth was concerned that Jess would lose it all if she kept playing.

'I can't leave it now, Beth, my luck is with me and that doesn't often happen. Trust me. I'm going to make a lot of money before

I leave this ship.' Jess chose not to answer the first part of the question.

Amelia and Beth looked at each other worriedly; they knew their friend had a deep-rooted problem and that they were going to have to keep a close eye on her for the rest of the cruise.

'How about you give us $9,000 to mind and you can play along with $1,000? After all, that is a lot more than you have ever had to gamble with before. I don't want to sound like a nag, Jess, but you have told me before to try and help if I felt you were having difficulty walking away.'

Beth was seriously concerned. It was an absolute fortune and to think that Jess could lose it all in a matter of minutes was quite frightening. She seemed to be losing control and was clearly in the casino a lot more often than they'd realised.

'I don't know, Beth, I'll think about it, but thank you for the offer.' Jess was now in serious danger; she had convinced herself that she couldn't lose.

The girls had no idea that she had actually spent $2,000 plus her winnings in order to get to the stage she was at now, and that she had no intention of stopping. She needed to win a lot more if she was to solve her financial problems at home.

'What's happening today? Is it the Acropolis?' Jess had the bible in her hand and was searching for information about buses.

'Apparently the hop-on hop-off buses come right down to the ship's docking area so why don't we take one of those, get off and do the Acropolis? If we have time, we can take in one or two other sights as well. Do you feel up to coming, Amelia?'

Beth had checked it all out when she was first up earlier in the morning.

'Yes, I am fine. We will be on a bus so, if I get tired, I will take a taxi back to the ship, but I don't envisage any problems.' She didn't feel like going, but knew she should.

'Okay, let's get ourselves organised and aim to be on the bus by

9.30am,' Beth said. She had appointed herself the decision-maker for the day and had allowed herself enough time to meet Kale for a quick chat before they left for their tour.

***

Kale was sitting beside the pool in the Solarium when Beth arrived. She had made sure to look her best and was wearing a Diane Von Furstenberg wrap dress in baby blue and white with wedges and light but expertly applied make-up. He stood up and kissed her.

'You look beautiful, Beth, I thought you weren't talking to me when you didn't come back last night.'

'Well, I need to talk to you now. Come and sit down beside me. I am sorry but I need to be quick, we are disembarking shortly to visit Athens. I spent some time thinking when I went walking after I left you and I have a few questions for you.'

'That sounds dubious,' he said, smiling meekly.

'I know nothing about you. I have told you a lot about me and my life and I need to know a little about you. I don't think that is unreasonable, Kale. What is going on with you and your wife? I can't understand how you have so much time free to spend with me.'

Kale looked startled by the force of her questions and the demand being made of him for answers. Beth noticed his hesitation.

'Maybe you feel I have no right to ask you this but if you feel that way then I will have my answer and there is no more to be said,' she stated.

Kale was older than Beth and his children from his first marriage were grown up. He had no children with his Lara, his second wife.

'I don't know what you are looking for, Beth, but things seem to be getting a bit heavy. I thought we were having fun together. My wife is not on the cruise; I am here with the dance group – I told you that soon after we met.' Kale was a little terse in his reply.

'Then how are things between the two of you? Do you have an open marriage or are you very happy?'

'Look, Beth, I really like you and I am enjoying our time together. My wife and I have an understanding that is complicated.'

'What do you mean by 'complicated'?'

'Okay, you're determined to get an answer so I will tell you, but it's not something I like to talk about. Lara is not very well; she has early onset dementia and is living in a nursing home. She doesn't recognise me anymore.' Kale had tears in his eyes as he spoke.

'I am so sorry, Kale, I didn't realise. It must be so difficult for you.' Beth was devastated for him. She felt humiliated and selfish and wished she had never started the conversation.

'Beth, I want you to know that you are very special and I felt something between us from the first moment we danced. Lara is still my wife, but dementia is a very cruel illness and she will never recognise me again. I know she would want me to be happy.'

They hugged each other and Kale kissed her. There was a new understanding between them now and nothing else needed to be said.

'I am in the final of the competition tonight. Will you come and watch?'

'Yes, of course.'

She smiled sympathetically and went back to her room.

***

As expected, the tour buses were waiting. It was just a question of which one to take. They picked the yellow one, paid €20 each and got on. They were soon on their way and drove around the suburbs and where they saw large, old mansions. Then the bus went through the city where they saw familiar high-street stores and restaurants along with some not-so-recognisable ones. Then they headed out of the city centre towards the Acropolis.

'I've just received a text from Meredith,' Beth announced.

Hi guys, just wondering if you are out and about. I'm heading for the Acropolis and would love to meet up. M

'What will I say to her? Do you want her to join us?' Beth asked, directing the question at Amelia.

'Yes, that's grand, we can meet her by the bus stop.' Amelia wasn't in the mood to have anyone join them but it was not in her nature to say no.

We'll see you in ten minutes at bus stop nine.

***

Meredith was there, waving as they walked towards the bus stop. It was hugs all around as if they hadn't seen each other for weeks. All suspicions about Meredith were put to one side for the time being. They bought their tickets and proceeded towards the steps that took them to the entrance of the Acropolis.

It was a very hot day and Amelia was feeling very uncomfortable.

'How could I not have known I was pregnant?' she said. 'I've had three babies already and feel so totally stupid. I have all the negative and unpleasant symptoms now that I've been told I'm pregnant and, yet, I was perfectly fine and happy a few days ago when I was in blissful ignorance.'

They chatted away as they walked around, marvelling at the beauty of the ancient rock and its archaeological history. There were signs displayed in front of different monuments explaining the history and they stopped and read each one as they went past. It was a very special experience and one that they would always remember.

Amelia began to get very tired and needed to sit down. When she said she was going to head back down, the others were happy to leave too. They decided to try and find a restaurant but there were none on site so they changed the plan and Amelia took a taxi back to the ship while the others got back on the bus to do a city tour.

***

When she arrived back at the ship, Amelia sent Sam a text.

Just back in the room, girls still out sightseeing. Do you want to have lunch?

Sam was delighted when he saw the text; it was an unexpected change to his usual solitary day.

I am just on my way back. I'm in the town so I'll hop in a taxi and meet you in your room in half an hour.

Amelia felt a surge of desire for the first time since the shock of her news and she smiled to herself, happy to know that she still felt the same about Sam despite everything that had happened. She was worried that the reality of the situation would have turned her off him, but she knew now that her feelings were very real. She hoped with all her heart that the baby was his so that her decision would be easier to make.

***

Meredith suggested that they get off the bus in the city centre and find a nice restaurant; it was no wonder she fitted in with them so well.

'What do you fancy, girls?' she asked. 'I think they pretty much have every type of cuisine here in Athens. Is there anything you're craving?'

'I would love some Chinese but it's not ideal in the middle of day. How about Japanese or Thai? Something Asian anyway, as they don't really offer that on the ship, apart from sushi.' Jess was very well educated when it came to food; she had eaten in all the top restaurants when travelling with her job.

'Alright, let's find the tourist office. I'm not sure I'd trust TripAdvisor for this.' Meredith wasn't a big fan of the internet and social media; she preferred communicating the old-fashioned way.

They were very helpful in the tourist office and sent them in the direction of Chinatown where there were numerous restaurants to choose from. They chose one that looked nice from the outside and that served dim sum. Once inside, they were delighted to see that there were a lot of Chinese people dining there, always a good sign. Once the wine was ordered, it was time to decide on the food. Because it was lunchtime they decided to go for the dim sum – Chinese tapas. The menu was endless and they ordered a few at a time so that they wouldn't have too much food.

'I adore this kind of food,' Jess said, clearly in her element. 'I know we should be eating Greek food but I really needed a Chinese fix.'

'Enough about the food, Jess, let's get on with the nitty-gritty. I want to hear all the latest news in your camp.' Meredith was being nosey again but they were used to it now. It was just the way she was and she already knew most of what was going on anyway.

'Jess won big money in the casino last night and is in the middle of a hot romance with the gorgeous Rick, so that's the good news,' Beth said, smiling at Jess who was surprised that she was willing to open up to Meredith. 'On the other hand, I am in a total state of confusion about Kale; hardly surprising really.'

'Why is it surprising, Beth?' Meredith didn't know Beth very well and didn't know her history with men.

'I am married with two gorgeous children and I am messing around with a man I hardly know who lives on the other side of the Atlantic.'

'Beth, you need to trust your instincts. I know I haven't got a very good track record but I have always followed my heart.' Meredith wanted to help but this was a challenging situation, even for her.

'Maybe you should forget about him. There are a lot of hurdles to get over if you want to make it work.'

Beth was furious; how dare this woman tell her to forget about Kale? It was none of her business. Jess looked at Meredith; she was sceptical too. What was this woman up to? One minute she was jovial and fun to be around and the next minute she was telling Beth how to run her life. They didn't really know Meredith and yet they had told her their innermost secrets. They had been very foolish to leave themselves so vulnerable; maybe Beth was right about her – they would have to pull back.

Beth certainly didn't like what she was hearing. Meredith had touched a nerve but she knew she was only saying exactly what Beth had been thinking herself. Jess was beginning to get concerned about who exactly Meredith was and what she wanted from them. She decided to put a stop to the conversation.

'I think we should get the bill and start heading back to the ship,' she announced firmly.

***

When they got back to the room, Amelia wasn't there. They sent her a text but got no reply.

'Do you think we should ring Sam's room to see if she's okay or leave it for the moment?' Beth asked in a worried voice.

'I think she's probably with Sam. She seemed fine when she left us and we need to give her some space. I'm going to read my book on the balcony for a while. Want to join me?'

'You're probably right, I'm just fussing. Thanks for the offer but I think I'll go for a swim and a think.'

Five minutes later, Beth left the room just as Jess received a text from Rick.

Jess, I know you normally have dinner with your friends but could I persuade you to have dinner with me tonight?

Jess was flattered but she was beginning to get nervous. All this talk about Kale and Beth was making her doubt her own situation. Were Rick's intentions true or was he just using her? There was no question that she was attracted to him; who wouldn't be? She loved being treated like a princess and God knows it was about time she had sex again, but was it all genuine? Everything felt right; in fact, it felt perfect but it was happening so quickly. How could she trust any man? She had always been hurt and couldn't go through it again. And there was one other thing – she had lied to him about the gambling because she knew in her heart that she had a problem.

Hi Rick, I'm sorry, but I always have dinner with the girls and unfortunately it is non-negotiable.

She sent the message, wondering if she had been a little short with him but, then again, there was no harm in playing a little hard to get; she didn't want to offer herself on a plate.

I understand, Jess. Would you join me at the captain's drinks party before dinner? Your friends are most welcome too.

Jess thought for a few minutes and wondered if the others would be happy to go to the drinks party. She thought they probably would but wasn't completely sure.

Thank you, Rick. I would love to come and I think the girls would like to come also but they are not here at the moment so I cannot ask them and they may have already made plans. What time and where?

Rick sent another text with the details and Jess lay back on the sun lounger planning what she would wear and how happy she was right at this moment. She knew she was falling for him and needed to put on the brakes. If he really wanted her, he could prove it once the cruise was over and she was back at home.

***

Beth had found herself a nice comfortable spot in the Solarium and settled down to relax and read for a while. Five minutes later, she sat up and put her book down; she ordered a cocktail and lay down again. She took out a pen and paper and started to write out the pros and cons of her relationships with Kale and Stephen.

Stephen
- Husband
- Father of Ed and wonderful stepfather to Bethany
- Good-looking
- Kind
- Funny
- Generous
- Caring
- Loving
- Protective
- Sex very good
- Argumentative
- Stubborn
- Difficult
- Unambitious
- Unromantic

And then a very interesting thing happened – she found that she couldn't list pros and cons for Kale because she didn't know him well enough. She could come up with a few but nothing exhaustive like she could with Stephen. Beth suddenly realised what had been staring her in the face; she didn't know this man and yet she was putting her marriage at risk for the sake of some great sex and learning new dance techniques.

On the other hand, she knew that her marriage was in serious trouble. She wouldn't be with Kale if everything was fine in her marriage, so she would have to go home after the cruise and talk to Stephen and, if necessary, go to counselling again. The strange thing was that she felt like a weight had been lifted from her shoulders once her decision had been made. She was going to enjoy the rest of the cruise and maybe she would enjoy some time with Kale (on her own terms) before going home to try and save her marriage.

***

Sam knocked and Amelia opened the door.

'You look gorgeous, darling, so much more rested and relaxed. Are you feeling better?' he asked.

'I'm fine. I decided to be sensible and take a taxi back from the Acropolis. There was no need to hang around and push myself unnecessarily and besides, I wanted to be with you.'

'Would you like to go up to the clubhouse and sit watching the world go by? There is no point in sitting inside on such a beautiful day.'

The sun was glittering in the sky and the waiter led them to a beautiful table at the aft of the ship where they had a view of both the sea and the port; it was simply perfect.

'We have never been able to have lunch together like this before, darling, and we couldn't ask for a more beautiful setting for our first one.' Amelia couldn't remember when she last felt so happy. When she was with Sam, nothing else seemed to matter.

They enjoyed a blissful, romantic afternoon that neither of them wanted to end.

'I know that I was furious with you when you told me that you had booked the cruise but it has been so special having this time together. I don't know how I'm going to go back to normal life.' Amelia looked at Sam with tears welling up in her eyes.

He took her in his arms and kissed her. They both knew where they were going as they walked away from the restaurant.

***

Beth went out to the balcony where Jess was still reading. 'We'd better start getting ourselves organised. The final of 'Dancing with the Stars' is on tonight and Kale is in it. I promised him I'd be there.'

'Rick sent me a text me earlier and invited us all to the captain's drinks party. It's on at 7.30pm. What time is the competition on?' Jess really wanted to go to the party but didn't want to let Beth down but she had totally forgotten about the competition.

'It's at 7pm so maybe we can do both. Did you ask Meredith to join us?'

'No, Jess, I'm getting a bit tired of her interference. I'm beginning to think she's a bit of a phoney. She doesn't know us and she is advising us on our lives.'

Beth was not usually critical of anyone but Jess knew that Meredith had gone too far with what she'd said to Beth earlier.

'I know what you are saying and I agree. I think there is something that she is not telling us. We seem to spend all our time talking about ourselves and never about her situation. There is definitely something going on with her and we need to find out what it is. I think we should step back a bit. We have revealed too much already, considering we don't know her from Adam.'

'Let's pull back completely. We don't need her and, God knows, we have enough going on without dealing with another challenge.'

Beth was delighted that Jess agreed with her. Now she could get on with enjoying her last few days before she went home to Stephen. She had made a decision to just have fun, enjoy the dancing and especially the sex, and forget about taking it seriously – she had made a new friend with fringe benefits!

Jess looked in the wardrobe and pulled out her favourite dress that she had been saving for a special occasion on the ship; she felt that the time was right to wear it. The dress was not the most expensive dress she had ever bought but it was gorgeous and she felt beautiful whenever she wore it. It was sky blue chiffon with shoestring straps and an empire line, and it fell magnificently to just below her knees. It had a wrap and bag to match and she looked like a goddess as it floated around her when she walked.

'You look stunning, Jess. I think all the officers will be falling at your feet tonight.' Beth was delighted that her friend had met someone. Whether it was serious or just a fleeting romance, she knew that she was truly happy for the first time in years.

'I normally find it difficult to accept compliments, Beth, but I do feel good tonight, so thank you.'

Beth was already dressed and they headed downstairs, not waiting for Amelia because they were afraid to miss the show.

***

Amelia and Sam had forgotten the time because it had been a very special day for them – their relationship had left the bedroom. They had not discussed the difficulties of their situation; instead, they had allowed themselves to enjoy each other and had put off talking about the inevitable problems that lay ahead.

'I need to get back to the others. I have been very neglectful of them, darling,' Amelia whispered.

'I know, sweetheart, it's been an amazing day and I can't wait to come home to you every night and have more days like this,' Sam said, assuming that she had made her decision.

***

Amelia went back to the room to discover that the others had already left. She tried to remember what they had said they were doing for the evening and suddenly remembered about the competition so she got dressed as quickly as she could and went downstairs.

Jess and Beth were happily watching the show and had held a seat for her.

'Where have you been? We were about to send out a search party!' Jess was smiling as she spoke.

'I have just had the best afternoon that I can ever remember.'

Amelia went on to recount her day with Sam and the romance of it all. The other two were delighted to see that she had perked up after the trauma of the past few days.

'Speaking of romance, we've been invited to the captain's cocktail party at 7.30pm so I was wondering if you would like to come along.'

'I will wait until the competition is over to give Kale support and then I'll join you if that's okay,' Beth said.

'I'll stay with Beth,' Amelia said. 'I'm not drinking and, otherwise, she will be on her own. Do you mind?'

'No, of course not, but please do come when it's over.' Jess gave them both a hug and went off to find the place where the party was on.

Kale and Dana were doing really well and there was no doubt that they were the best dancers so it wasn't a surprise that Marcus finally announced them as the winners. Beth was over the moon for Kale but she decided to sit and wait for a while to see if he came over to her. She ordered another drink and after about fifteen minutes she noticed that he had gone.

'Do you think I should text him, Amelia?'

'Well, there's no harm, I suppose. Maybe just congratulate him and wait for a response.'

Congratulations, Kale, you were amazing!

Beth sat back and waited for a response as she silently wondered why Kale had ignored her.

***

When Jess walked into the room she was slightly overwhelmed by the number of people there. There was a lot of chatter and she was offered a glass of champagne immediately. She looked around, her eyes searching for Rick, but she needn't have worried, he was beside her within seconds.

'My darling, you look exquisite.' He kissed her on both cheeks and linked her arm proudly as he led her over to the captain.

Jess stopped in her tracks. As she was walking towards the captain, she saw Meredith standing beside him, laughing. What on earth was going on? She'd never said that she was friendly with him. Meredith looked a bit startled but covered it up well.

'Jess, darling! How fantastic to see you. Allow me to introduce you to the captain.'

'Thank you, Meredith, but we have already been introduced. Good evening, Captain.'

'Good evening, Jess, how very lovely you look. How has your day been in this wonderful city? It is my home town.'

'We had a wonderful but somewhat tiring morning visiting the Acropolis, but it was well worth it. Then we went sightseeing and had a long, lazy lunch. In fact, Meredith was with us. Athens is a truly beautiful city in a stunning country. You must be very proud.'

'Yes, indeed, I have to agree, although I travel so much on the ship I don't see much of it these days.'

'How do you know the captain, Meredith?'

'Oh, we go back a long way. That's another story for another day, my dear,' she said as she looked at Captain Jean Claude.

***

Meredith had been horrified to see Jess and was proud of herself for reacting so well under the circumstances. It should have occurred to her that Jess might be at the party now that she was dating Rick, but she'd had too much on her mind and was getting more and more nervous about Jean Claude's plan.

***

Beth was finishing her drink when her phone beeped.

Sorry for the delay in replying. I had to go for a quick meeting with Dana and the other dancers but I am free now if you want to meet or I can meet you after dinner?

Beth was happy; she had been a bit worried that she wasn't going to get a reply.

Do you want to join me for the captain's cocktail party? I am heading up there now.

Her phone beeped again.

Sure, Jean Claude mentioned it to me earlier. I'll see you there in about ten minutes.

'Have you told Sam that we are going to the cocktail party, Amelia, or do you want to ring him?'

'I'll text him now.'

***

Amelia and Beth had no trouble finding the room which was just behind the reception area on deck three. They went straight in and spotted Jess amongst the circle of uniforms. She was relieved to see her friends. Even though she was with Rick, she felt quite intimidated by all the officers, which was strange considering she would be well used to officers in uniforms from working in an airline.

Kale arrived followed closely by Sam and they had a great time chatting with the officers. Kale already knew quite a few of them so between himself and Beth and Rick and Jess, they were well and truly considered VIPs by the end of the party.

Jess noticed that Meredith seemed a little uneasy, there was definitely something strange going on with that woman and she was determined to get to the bottom of it. Why had she not said that she knew the captain? By the looks of things, she knew him very well.

They made plans to meet the guys after dinner in the Morello Bar. By popular demand, there was another Abba night starting at 11pm in Panorama Nightclub and the girls were determined to attend. Before they left the party, Rick beckoned to Jess to move away from the others.

'I want to spend more time alone with you, Jess, can you get away?'

'I understand, Rick, but I came on the cruise with my friends and I want to spend time with them. Why don't you come to Abba with us and then afterwards we can spend some time together on our own? Besides, I would like to check out your dancing skills and make sure they are up to scratch.'

'Okay, I suppose I will have to settle for that.'

Jess felt butterflies run through her body. She knew that Rick was a bit of a charmer and she had to keep him on his toes. She needed to protect herself from getting hurt but, at the same time, she knew she had to give him a chance.

***

The girls were looking forward to dinner because they were going to Caprice, one of the speciality restaurants. It was known for its service and waiters who loved to show off by using techniques such as flambé. The setting was magnificent, with candlelit tables, linen tablecloths and low lighting from crystal chandeliers; there was certainly no expense spared when creating this lavish dining experience.

'That is without doubt the best meal we have had so far,' Beth said, as they ate.

'Did either of you notice that Meredith was acting a bit strangely at the party earlier?' Amelia asked.

'Yes, and I didn't know she knew the captain so well. I, for one, have had enough. I think it's about time we found out a little bit more about her.' Beth replied, not at all happy with their new friend's demeanour.

'Are you meeting Rick, Jess?' Amelia asked.

'Yes, I told him he could join us on the dance floor at Abba and that I wanted to spend time with you two beforehand.'

***

Panorama Nightclub was so busy that they were lucky to get a seat. Normally it would only be half full but, obviously, Abba was a massive draw for the guests on the cruise. The band was a very good cover band; if you closed your eyes you would have thought you were listening to the real thing. Beth and Jess danced all night with Amelia joining them every so often; it was driving her mad that she had to take it easy. Rick was mindful of what Jess had said about being with her friends and only got up to dance every now and again.

Later on, Rick led Jess out the door. She smiled at Amelia who winked back approvingly. Sam was beside her so she was very content. They were about to head to bed and as she looked around to say goodnight to Beth, she noticed that she, too, had disappeared. It looked like stateroom 8227 was going to be empty for the night with all promises forgotten!

DAY NINE

AT SEA (EN ROUTE TO VALLETTA)

It was an at-sea day and everyone had agreed that there was no pressure to get up early but when Jess opened the door she was a little surprised to see that the room had been left totally empty all night. She thought about it for a minute; this was a holiday for three best friends to celebrate their friendship by spending time together and here they were, trying to fit time with each other around shagging their various men! They had lost the run of themselves completely; three menopausal women with men falling at their feet! All the same, it was not bad going at their age – they certainly had no problems pulling handsome men!

She was thinking about the casino. She knew it would be open again all day when they were at sea. This was her opportunity to win more money, but she would have to be careful as the girls were keeping a close eye on her.

Beth arrived back, still in her dress from the previous night. Jess had changed so it wasn't obvious that she hadn't come back either.

'Good morning to you, my dear, I have to say it is a bit odd to see you in your finery at this time of day. Did you get any strange looks doing the walk of shame?' Jess grinned at her friend, secretly delighted that she hadn't been caught out herself.

'One or two, yes, but I couldn't care less. Are you going to tell me about Rick or do I have to drag it out of you?'

'We had an amazing time. I can't explain it but he seems to understand me. He is so gentle, Beth, but I am afraid of getting hurt. I am afraid that I am falling for him too quickly. When I met James, it was just like this – it was literally love at first sight. I couldn't stop thinking about him and wanting to be with him every waking moment. I feel like that with Rick but can it be possible to meet someone and fall in love so easily again?'

'I think it can when it is your destiny. I truly believe that there is more than one person out there for each of us. You wear your heart on your sleeve, Jess. It is exactly how I would see you falling in love again, because you are true to your feelings and know how to show love.'

'Thanks. Beth, I feel a lot better knowing that I have your support.'

'You have Amelia's too, I know that.'

Beth meant every word but she couldn't help thinking about what had happened to Jess all those years ago. She wondered if it had in some way affected her relationship with James. Jess was very insecure despite the air of confidence she portrayed.

***

In the summer of 1982, Jess, Beth and Amelia had met for the first time when their parents had sent them to Irish College in the Gaeltacht (Irish speaking part of Ireland). They had shared a cubicle in the main dormitory and had hit it off immediately. It wasn't long before they were inseparable. During the day, they had classes and sport, and every night there was a céilí dance. The girls always looked forward to dressing up, hoping that the boys they fancied would ask them to dance.

Jess wasn't interested in the boys because one of the younger teachers had taken a shine to her and had no intention of taking no for an answer. It had started out innocently at first and Jess thought that he was simply being nice to her and that she was the class pet. Then he started to ask her to stay back after class on her own and, after a few days, he told her he wanted her to sit on his knee. She was flattered but nervous and didn't know what to do; the next thing she knew he had his hand inside her blouse and was kissing her. She liked it; it made her feel grown up and gave her a funny feeling inside.

This continued every day after school for a week. Then he arranged to meet her in a secret place one night, but made her swear not to tell anyone about their plan. Jess had been excited and but hadn't told her friends anything. Later that night, when she found herself alone in the woods, having had her innocence brutally ripped from her, she wept as she thought about what had just happened. She was terrified and in pain and it took her a while to find her way back to the dorm. When her friends saw the state she was in, they wanted to report it but Jess refused, blaming herself and worrying that no one would believe her. And so it became their sworn secret. Jess had learned to live with it but she had clearly never really recovered and had very little trust in men.

***

'What are the plans today? Have you checked the bible? I absolutely adore the at-sea days.' Jess was loving everything about the cruise, but the idea of a whole day without having to get off the ship was lovely because it meant there was time to really enjoy the facilities and entertainment on board.

'Well, we have booked a long lunch in Caprice and some spa treatments for this morning, so we just have to plan the rest of the day. I hope you're not intending to blow all your winnings in the casino.' Beth was not joking; she knew it would be open all day and night while they were at sea.

Amelia arrived out onto the balcony.

'Hi you two, I can only assume we all had a very pleasurable end to our evening yesterday?'

'Now that you have brought it up, Amelia, I just want to put it on record that I think we are a bloody disgrace! Imagine if any of our friends or family could see what we have been up to.' Jess was laughing but they all knew that she was right.

'I found this outside the door in our mailbox,' Beth said, holding up an envelope. She opened it.

MS AMELIA BRADY, STATEROOM # 5227
We are delighted to inform you that you and Jessica Jones have been chosen to play together in 'Who wants to be a Millionaire' this afternoon at 4pm in the Santana Theatre on deck four where you will have the opportunity to win a cruise amongst other fantastic prizes! Please phone ext.323 to confirm your participation by 11am. Good luck!

'Oh my goodness, you two have been chosen to play 'Who wants to be a Millionaire' this afternoon as a couple,' Beth said.

'You're joking! I can't believe it. I mean, we only put our names down for the craic. I never thought we would be chosen. Are you included, Beth?' Jess asked excitedly.

'No, it is a couples' one this time and that means they don't need three of us.' She was a bit disappointed, although she was delighted for her friends.

'Well, it doesn't matter anyway. Whatever we win, we will split three ways!' Amelia piped up.

Jess dialled the number and asked for a few more details. She was told to be in the theatre thirty minutes in advance of the quiz. There would be two other couples and the allotted time for the show was ninety minutes. The first prize was a seven-night cruise for two people anywhere in Europe.

Amelia was very excited. 'Okay, the deal is that all three of us are going on the cruise if we win and we will pick a fab itinerary. Now all we have to do is make sure we do win!'

'It's practically impossible to prepare and practise for this but at least with two of us playing, it should be a bit easier,' Jess said cheerfully.

'I have a massage booked so I'm off to relax now while you two plan your strategy. Don't forget to tell the boys to come along; the more support we have the better.'

Beth was happy that they would all be going on the cruise if they won, so she didn't mind not being on the stage – she would be able to give them a terrible slagging if they didn't win.

Amelia went for a rest while Jess headed off to the casino; she had been thinking about nothing else since her big win.

***

The minute she arrived in the spa, Beth immediately fell under the spell of the beautiful aromas that enveloped her. She was offered a beautifully folded fresh robe and was guided towards the treatment room where her therapist, Adele, left her alone to get ready. She loved having beauty treatments, especially massages and facials, and tried to have them at least once a month. She had been to many beautiful spas in her time and this one was up there with the best of them; no expense had been spared in creating a sanctuary where you could have the best signature treatments – and pay dearly for the pleasure!

She took everything off and lay naked on her stomach with just the towel over her. As she lay there, she began to dream about the girls winning the cruise and where they might go.

***

Jess thought about contacting Rick when she was on her way down to the casino. She was in two minds about asking him to join her but she decided to text him.

Good morning Rick, I am on my own for a change and thought it would be nice to see you. Are you free for half an hour? Jess xx

She was walking down the stairs to deck four when she heard her phone beeping.

Good morning, gorgeous! I would love to see you. I just need to finish some work and I can be with you in ten minutes. Where will you be?

Jess decided that she was going to find out if her gambling was a deal-breaker for Rick. She had been wondering about what he had said about her having a gambling problem and she needed to clarify the situation. She took the bull by the horns and started typing.

I am just arriving in the casino, going to have a little look around before I play. Are you in the mood for a flutter?

Jess had pressed 'send' before she read the text through properly; she hadn't realised what she had suggested. She was mortified!

I most certainly am in the mood. See you in a few minutes!

Jess found the casino an extremely enticing place, full of excitement, glamour, risk and cash – lots and lots of cash. She decided to wander for a bit. She didn't want to choose a table until Rick arrived in case he wanted to play too. She had been thinking about what Beth had said about giving her the $9,000 to look after; she would give it to her later on.

When Rick found her, he kissed her and they held hands as they walked together around the packed room.

'Did you say you wanted to have a flutter with me?' he asked, winking.

'No, what I said was would you like to have a flutter with me,' Jess replied. She felt her cheeks burning bright red.

'Well, maybe we should have a flutter together!'

They both laughed and he kissed her again.

'How about a bit of blackjack to get the fluttering started?' Jess giggled.

'That sounds pretty good to me. Lead the way, Madame!'

They played for about half an hour and were down about $100 so they decided to go for a coffee.

'I want to ask you about something you said to me the other night, Rick,' Jess said uneasily.

'Yes, of course. What is it?' Rick replied, a little on edge.

'You asked me if I had a gambling problem.' She looked at him, trying to read his expression.

'That's right.' He didn't elaborate.

'Why did you ask me that?' she said.

'My father had a serious gambling addiction that affected us all growing up and my mother had a terrible time with him. I was worried when I saw you gamble such a large sum of money on one bet.'

Jess took both his hands in hers and looked into his eyes. 'I am really sorry that you had such a difficult time with your dad's problem but I don't have a gambling problem. Casinos are illegal in Ireland, for goodness sake! Look, Rick, I know you saw me do a very irrational thing when I placed that bet, but I promise you I have never done anything like that before. There is a private members club in Dublin that sort of gets around the illegal gambling rule and I have played and lost money there. I did come on the cruise hoping to win some money. To be fair, I don't think anyone goes to a casino with the intention of losing. I will be honest with you and say that I love the buzz of the casino and the thrill of the win. I would happily spend hours here but I know that it is not real life and I am not a millionaire with money to burn. I am also aware that I have the potential to develop a problem and I have to be careful, which is why I am going to give $9,000 of my winnings to the girls to look after for me.'

Jess had been economical with the truth as she didn't want to frighten him away. She decided that she would tell him the full truth when she knew him better.

Rick said nothing; he simply smiled and squeezed her hands so she continued.

'I know that we don't know each other very well and I know that I am asking a lot when I ask you to trust me on this, but if you want to be with me you have to take me as I am. Beth agrees with you that I was a bit insane when I placed the bet and I am going to listen to her and to you and make sure that I never do anything like that again. I can't say fairer than that, can I?' Jess smiled meekly, her eyes watering up.

'No, I most certainly can't ask for more than that. Thank you for explaining, Jess.'

'I think you may be a good influence on me, Sir! Guess what?' Jess had pulled herself together and was almost giddy as she spoke.

'I've absolutely no idea. What?' Rick found her enchanting.

'Amelia and I have been chosen to play in 'Who wants to be a Millionaire'!'

'Wow, that's fantastic! That's today, isn't it?'

'Yes, it's at 4pm this afternoon and the first prize is a cruise. Will you come and support us? Beth will be in the audience because she didn't get chosen.'

'Yes, of course, how exciting.'

Rick was delighted to have had the chat with Jess. He felt more relaxed about things now and was looking forward to the quiz in the afternoon.

***

Rick's wine business had really taken off over the past two years and he knew that he was ready for a relationship again. He had employed another five staff in the past six months and the cruise contract had been a huge addition to his growing client base. His marriage break-up had nearly destroyed him; his family meant the world to him and he couldn't believe it when he came home from work one day and found his wife in bed with another man. She had thought that he was in France on a buying trip, but Rick had his suspicions that she was having an affair so he had decided to set a trap and she had fallen for it. It had been very acrimonious initially but, for the sake of their daughters, they agreed to be civil and things were now quite amicable between them. His wife had gone on to marry her lover and he knew that it was time for him to move on with his love life also.

***

'Here she is; our very own little wanderer!' Beth said with a laugh when Jess arrived back in the room. 'So, did you win?'

Jess was a bit taken aback that Beth would have assumed that she had been in the casino.

'No, but I met Rick and we only lost a small amount between us. He told me that his father had a very bad gambling addiction that had affected his family all their life, and he was worried that I had an addiction too.'

Jess had decided to be truthful with the girls; it was the only way and there had been enough secrets over the past few days. 'I want you to take the money and look after it for me, Beth, just like you offered. I need a bit of help but I don't want you to stop me going to the casino altogether, I need some play money!'

'Absolutely, Jess, I am so proud of you and it looks like you've found a good man in Rick.' Beth gave her friend a big hug. 'Let's go to lunch.'

'We need to take it easy with the drink if we are to be at the top of our game for the quiz this afternoon. There is a cruise at stake and I really think we can win it.' Jess was very confident and her excitement was infectious.

'I love your enthusiasm. I hope you'll put your money where your mouth is because I don't think my general knowledge is all that great, Jess.' Amelia was feeling very nervous and starting to wish she wasn't doing it. 'Do you think that you could do it instead of me, Beth?'

'I'd be happy to, Amelia, but I imagine that they will be using our ship pass as ID and we won't be able to transfer. We can ask, though, there's no harm in that.' Beth was thinking that she would love to take Amelia's place, but it probably wouldn't happen.

***

They had a delicious lunch with just a couple of glasses of wine and went back to the room to relax. Later on, they went down to the theatre which had been set up to look exactly like the set of the real show. It was incredibly authentic and a feeling of excitement and anticipation started to rush through Jess. They went to see if Marcus would allow them to transfer Amelia's place to Beth but, unfortunately, he told them that because the paperwork had all been finalised, it wasn't possible.

Beth had known that this would probably happen so she was prepared and didn't mind, but Amelia started to get really nervous and wasn't sure if she could do it.

'I am really scared. The idea of getting up there in front of all these people is freaking me out.' She was actually getting terrified.

'Okay, Amelia, sit down here and I will go back over to Marcus and explain your situation. You never know, it might make a difference.'

Jess stayed with Amelia while Beth went over to Marcus who was rushing around the place trying to organise everything; it looked as if he was under serious pressure.

'Marcus, I'm sorry to be asking you this again, but our friend is not well. She is pregnant and has really high blood pressure, so I don't think it would be a good idea for her to go on. I know the paperwork has been done so why don't I go in her place? You need another person anyway now and nobody will be any the wiser.' Beth was very calm and persuasive and Marcus didn't have time to find a substitute at this late stage so he agreed. It was all sorted.

Backstage there were lots of people walking around with clipboards. The girls were asked to sit down and to give a bit of information about themselves for the introduction on stage. After that, the six contestants were brought together and told how everything would happen. The names had been drawn for the order of play; there would be no 'fastest finger first' unless there was a tie-breaker. The girls would be on second. The 'phone a friend' would be one of the crew and they would have a choice from five people. It was pot luck really, though the contestants were assured that the five staff were all quite good at general knowledge.

The audience was given coloured cards with the letters A, B, C, D on them. The producer would take the majority showing of cards as the answer. The questions had been taken randomly from previous productions of the show and they had the presenter from Australia's 'Who wants to be a Millionaire' as the host. All in all, it was as close to the real thing as you could possibly get.

Jess and Beth were sitting together, waiting for their turn, when they heard the music start. Marcus introduced Eddie McGuire, the host for the show.

'It's all beginning to feel very real,' Jess said. 'I didn't realise they were going to do it so authentically.' She was a bit nervous but was trying to hide it.

'I know, Jess, I thought it would be quite amateurish so I am very surprised. I don't know how you're feeling, but I'm starting to feel a bit jittery.' Beth was beginning to wonder why she had volunteered to swap with Amelia.

'Try not to dwell on it. We'll be grand,' Jess replied. She knew that Beth could get herself very worked up if she didn't nip it in the bud. 'Try to focus on winning that cruise.'

They both squeezed hands and sat in silence as they watched the show on the screen backstage.

***

The first couple, a husband and wife in their sixties called Jack and Vera, was from Florida. Jess started to laugh and relax as she remembered the characters from *Coronation Street* who had the same names. The questions weren't easy but Jack and Vera managed to get to $16,000, which was very good. It was going to be tough for the girls to beat them.

'And next we have Jess and Amelia from Ireland,' Marcus announced, forgetting that it was Beth.

The girls came out onto the main stage and sat on the high chairs in front of Eddie. He whispered to them to relax before the music stopped. They both looked down at the audience, searching for their friends, but they couldn't see anything because of the lighting. Eddie introduced them asked them a little about themselves before getting on with the quiz.

They had no problems getting to $1,000. The first hurdle was the $2,000 question which was a geography one. They had to use up their 50-50 lifeline, which knocked their confidence but after that they got as far as $64,000 before being knocked back down to $32,000 on an American history question.

This meant they were in the lead and it all hung on the next couple who were from Sydney, Horo and Tan. They were in their late fifties and Tan was very glamorous; she looked as if she should be on a catwalk more so than on a gameshow.

'Do you think they'll be any good?' Beth asked, as if expecting Jess to know the answer!

'This is going to sound totally bitchy and nonsensical but I think that she will be useless because she can't possibly be brainy as well as beautiful,' Jess answered. She was laughing but she meant every word.

The music started again and Horo and Tan took their seats. Things were going really well and they got to $16,000 with one life still left. Jess and Beth started to get excited backstage.

'I am afraid to even think that it might be within our reach. We just need them to miss one question and lose that life and then we're in with a serious chance!' Jess said, grinning like a Cheshire cat.

'You are going to jinx us. Shut up, Missus!' Beth was very superstitious in everything she did.

Horo and Tan got to $64,000, then they got a question about a US daytime TV show which was very tricky for them, just as the American history question had been very difficult for the girls. They didn't know the answer and were back down to $32,000, just like the girls.

Marcus returned to the stage.

'We have a tie-breaker situation, ladies and gentlemen, so we are going to go to sudden death using 'fastest finger first'. Each of our couples must choose one partner to represent them. We will take a break and see you back here soon for the exciting finale.'

'Oh God, I can't believe this is happening!' Beth was nearly sick with fear and excitement. 'Will you do it, Jess? I really don't think I could cope.'

'I will, Beth, but I think your general knowledge is better than mine.' Jess looked at her with a very serious expression on her face.

'This is about time and pressure more than anything else. You know the way you have to put things in order? That's what we have to do and you are so good at that,' Beth explained,

'Okay, I'll do it.' Jess felt complimented by Beth's comments and forgot her nerves for a moment.

***

Amelia, Sam, Kale and Rick were in the audience and couldn't believe what had just happened.

'I've never seen such a nail-biting game show in my life,' Beth joked as they went out to the bar for drinks.

'I think that has something to do with you having a vested interest in the contestants,' Sam remarked, laughing.

'I am very impressed with their knowledge, especially considering the fact that the questions have been so varied and international,' Rick said.

Amelia was delighted. She felt very proud of her friends, and even if they didn't win, she knew they would be booking another cruise.

'It's just about to start. We'd better go back in,' Kale said when he heard the drum roll.

***

The stage had been changed around so that there were two chairs lined up perpendicular to the audience and there was a keypad to the left of each chair. Jess and Horo had been chosen to play. Their partners were sitting on chairs near the back of the stage, out of sight of their team member but within view of the audience. Marcus introduced Eddie again and he, in turn, explained the rules. The question was about rivers in Asia and the contestants had to put them in order of longest to shortest, beginning with the longest. Horo and Jess answered the question as well as they could.

'It looks very close,' Marcus announced. 'I will have to play it back with the producer and we will announce the winner at 7pm this evening. Thank you all for participating and making it such a fantastic game. I hope you all enjoyed it.'

The girls had a quick word with Marcus and Eddie to thank them both and then they went to find the gang, who were waiting for them in the bar just outside the theatre.

'You two were amazing,' Amelia said as she hugged her friends. 'Do you think you've won?'

'I haven't a clue,' Jess answered. 'I did know the answers so it's all about the timing. Maybe we are in with a chance.' She was beginning to get very excited.

'I know we should go and get ready for dinner but I just want to stay down here.' Beth was in the mood for going drinking and when she was like this she was unstoppable.

'We can do what we like so if you want to stay here, then that is what we shall do, my dear,' Jess answered.

'I just want to wait for the result; the suspense is too much. I have never won anything in my life, much less been in any sort of a quiz or competition.' Beth was on a complete high.

Rick had to go back to work but he assured Jess that he would be back for 7pm to hear the announcement.

They made their way into the grand foyer and found some seats. The Flutes were playing and quite a few people were enjoying the music as they waited to hear the result of the show. Jess spotted Horo and Tan sitting over by the window and she gave them a friendly wave.

Marcus arrived and headed over to where the band was playing. When the song had finished he took the microphone.

'Ladies and gentlemen, you are all very welcome. As some of you may know, we had a fantastic game of 'Who wants to be a Millionaire' and it was a nail-biting finish in the end. I had to get our adjudicators to look into the results and am now delighted to announce that the winners of the superb cruise are Jess and Amelia from Ireland! Please come and join me, ladies.'

The girls were totally overwhelmed as everyone clapped and cheered them on. Marcus congratulated them and handed them their prize.

'Congratulations, it was a very well-deserved win and I hope you enjoy yourselves on whatever cruise you choose,' Marcus said. 'Who knows, you might come back to me on the *Santana*.'

Marcus had remembered it was Beth who was on stage but he decided to call her Amelia for the sake of continuity and ease; the paperwork involved in changing the names would have been a nightmare.

'Thanks Marcus. We are so excited, I can't believe this is happening!' Jess said, jumping up and down.

She grabbed Beth and they ran back to the others.

Rick had arrived just in time to see the announcement. 'I think celebrations are in order. My best champagne will be organised later on, just leave it to me.'

'Where are we going to go next? Not only have we won a cruise but we will be getting a suite on the ship; we won't know ourselves!' The girls had never seen Beth so excited before and it was quite endearing. 'I can't wait to start planning it,' she declared.

'I think we should go back to the room and get ready and then head to dinner. The excitement is getting too much and you don't want me to go into labour!' Amelia joked.

***

They were dressed in all their finery as they headed down to Kiko; they had been dying to try it since the cruise had started. As soon as they entered the restaurant, they were shown to their table and each handed an iPad which contained the menu. The food on offer was divided into regions of the world, with China, Japan, Mexico, the Mediterranean, India, Persia, North and South America represented. The idea was to order a few items at a time – a bit like international tapas.

After they'd eaten a delightful meal, Jess' phone beeped.

Hi Jess, are you and the girls finished dinner? I was wondering if you would like to meet in the Cave Wine Bar?

'Rick has just sent me a text asking if we would meet him in the Cave. What are our plans?'

'We didn't really make any this morning what with all the commotion of the gameshow,' Amelia replied. 'What would you like to do, Jess?'

'Well, I'd like to meet up with him at some point but, more importantly, I want to celebrate our win together and start planning our next cruise.'

'What about you, Beth?' Amelia wasn't sure if Kale and Beth had arranged to meet up; their relationship was getting a little confusing.

'I want to party with both of you and I don't mind whether the men are there or not; this is about the three of us.' Beth was on a complete high; if Amelia didn't know better she would have said she had taken something.

'Okay, my suggestion is that you text Rick and tell him we will meet him in the Cave and we'll take it from there. Does anyone know if there's anything special going on in the Panorama Nightclub?' Amelia was tired but she knew they only had a few nights left and she wanted to make the most of them.

We will meet you in the Cave in five minutes. We're open to suggestions for partying the night away!

Jess grinned to herself as she pressed the send button. Rick was thrilled; he couldn't believe how much this woman was starting to mean to him and he wanted to spend as much time with her as he could.

I'll be there. xxxx

'I checked with reception and you're not going to believe what's on tonight in Panorama – Madonna!' Beth announced, as excited as if Madonna herself was going to be performing.

***

Sam and Kale arrived. Rick had organised the champagne and the celebrations were soon in full swing.

'Well done, ladies,' Meredith said as she arrived to the table with a glass of champagne in her hand. 'I heard all about your win today. It seems you're the talk of the ship.'

She was smiling but Jess wasn't sure if she was being sincere.

'Yes, we're celebrating, we can't believe it!' Beth said. She continued in a slightly sarcastic tone. 'Do you want to join us? Maybe you can tell us all about how you know the captain.' The girls were starting to realise that Beth was very drunk.

'Yes, thank you, I would love to join you,' Meredith responded, ignoring Beth's remark.

'Well, then, what is the story, Meredith?' Beth was determined to get the truth from her.

'The captain and I have known each other for years, there is no big secret, Beth, you are making a big deal out of nothing.' She looked at Kale who acknowledged her with his eyes, but said nothing.

'There's something you're not telling us, Meredith,' Beth said. She left it at that but her mind was made up about this woman.

DAY TEN

VALLETTA

Amelia was up first. She knew the captain was sailing into Valetta a little later than usual to afford people the opportunity to enjoy the experience. She was really looking forward to Valletta. She had been there a few years before with Paul and the kids and they had loved it. She took the bible out on to the veranda and stood leaning over the balcony, watching the ship sail into the port. It was a magnificent day. The sky was blue and the water was clear and sparkling. Amelia pinched herself; for a moment she felt like she was in a dream.

'Good morning,' Jess said as she came out onto the veranda.

'You're just in time, Jess. Is Beth awake? She would love to see this.' Amelia pulled back the curtain a little and looked into their room.

'I'm coming now, don't fret!' Beth replied.

They were all speechless as they watched the ship glide towards land. As she moved inside the port, she seemed to turn around as if preparing to head back out again.

'What is the captain doing, Jess?' Amelia asked. 'Are we leaving again?'

'No, he is turning so that he will have a different side of the ship against the wall today to try and make it fair for the guests. Sometimes he docks portside and at other times he docks on the starboard side,' Jess explained.

Once the ship had finished turning, it started to reverse into place. The crew were running around madly and it was incredible to watch the skill involved in the procedure. When they had tied up and the engines were finally switched off, the girls sat down.

'That was amazing – one of the highlights of the trip for me,' Amelia said with a smile.

'I only wish I had seen more of the ship cruising into port,' Beth stated.

'I know, but they always arrive too bloody early. It's something I think they should look at changing. We can't be the only ones that want to watch it at a more civilised hour. I think it's something to do with the excursions. A lot of them leave very early so the ship needs to facilitate that,' Amelia said knowledgeably.

'That makes sense, Amelia,' Beth said jovially before changing the subject. 'Valletta is one of the places I really want to see so I want to get off the ship as soon as possible. I don't mind going on my own if you two want to take your time.'

She was not usually so keen on sightseeing and the girls were quite amused by her comments.

'Well, excuse us! This is slightly unusual for you Ms Carmody. Why the mad desire to see Malta?' Amelia was grinning as she winked at her friend. 'Are you planning a romantic rendezvous or something?'

'Oh, for God's sake, Amelia! Not everything I do revolves around men. I have always wanted to see Malta – that's all!' Beth was indignant as she spoke.

'Relax! I'm only joking.' Amelia felt she had hit a nerve.

Kale had sent a text to Beth earlier that morning but, as her phone was on sleep mode, Jess and Amelia didn't know about it.

I know you are excited about Malta today. I have been there a couple of times so if you can spend some time with me today I would love to show you around. Kale xxx

Beth didn't know how to handle the situation with the girls, especially after the comment Amelia had just made. Maybe she should just come out with it and tell them the truth? After all the things they had kept from each other so far, it was uncharacteristic of them to keep secrets like this.

'Okay, you're right, Amelia, Kale sent me a text saying that he would like to show me around Malta. He's been here before. How is it that you can read me like a book? It's very annoying.'

'It's called friendship,' Amelia said. 'We go back a very long way, Beth, and I wouldn't change you for the world. I think you should meet him if that's what you want. We only have two days left so we have to make the most of them. In fact, I have a suggestion.' Amelia was going to take a chance on saying something she hoped would go down well.

'Maybe today we could spend some time with the guys. I know it is breaking our own rules but now that each of us has a man on board, surely there is no harm in it and it will give us more to talk about over dinner later. What do you think?' She was hesitant as she spoke.

Beth and Jess looked at each other and smiled. 'Would we ever have imagined this situation ten days ago?' Jess giggled. 'I think you have your answer, Amelia.'

Texts were sent and arrangements made before the girls set off for breakfast in the Wayfarer.

***

When Amelia arrived at Sam's room at 9.30am, he couldn't believe how beautiful she looked. Maybe it was the pregnancy, or maybe it was just his sheer love for her, but there was one thing he knew: he was never going to love any other woman.

'I want to make the most of this day, darling, we have never had time like this together and I want it to be very special. I know you have been to Malta before. Is there anywhere in particular you would like to go?'

Sam liked to spoil and pamper Amelia but in this instance Amelia knew the place and he didn't.

'I think we should do a little bit of sightseeing with a private taxi and then I want to take you into Sliema where we can walk around and look at the shops and find a nice place for lunch,' she said. 'There is a restaurant I have in mind, but I'm not sure if it is still there so we will wait and see.'

They didn't notice the forty-five minute journey to Mdina because they were so engrossed in each other's company. Once they arrived there, they walked around, enjoying the spectacular setting. They noticed a large group of beautifully dressed people standing outside a church and realised that a wedding was about to commence. A white, vintage Bentley drove up and the bride and her father got out. Amelia was transfixed; what girl doesn't like watching a wedding and looking at the bride?

'This is such a romantic place for a wedding, Sam, and she looks radiant. I don't think I will ever forget today.'

'Look Amelia,' Sam said, pointing, 'it's Meredith.'

Standing beside the cruise ship's captain, Meredith was wearing a stunning silk dress in three shades of blue that looked very much like a DVF number. She had a signature Philip Treacy hat and Jimmy Choo shoes to finish it all off.

'Wow, she looks fantastic, Sam, that dress really flatters her,' Amelia said. 'What is she doing here, though, and why is she with the captain? Do you think we should go over and say hello, or would that be out of order?' She was out of her mind with curiosity but she was well mannered and would never like to do what she considered the wrong thing.

'No, darling, I don't think we should go over. You can find out all about it later.' Sam was curious too but he was more interested in spending time with Amelia.

Just as they were about to leave, Meredith spotted them. She whispered in Jean Claude's' ear that she was going over to talk to the Irish girl.

'Amelia! Sam! Hi!' Meredith called to them. She had no idea how she was going to handle this unexpected situation.

'Hi Meredith, I didn't know you were going to a wedding, especially in such a beautiful place,' Amelia said in a sarcastic voice.

'The bride is the captain's daughter and he invited me,' Meredith replied in a noncommittal tone.

Amelia didn't want to seem too nosey in front of Sam, but she felt Meredith owed her more of an explanation than that.

'You must be great friends with the captain.' Again Amelia was being sarcastic, something which was obvious to both Sam and Meredith.

'As I said, we go back a long way. What are you two up to?'

Meredith was clearly not going to go into the details of her relationship with the captain and Amelia was frustrated. Beth was right; they had all confided in her and laid themselves bare, and she had told them nothing. She knew she wasn't going to get any further with the Texan, so she very reluctantly dropped the topic.

'We're going to go down towards Sliema to take a walk around and find somewhere romantic to have lunch,' Sam said. He smiled as he looked lovingly at Amelia and Meredith felt sick with jealousy.

'Well, enjoy, I'm off to the reception which is taking place on the ship,' Meredith said as she walked towards the wedding party.

'I wonder if they are all staying on the ship?' Amelia commented. 'It's weird that Meredith never mentioned anything about this wedding before. I can't understand it. I think it's a big deal to be part of the captain's daughter's wedding; it will probably be a major event back on board.' She felt quite annoyed with Meredith but she was curious as well.

'Well, you are just going to have to wait to find out more, my little nosey parker!' Sam replied. He gave her a warm hug and they got back into a taxi and went to Sliema.

***

It was a gorgeous drive along the coast after they had left the hillside areas of Mdina and Rabat. Once in the town, they asked the driver to drop them in a central location. They walked hand in hand through the streets, stopping every now and again to peruse the menus in different restaurants. They finally found a pretty little restaurant that offered Maltese/Italian food. They sat down, both tired after the morning of sightseeing.

'Malta is really lovely, Sam, I would love to come back again for a longer holiday. I don't know how I'm going to face reality when we go home; it's all so heavenly and I can't bear what lies ahead.' Amelia was starting to remember the predicament she was in.

'I know, but let's enjoy today. We won't have this time together again for a while.' Sam looked at her lovingly as he reached out his hand and put it on hers reassuringly. 'I am here, we are in this together.'

They lost all sense of reality as they enjoyed their romantic lunch.

***

Beth met Kale on deck four where they were disembarking. She didn't know what he had planned, but she was very excited. They had to wait a while for a taxi and the minute they arrived at the top of the hill they saw the horse-drawn carriages.

'Would you like to take a horse and carriage, Madame?' Kale asked. 'We could do a trip around Valletta.'

'I would love that, Sir. Please lead the way!' Beth answered happily.

They walked over to where the horses were lined up. Kale did a deal and they were soon on their way. The driver spoke quite good English and Kale asked him to show them the most interesting sights, as well as throwing in something special so he gave them a bespoke tour, finishing off in the Barrakka Gardens with their magnificent views over the harbour.

'That was wonderful and I loved every minute of it,' Beth said and kissed him affectionately. 'I know we said you were in charge today, but having seen a bit of the place now I think it might be nice to do some people-watching down by the waterfront.'

They walked happily along the street before wandering down the steep hill towards the sea, stopping every now and again to take some photos and admire the beauty of the setting and their gorgeous ship in all her splendour out it the water. They perused the menus of quayside cafes and restaurants before deciding on a lovely waterside table in a little Italian bistro.

Beth and Kale enjoyed watching the comings and goings of the *Santana* and another cruise ship in the port. They noticed a red carpet being laid at the entrance to their ship and wondered what was going on.

'There seems to be a wedding down at our ship,' Beth remarked. 'I can see a bride and lots of people all dressed up getting out of buses. Did Marco tell you there was a wedding happening?'

'No, he didn't. I had no idea and there has certainly been no sign of any celebrations so far, so maybe they are only joining us on board now. This could be fun, maybe they'll lay on fireworks or something like that. When I was on a cruise before, there was a wedding and they had fireworks every night for a week,' Kale replied.

Beth's phone beeped.

Hi ladies. You're not going to believe it but we just ran into Meredith with the captain. She was at his daughter's wedding in Mdina and they are going back to the ship for the reception. P.S. Hope you're having fun!' A xx

'Well, I have the answer, Kale. You're not going to believe this. The captain's daughter is the bride and she just got married in the church in Mdina. Amelia and Sam met Meredith who is at the wedding as a guest of the captain! What the hell is going on with that woman? I knew she was not being straight with us. How does she know the captain and why has she not told us about the wedding? If I was going to a beautiful wedding in Malta as a guest of the captain, I would be shouting it from the rooftop.' Beth was prone to exaggeration from time to time.

She sent a text to the others.

We're sitting here at the waterfront having lunch and they are all getting on the ship now. We were wondering what was going on, Amelia. Meredith is certainly a very secretive woman. B x

Beth and Kale headed back to the ship, curious to see what was going on. As they arrived, they saw Meredith disappearing inside the ship.

***

Meredith was furious that Amelia had seen her at the wedding. She should have been more careful and should have known that there would be people from the cruise visiting Mdina. How was she going to explain it to the girls? She knew they were suspicious of her already and she was not going to get away with fobbing them off. She was annoyed with Jean Claude, too. What had he turned her into? She had been a normal, law-abiding person before she'd met him.

***

Jess was meeting Rick at 9.30am at the casino; it seemed as good a place as any. He hadn't said anything about the itinerary he had planned for the day, but Jess knew it would be a special day for both of them. When she arrived, there was no sign of him, but she needn't have worried – he arrived seconds later and she started to have that butterfly feeling she'd been getting since she first met him.

'I can't believe we have this day to spend together, Jess, let's get out of here.' He grabbed her hand and she followed him, as if hypnotised.

'Have you been to Malta before, Jess? I know you've travelled a lot?'

'Funnily enough, it is one of the few places I haven't seen and one of the reasons we chose this itinerary was because Beth and I have never been here. I've been really looking forward to it so I hope you know where you're going.' Jess was feeling very relaxed and happy.

'I know Malta very well. In fact, I spent a few months living here a few years ago and I was considering exporting some of their wine but, after doing some market research, I felt it wouldn't sell well so I abandoned the idea. If you are happy to leave things in my hands, I will show you the best of the island, allowing for the time constraints of the ship, of course.'

'I would be delighted. Lead the way, kind Sir!' Jess said, smiling. 'Where are we going?'

'Sssh! Patience is a virtue and I'm not sure you have much of it,' he said teasingly.

He led her down to the pier where their own private gondola was waiting for them. There were other boats lined up that could take up to eight passengers, but Rick wanted to really spoil her.

'This is amazing, Rick, thank you.' Jess gave him a long, lingering kiss on the lips.

The boatman went around all three harbours and explained everything in perfect English. Jess decided that she was hooked on Malta even thought she had only just arrived.

When they returned to the waterfront, there was a limousine waiting for them.

'You certainly know how to treat a lady, Rick. You had better be careful, though, because I could get very used to this!'

They got inside and Jess sat back while Rick poured the champagne. They drove for a while and then stopped for a wine tasting in a family-owned winery that was well known for producing award-winning wines. Jess adored the whole experience; she'd had wine tastings in many countries and it was always a joy to learn about the different methods used in wine production in the different regions.

When they were done, they jumped back into the limo and drove through the hills and countryside before having a quick stop in Mdina and then driving along the coast.

'I never want this day to end, Rick. How do you know what I like? It's incredible.'

Jess lay back in his arms and felt a warm glow rise through her. She was really aroused and turned to kiss him. He returned her kiss hungrily and they moved closer, forgetting where they were. The driver was separated from them by glass, but they knew it was inappropriate to behave in this way so they pulled away from each other reluctantly.

They finally reached St Julian's where they stopped for lunch. The limo pulled up outside Paranga and the driver opened the door. Rick got out and then helped Jess out. He told the driver he would call him when they were ready to go home. Paranga was a small, long restaurant, built out over the sea and specialising in seafood. The tables were mostly waterside but one table was located in its own glass room, with glass flooring and the sea visible on all sides and beneath the diners. Unbelievably, Rick had managed to book this very special space at short notice.

When they were seated and the wine had been poured, Jess looked at him.

'I have been many places in the world, but this is definitely the most romantic restaurant table I have ever sat at. Thank you. It is hard to put into words how much I am enjoying today.'

Just as she finished speaking, Jess heard her phone beep.

Hi ladies, you're not going to believe it but we just ran into Meredith with the captain. She was at his daughter's wedding in Mdina and they are going back to the ship for the reception! Hope you're having fun! A xx

'I don't believe it,' Jess said to Rick, 'Amelia and Sam have just seen Meredith with the captain at his daughter's wedding in some church in Malta!'

'Well, you did say you thought something strange was going on,' he responded.

'Did you know they were going to a wedding?' she asked.

'God no, I would have told you if I did,' Rick replied, a bit puzzled as to why Jess thought he might have known about it.

'Sorry, I just thought that because you know the captain you might have known about it, especially if the reception was on the ship. Surely more champagne and wine would need to have been ordered? Maybe they don't drink, or maybe they have a secret stash! I wonder what's going on and why Meredith did not say anything? She made out to us that she was on the ship on her own, recuperating from a broken marriage.' Jess was dying to get to the bottom of things. 'I suppose I'll have to wait until later to find out more. Let's order the food.'

'I know we won't get the chance to have time like this on the ship,' Rick said. 'You are with your friends and I fully understand that, but we have something very special and I want to make plans to see you over the next couple of weeks.'

Rick couldn't believe how he had fallen for this Irish girl; he was totally smitten and spent every waking moment thinking about her.

'I fly the LAX route and it is direct, so I don't pass through the UK ever, really,' Jess said in an unintentionally flippant way.

'Well, I can come and see you. I have some clients in Dublin so I go there regularly and maybe you could come with me on some of my trips to France and Spain. What do you think?'

Jess didn't want to sound too enthusiastic. People always said that you should treat them mean to keep them keen. 'I'd love to show you Dublin when you're next over,' she offered.

Rick wasn't sure if this was a brush-off or whether she was just protecting herself from getting hurt, but he was determined to get this girl, no matter what it took.

'Am I taking things a bit too quickly, Jess?' he asked, somewhat nervously.

'No, Rick, it's just that you are the first person I've dated since my marriage ended, and I suppose I am out of practice. I find you very attractive and I adore your company. I would love to see you again soon in Dublin. I know we have something really strong here but I don't want to rush things, we have both been hurt and I, for one, have a fragile heart. The cruise is a holiday environment and I need to be sure we both feel the same way when we are back home.'

'I'll be in Dublin in two weeks' time and I will stay in my usual hotel and we can take it from there. Does that sound good?' he asked, smiling.

Jess beckoned to him to lean forward. She kissed him gently, giving him the answer he was looking for. 'This has been a very special day, one that I will never forget. Thank you.'

'Shall we go back to the ship?' Rick was grinning.

'Do you need to ask?' Jess thought she would burst with desire. Just at that moment she heard her phone beep.

I hope you're having a lovely day in Malta. I see you've been spending some time with the boys. I would love to get together for a drink in the Cave Wine Bar at 6pm if you can make it. I am at the wedding but I will slip away. Meredith

Jess couldn't believe it. They had all been curious about Meredith and Beth had been particularly disturbed by her behaviour but it seemed they were going to get some answers at six o'clock! She decided to text the other two:

Hi guys, hope you've been enjoying the day. I can't believe the goings-on. We're on our way back to the ship now and should be there in about five minutes. Will I see you back in the room? J

***

Back in the room they had so much to talk about, they didn't know where to start. All three went out on the balcony and sat down.

'Well?' Beth asked, grinning as she looked at them both.

'I had a fantastic time and Rick treated me like a princess.' Jess went on to tell them all about the day she'd had with him, and the other two were speechless with envy.

'You deserve it, Jess. God knows you've had a shit time over the past few years. I really hope this all works out with Rick,' Beth said warmly.

'What about you, Beth? How did it go with Kale?' Jess asked.

'It was a lovely day. Nothing as fancy as yours, but I really enjoyed it.' She told them about the horse and carriage and the relaxed time they had spent together and how it all felt very effortless and natural.

Then they both turned to Amelia.

'I think you are the one that had the interesting morning! What happened?' Beth was both amused and curious.

Amelia told them about Mdina and about Sam and the lovely romantic time they had. She explained that, just as they were leaving, they saw the wedding and Meredith with the captain. It was clearly a very upmarket wedding, judging by the style, and they enquired of a few local people who told them that you had to be very rich to hold a wedding in Mdina. But it was the fact that Meredith was there with the captain, and that she hadn't mentioned it before, nor had she mentioned her obviously close relationship with him, that didn't make sense.

Meredith had chased their friendship throughout the cruise and they had felt sorry for her being on her own and had included her as much as they could, confiding in her in a very personal way. They were now feeling a bit foolish that she clearly was not who she had pretended to be.

'How did she react when she saw you, Amelia?' Beth asked.

'She was really shocked and whispered something in the captain's ear before coming over to us. I don't think she expected to see anyone that she knew around and she wasn't prepared for it. She told us it was the captain's daughter that was getting married. What do you think her connection is with him and why has she wanted to keep it quiet?' Amelia was not normally bothered by things like this, but she found this story fascinating.

'I don't know what's going on, but it's intriguing. It's not the fact that she knows him that I find interesting; it is the fact that she didn't want us to know. Well, it seems she is going to tell us something at six. Whether it's the truth or not is anyone's guess,' Beth said.

'I think we should get dressed for dinner now and head down so we don't have to come back up afterwards. I get the feeling it's going to be a peculiar and possibly eventful evening,' Jess said.

***

The girls had been sitting in the Cave Wine Bar for about five minutes when Meredith arrived, bang on time. She looked stunning, but was a little on edge.

'You look gorgeous, Meredith. How is the wedding going?' Amelia asked nicely.

'Thank you, Amelia. It's been a great day so far. Look, girls, I just wanted to explain, I feel you should know what is going on.' Meredith was looking a bit pale as she spoke.

'The captain is my brother-in-law and it is my niece's wedding. My sister and brother-in-law were divorced very acrimoniously and, sadly, my sister died two years later from cancer. When she died, I spent a lot of time with him and the children and we became close and ended up having an affair while I was still married. We both felt it would be better if we ended it as we didn't think it would be fair on my sister's children, but my marriage did not survive. I hope you can understand why I have kept this quiet.'

'I am sorry that there is sadness attached to such a happy occasion, Meredith. It must be difficult for all of you.' Beth was feeling a bit guilty for thinking suspiciously about Meredith, though she still wasn't happy with the answer. Something just wasn't adding up.

'I wanted to explain. I'm sorry for not telling you before, but it's not something that I talk about. I hope you understand. I have to go back in now, but maybe I'll see you later or, if not, tomorrow.' Meredith smiled meekly and left.

Once she was safely out of view, Beth turned to the others and spoke. 'There is more to that story, I'm sure of it.'

'What do you mean, Beth?' Amelia didn't quite understand why Beth had a problem with what Meredith had said.

'Think about it. She has told us a story about three failed marriages and coming on the ship to recover from the last one. The next thing we find her at the captain's party and she doesn't say anything about how she knows him and he turns out to be her brother-in-law. What's more, he didn't say anything either, come to think of it. We pour out our hearts to her and yet she doesn't even tell us that her niece is having her wedding reception on board, never mind the fact that the girl's father is her ex-lover! You then see her at a sophisticated wedding in Mdina with him. It's also highly unusual for a party of people to board the ship in the middle of a cruise, unless it's an official embarkation point. I know Jean Claude is the captain and I'm sure rules can be bent but, still, things are not adding up here, I'm telling you. Where were all these people beforehand? Surely the bridal party needed to check in before the wedding but, instead, they all just rocked up and got on a major cruise ship. Any cruise weddings I've ever heard about are totally on board; not in a church for the ceremony followed by the reception on the ship. The logistics are inconceivable.'

'You seem to have worked it all out, Beth. How do you know they hadn't checked in already?' Jess asked.

'I saw the baggage being taken off the coaches when we were having lunch, but the guests never went through the check-in process that we went through – they all stepped off the coach and up into the ship. That shouldn't happen. Everyone has to go through passport control, including crew, when they start a cruise. Security is watertight on cruise ships. Our photo comes up on a screen every time we use our ship pass. There is something going on. All that luggage and all those people have boarded without security checks and that makes me very uneasy.'

'Do you think Kale or Rick could find out anything?' Amelia was a bit startled now that she was beginning to see where Beth was coming from.

'They would have had to use the scanner at least, surely, Beth, and they would have had to have ship passes,' Jess said, trying to calm things down a little.

'Oh God, yes, I would hope so, unless there is some sort of crew conspiracy going on. But that means nothing if all the luggage has gone on without being scanned. I'm sure fake ship passes could always be arranged in advance,' Beth replied.

'Are you suggesting there is something corrupt going on, Beth?' Jess looked at her friend in horror.

'I don't know, but it smells, and I really don't think I'm overreacting here. I'll send Kale a text and ask him to come down. Actually, come to think of it, maybe all the boys should join us under the circumstances.' Beth was growing very concerned, she couldn't put her finger on it, but there was something dodgy going on; she was sure of it.

'I'm not saying you're over-reacting, Beth, but do you not think that maybe there is a simpler explanation? This is all very dramatic stuff and maybe we shouldn't get involved.' Amelia couldn't believe what Beth was saying.

Kale, can you come to the Cave Wine Bar? It is very urgent.

Just before she pressed 'send', she stopped and suddenly bells started to ring. Maybe Kale was in on the whole thing? It would make sense, considering his situation. It was all starting to add up now: Kale and Meredith knew each other and Kale knew the captain. Her imagination was going into overdrive.

Ignoring Amelia completely, Beth said: 'I don't know how to say this but I am not going to ask Kale. I have a sick feeling that he could be involved in all of this.' She went white then suddenly left and ran to the loo.

While she was gone, the others agreed that she was over-reacting and that they needed to calm her down; it was all getting very silly at this stage.

When she returned, Beth looked a lot better. Just then, Sam arrived. He sat down beside Amelia and looked at the three disturbed faces.

'Good God, what is going on?' he asked.

Jess told him everything and they all looked at him, eagerly awaiting his response.

'I too, have felt that there was something odd about Meredith, and that she was hiding something, but I don't think it's anything that affects us.' Sam spoke very calmly.

'I don't agree,' Beth said softly. 'I think it's people trafficking, and when you think about it, it's an ideal way to do it, but I will leave it be and hope to God that you are all right and I am wrong.'

They talked for a while longer and decided to leave things be for the moment as they had nothing substantial to go on.

***

After dinner in Orchid, they went to the theatre where there was a Moulin Rouge-style cabaret show on. Jess sent a text to Rick and he joined them for a lovely evening where everyone did their best to forget about Meredith and the captain.

After the show, Amelia and Sam went to bed while the others went up to the Panorama Nightclub. Beth spotted Kale dancing with his dance partner, Dana. He looked up as she came in and waved. As soon as the song ended, he came over.

'Hi guys, how has your evening been? Did you two have a nice time in Malta?' he asked Jess and Rick.

'We had a fantastic day. I absolutely loved Malta and can't wait to go back. Beth said you had a lovely day too.' Jess was giving Kale the benefit of the doubt for the moment.

'Yes, it was wonderful and now I think we should dance. Beth?' Kale took her by the hand and led her onto the dance floor.

Beth didn't know what to do. She was feeling uneasy but, at the same time, she thought that maybe she was wrong. Surely Kale wouldn't have had time to spend the day with her if he was involved in a big smuggling racket? She was totally confused and needed to calm her mind down.

Jess turned to Rick and asked him how well he knew the captain. Just as she finished speaking, Meredith walked in and made her way over to them. Jess could feel her chest tighten as she grabbed her drink.

'What's wrong, Jess?' Rick asked, puzzled.

'Nothing, I'm fine. Hi Meredith, how is the wedding going?' Jess spluttered.

'They are all still partying, but I've had enough. I thought I'd rather spend a bit of time with you guys. I see Beth is dancing. Where's Amelia?'

'She's gone to bed; it's been a long day. Tell us more about the wedding. Your niece is beautiful and it's sad that her mum wasn't there to see her. Are there many guests at it?'

Jess started asking question after question. Without realising it, she was beginning to give the game away that they didn't trust Meredith.

Meredith answered her questions and eventually joked that she would be asking her what kind of underwear she was wearing next. Jess got the message and stopped. She felt that Meredith had fobbed her off with her answers. She had tried her best to find out what was going on and failed. For the moment.

Rick pulled Jess onto the dance floor. 'Excuse us Meredith, I love this song,' he said. Jess looked at him gratefully and they danced together, oblivious to everything and everyone around them.

***

When Beth and Kale finished dancing, he walked her back to her room. When he had gone, she discovered that she had left her ship pass inside the room and couldn't get in so she headed down to reception to get a new one.

DAY ELEVEN

TAORMINA

When Jess woke up and looked around, she noticed that Beth had not come back. She went out onto the balcony and saw that they had anchored in Taormina in Sicily. They had only two days left; the next day they would be in Naples and after that it was back to Rome and then home. How she wished it could go on for longer. She couldn't believe that she had met Rick and right at this minute she was happier than she had been in a very long time. She knew it was very early days and that she should be careful not to rush into anything, but she had a good feeling about him and he seemed to be very keen on her.

Amelia was relaxing on a sun lounger.

'Good morning, Missus, do you know where Beth is?'

'No, she didn't come back last night,' Jess said wearily. 'I thought she said she was going to come back to our room to sleep, given her suspicions about Kale.'

'I know. I think we should ring her.' Amelia was a lot more anxious than she was letting on.

Jess dialled Beth's number and she heard a phone ringing in the room.

'She left it here, blast it!' Amelia said, highly irritated.

'Okay, let's not overreact. Why don't we get dressed, go to breakfast and if she's not back by the time we return, we'll rethink the situation.'

Jess didn't know why she felt so uneasy, but after the events of the previous day, she felt that something was not quite right.

***

The girls had been back in the room for fifteen minutes after breakfast and there was still no sign of Beth.

'I know you are going to think I am reading too many thrillers, Amelia, but I think something has happened to her,' Jess said, looking very concerned.

'I can sense there is something not right too, Jess. I can't explain it but it's the whole thing with Meredith yesterday. I tried to find out more about her last night but she was very cagey. Beth definitely told me she was coming back last night, and I don't think she would have forgotten that she had said that. Do you think Kale and Meredith have something to do with it?' Amelia was getting stressed.

'I don't know about Kale, but it's highly likely that Meredith does. I think we should call Sam. Three heads are better than two and we need to work out who we can trust on this ship so that we can find her.'

Jess could see that Amelia was getting stressed and she was worried about her blood pressure.

***

Sam came to their room straight away and joined the two girls on the balcony to discuss the situation.

'Going by your usual routine during the cruise, she certainly would have been back by now, so it's not looking good,' he said.

'Added to that is the fact that since the events of yesterday with Meredith, she was very concerned about the situation and wasn't sure if she could trust Kale, so there is no way she would have stayed the night with him. We have to report her missing, but we also have to be careful who we talk to because we don't know who we can trust. There is something very strange going on that we know nothing about. We could try calling to Kale's suite, but I don't know if that is a good idea.'

'We could contact the police in Taormina,' Amelia suggested cautiously.

'Yes, but we don't really have any evidence and they would probably laugh at us,' Jess said, not meaning to dismiss Amelia.

'I wouldn't rule out the police, but Taormina is a small town and I'm not sure how much use they would be,' Sam replied. 'I think we should try Kale's room first.'

**

When they knocked, there was no answer from Kale's room.

'Oh God, where is she?' Amelia was starting to feel sick.

Sam and Jess looked at each other.

'Amelia, I think you should lie down for a bit. You look quite pale,' Sam said. 'I will talk to Jess and try to work out a plan.'

Amelia knew her body was telling her to rest and that Sam was right, but she hated not being part of things.

'The other issue here is Stephen,' Jess said to Sam. 'We need to think about whether or not we should tell him what's going on.'

'I agree, Jess. Ultimately the decision is yours and Amelia's, but I think it's a bit soon. Let's wait until lunchtime to see if she returns.'

'Okay, you're probably right, Sam. What are we going to do now, though? Do you think Rick would be of any help? He doesn't work for the cruise line but he knows a lot about the inner workings of the ship and he knows some of the senior officers. He might know who we should report it to, or what we should do next.'

'We might have to take a chance, Jess. We are thinking about the worst possible scenario here; it might all be nothing and we should be mindful of that.' Sam spoke very calmly and Jess felt slightly better now that he was involved but she was still frantic with worry about Beth.

She sent a text to Rick.

URGENT. Rick, please call me ASAP in the room.

Two minutes later, the phone rang. Jess told Rick what had happened. He asked her not to panic and said he'd come to the room immediately.

***

When she opened the door, Rick held her in his arms as if they had been a couple for years. With him, she had a feeling of security she hadn't had since she'd been married.

They all sat down in the room while Amelia propped herself up on the bed. Sam told Rick what they had discussed and asked him what his thoughts were. Rick was horrified by what had happened and was determined to use whatever contacts he had to sort things out.

'I was thinking about it as I was on my way up here, trying to work out who would be the best person on the ship to talk to. You might be surprised when I say this but I think Marcus – the cruise director – is a sound guy and very trustworthy. The nature of the job he does demands nothing less. Aside from that, he would have been around late last night and might have seen something that could be of help.'

Jess looked at Amelia and Sam. 'Are you happy for Rick to talk to Marcus?'

'Yes, I think so. We sort of know him from the 'Who wants to be a Millionaire' show,' Amelia said nervously.

'Absolutely, I think it's a very good idea,' Sam said.

Rick said he would go and find Marcus and come back as quickly as he could but an hour passed and there was no sign of him.

'Where is he, Jess? I thought he'd be back by now?' Amelia was pacing the floor, her stomach churning; if she didn't go into premature labour now it would be a miracle.

The phone rang and Jess answered it. Rick was calling from the cruise director's office.

'I'm sorry for taking so long, Jess, but I'm with Marcus now and he says he saw Beth late last night leaving Panorama Nightclub with Meredith. He is extremely concerned that Beth hasn't come back this morning and says he would like to meet you to discuss it.'

'Should we come down now, Rick?' Jess asked.

'Yes, he'll meet us in a private meeting room on deck three. I'll meet you outside the theatre and we can go there together.'

***

As cruise director, Marcus was one of the most senior officers on the ship. He was responsible for the entertainment and activities programme on board, and was the most visible officer on the *Santana*. It was not an easy job, but he was known to be one of the best in the business.

When they arrived, he was waiting for them and showed them into a small meeting room.

'I am so sorry about Beth. You must be extremely concerned,' he said, opening the conversation.

'Thank you for meeting us, Marcus. We don't know what to do. Our main concern is that the security on the ship must have been compromised in some way. Did Rick explain?' Jess asked nervously.

'Yes, he has told me everything and I think I understand what the issues are. Am I right in saying that you feel sure that Beth would not have stayed with Kale last night?'

'Yes, absolutely. She had begun to mistrust him and there is no way she would have put herself at risk,' Amelia answered. 'We had also made a pact between the three of us to come back to the room to sleep last night.'

'So we can pretty much assume that something has happened to her. The question is what?' Marcus commented.

Jess was a bit confused. 'What are you suggesting, Marcus? If she wasn't kidnapped by Meredith, the only other thing that could have happened is that she could have fallen overboard. Is that what you are saying?'

'No, Jess, not at all, but you need to be mindful that it is something that can't be ruled out,' he replied in a gentle voice. 'We need to look at all the possible scenarios. Would you be happy for me to bring our customer relations manager into the meeting? I feel she would provide great support to you at this time.'

Jess looked at Amelia who nodded in agreement.

'Yes, Marcus, thank you, that would be very helpful. I think we met her earlier in the week – Paula, isn't it?'

'Yes, that's right, Jess, I'll ring for her now.'

He was about to continue talking when Jess interrupted.

'Marcus, I am sorry to interrupt but I want to be clear about one thing, Beth would NOT have fallen or thrown herself overboard and I, for one, do not want to focus on that possibility.' Looking at Amelia and gripping her hand tightly, she continued. 'I think I speak for both Amelia and myself when I say that we know that this whole thing involves Meredith.' Amelia nodded in agreement.

'Okay, I understand, Jess, please excuse me for a few moments,' Marcus replied as he went outside to talk to Paula.

When they came back into the room, Paula spoke gently.

'I want you to know that I am here to support you. We will make every effort to find out what is going on. I am sure you are shocked and concerned about Beth's safety and I want to reassure you that the matter is being taken very seriously.'

'Do you think we should contact the police?' Amelia asked.

'I don't know, Amelia, I think our priority is Beth's safety, so we need to be careful.' Paula looked at Marcus nervously.

'I agree, Paula. I think that the police could do more damage than good at the moment,' he replied calmly.

'The other issue is her husband. Do you think we should inform him that she is missing? Maybe he has a right to know?' Jess asked.

'I think so, Jess. He is her next of kin,' Paula replied.

This was her area of expertise and although she had never dealt with a kidnapping on a ship before, she did have years of experience in tricky situations, including the deaths of passengers while on board.

'Okay, let's do it now,' Jess said. She was finding it difficult to think clearly and her head was spinning.

Without waiting another moment, Amelia dialled Stephen's number. He answered straight away.

'Hi Stephen. Please don't be alarmed because it's probably all a big misunderstanding but I need to tell you that Beth hasn't been seen since midnight. We woke up this morning and she hadn't come back to our room.'

'What? Jesus, Amelia, what the hell is going on?' Stephen sounded angry.

'Please try not to worry. We are trying to sort it all out and we are with two of the ship's senior officers at the moment, but we needed to tell you what was going on. I had better go now. I will ring you again as soon as I have an update. Please don't do anything until you hear from me. It's a very delicate situation and we think she may have been kidnapped. I promise I will be in touch as soon as I have any news.'

She hung up, not giving Stephen the opportunity to say another word. Her phone rang immediately; it was Stephen. She didn't answer and switched it off. A few minutes later, she turned it back on when she remembered that it might be needed.

***

Meredith was wondering what to do next, she hadn't planned on things getting so complicated and was feeling a bit out of her depth. They had been over the plan several times and it had seemed so easy; how did she end up taking this bloody Irish girl hostage? What were they going to do with her? They couldn't let her go now that she knew what was going on, but her friends would be looking for her so something would have to be done. She picked up the phone and dialled the captain's suite.

'Jean Claude, I need to see you. We have a problem.'

***

Meredith sat down on the sofa in Jean Claude's suite, fear etched all over her face.

'I thought you had taken care of everything, Meredith. Why the hell did you have to get so friendly with those girls?'

'I was bored. It's a long cruise with nobody to talk to or hang out with. It's alright for you, your life goes on as normal but, for me, it's very lonely so I didn't see the harm in making some friends.'

Meredith was trying to explain herself even though she knew there was no point. She found Jean Claude very attractive but he had never shown any physical interest in her – the story she had told the girls was a huge lie.

'What in the name of God happened, you bloody idiot? How did you end up taking her hostage?'

'I was walking down the corridor near reception at midnight last night when I ran into Beth, the girl that has been seeing Kale. She told me she was locked out of her room and had come down to get another key so I asked her if she wanted to go for a nightcap. We went back up to the Panorama Lounge and were talking when, out of the blue, she asked me if we were involved in something illegal. She said she knew that all the wedding party had boarded the ship without security checks and that she thought we were dealing in drugs or human trafficking. I was totally shocked and taken aback by her question. She knew by the look on my face that she had her answer.' Meredith stuttered as she spoke.

'And where the hell is she now?' he shouted.

'I spiked her drink and told her there was a party in one of the officers' rooms and then locked her in room A101.'

'What are you going to do with her?' Jean Claude shouted.

He was livid with Meredith and she was furious with him.

'What do you mean? She is your problem as much as mine. We are in this together, in case you'd forgotten,' she shouted.

'This was not part of the plan, Meredith, and you know that. How do you expect me to help you sort it out?'

'You're going to have to think of something, because if I go down, I'm taking you with me,' she snarled.

She went back to her room feeling a mixture of aggravation and anguish; she had no idea what she was going to do.

***

Beth felt sick when she woke up. She couldn't believe the nightmare she was in. She tried to remember what had happened but her head was aching. The room was pitch dark and she couldn't see a thing. Slowly she began to recall what had happened. She'd been in Panorama Lounge talking to Meredith about the wedding and all the people coming onto the ship. The next thing she knew, she was being dragged down a corridor and thrown in a room. Everything after that was a blur.

She was really scared now: what if they didn't find her? She had read books where the hostages never again saw the light of day and were eventually murdered before they were found. She shouted out many times but no one came. After what seemed like hours, a door opened, a light was turned on, a bottle of water was thrown across the floor and the door slammed again.

Beth crawled around the room carefully, feeling her way. She figured that she was in a much smaller version of her own room but she couldn't find a window. There was a door at the end which opened into another small area that had a toilet, shower and sink. She worked out that she was probably somewhere in the crew area below deck because there was no window but, then again, it could have been an inside cabin in the guest area. Her mind was working overtime.

She heard footsteps coming along the corridor and shouted out again, but they went by without stopping.

**

Back in the meeting room, everyone was getting frustrated that things were going around in circles.

'Do either of you know anything about Jean Claude? Did you know his daughter was having her wedding reception on the ship?' Jess directed the question at Marcus and Paula.

'No, this is his first season on the *Santana* so I don't know him at all. What concerns me is that none of the crew was aware of the wedding reception, not even the executive chef, Tito. He told me that he was informed yesterday morning that there was a late request for a local corporate reception that Jean Claude felt would be good marketing for the company. He asked Tito if he had sufficient supplies on board to cater for it. Tito thought it was very odd and asked me if I knew anything about it,' Marcus said. 'Jean Claude never told him it was his daughter's wedding reception. Why would he want to keep it a secret when it should have been a mammoth celebration? How many brides have the opportunity to get married on a cruise ship on which their father is the captain? It doesn't add up.'

'I worked with him on another ship and always found him to be very professional but he kept his distance and didn't make friends with the officers,' Paula added.

'I think we can pretty much assume that there are very few senior crew aware of what's going on but, as you have already pointed out, Jess, the director of security most definitely is, and so we need to be extremely careful,' Marcus said.

He'd made sure they were using a room that had no security cameras – such rooms were regularly requested by people for confidential meetings.

'First and foremost, we need to find Beth and, to be honest, I don't really care what happens after that,' Jess said.

'Meredith will know that we will be looking for Beth by now so she is probably going to make a move,' Amelia said to Jess in a matter-of-fact tone of voice.

Rick and Sam had been staying quiet; Marcus and Paula were there now and there didn't seem to be any need for them to speak.

Amelia's phone beeped, alerting her to an incoming text.

Beth is with me. She will be held safely and will be well looked after until the ship reaches Rome as long as there is no interference from yourself, Jess, or anyone else. If you choose to disobey this instruction, Beth will not disembark in Rome.

'Oh my God! They are going to kill Beth if we get involved.' Amelia started ranting hysterically. 'I can't believe this is happening. All we did was book a holiday!' She ran to find a bathroom.

Ignoring Amelia's hysterical disappearance, Marcus spoke.

'We now know that you were right about Meredith. It's clear we are dealing with a very serious situation. We have to tread very carefully if we are to ensure Beth's safety.'

He was surprised at how serious things were turning out to be.

***

Meredith knew they were nearly there; just two more days and they would be in Rome. Then it would all be over and she would be rich beyond her wildest dreams. She was not going to let those Irish bitches ruin everything that she had worked so hard for. This operation had taken two years to plan and the set-up hadn't been easy. They were so near the end now and it had all been so smooth. She kept asking herself over and over why she had taken that stupid girl who probably wouldn't have done anything as she was just being nosey. Now what was she going to do with her? She asked herself what Jess and Amelia would do – would they sit back and wait for Rome, or would they try and find Beth?

***

Jean Claude couldn't believe the stupidity of the woman. What sort of an idiot was she? No wonder he had never fancied her even though he knew she was his for the asking. He wondered how she could have taken a guest hostage, and just when they were so near the end and everything had been going so well. This could be a real problem; this could actually scupper the whole deal.

He figured out that he was going to have to dock in Rome a bit earlier than planned because of this issue. They would have to get everything off the ship before daylight. He needed to talk to Ralph about the security issues in Rome. He would handle the port staff himself en route to make it look less conspicuous.

If he changed the arrival time now if would look odd. Ralph was responsible for ease of access on and off the ship so that was not going to be his concern for the moment; there was a team involved and everyone had a specific job to do.

***

Beth was starving, as well as bored and frightened. She thought about Stephen and the children and how desperately she wanted to see them. She had been thinking about Stephen a lot over the past few hours and one thing she knew was that she loved him and didn't want to lose him. Would she ever see him again or would she be killed here in this room? She couldn't stop her mind from thinking negative thoughts so she closed her eyes and tried to sleep. Suddenly the door opened and Meredith came in.

***

Back in the meeting room, they were all coming up with different suggestions about what they should do next, but nobody really had a clue. Paula was great at comforting the girls, just as Marcus knew she would be, and that helped keep the situation calm.

'I think we need to respond to Meredith in some way. We can't carry on for the next two days leaving Beth on her own in some awful room,' Amelia said eventually, tired of listening to all the suggestions. 'I think we should reply and maybe saying something like this: *Meredith, we are horrified by your actions especially because we thought you were a friend. We are devastated by Beth's incarceration and want to see her. You can't expect us to wait until we get to Rome to know that she is alright.*'

'I agree, Amelia, let's do it.' Jess went over and sat beside her, neither of them waiting for approval from anyone in the room.

Beth was their friend and they would make the decisions.

***

'Hello Beth,' Meredith said as she approached the hostage, carrying a tray with some lunch. Her phone beeped.

'What am I doing here, Meredith? What is going on? I want to go back to my friends. Please let me go,' Beth implored.

Meredith looked at her phone. The message had just come through from Amelia and she was quite surprised by the tone; they obviously had no idea how serious the situation was. She realised reluctantly that she would have to meet them.

'It's your own fault for meddling, Beth, if you had kept your mouth shut and your nose out of what was not your business you wouldn't be here now.'

'What's going to happen to me?' Beth asked in a trembling voice.

'I don't know yet. That all depends on the behaviour of your friends,' Meredith replied as she turned and walked out the door, closing it quietly behind her.

Beth found that the appetite she'd had vanished. She felt sick with fear as she sat on the bed with tears running down her face. What was going to happen to her?

***

Meredith went back to her room and started thinking about what she should do next. From her limited knowledge of the girls, her instinct was telling her that they wouldn't contact the authorities if it would put Beth in danger, but they would leave no stone unturned until they found her. She felt that they could probably be persuaded to keep quiet, but she wanted to be sure.

Should she organise for them to be denied disembarkation in Naples tomorrow and also take their phones? Should she bar outside calls from their room? Should she take them hostage, along with Beth?

She decided to discuss it with Jean Claude before making her decision.

***

He was not impressed.

'Jesus, woman! You have brought all this trouble on us and now you want me to sort it out for you.'

'No, Jean Claude, I am happy to take on the responsibility. I just didn't want to go ahead without telling you what I was doing.' Meredith was feeling very stupid. She had wanted to impress Jean Claude but, instead, she had made a fool of herself.

'Fine, do whatever you think, Meredith, but be aware that you are not answering to me alone. There are other people who will be extremely unhappy if you are the cause of the failure of this deal. What do you think is going to happen when the girls are eventually released? They are hardly going to let you away with having ruined their holiday and causing them untold distress.' Jean Claude spoke very sternly

Meredith had never seen this side of him before.

'What do you mean?' she asked timidly.

'Don't be stupid. You know that Ralph is a major player in the deal and his brother is coordinating things in Rome, so there is a chain of people who will be affected if things don't work out. I will not be able to protect you. My strong advice is that you sort this out. I really don't care how you do it. I suggest that you use whatever friendship you have with them to fix things, and fast. If you don't, you will be arrested soon after the ship docks.' Jean Claude knew he was being harsh, but he had to make her understand.

'Fine, I will sort it,' she said with a mixture of determination and fear.

She left his office and went back to her room to think.

***

Amelia's phone beeped, it was Meredith. She read out the text.

I think we should meet. Maybe we can come to an agreement.

'I don't think it's a good idea to meet with her,' Marcus said. 'Ask her to discuss the agreement on the phone. Tell her you want to speak to Beth to know she is alright.'

Amelia started writing her reply.

I will talk to you on the phone. I do not want to meet. I want to speak to Beth to know she is okay.

There was no reply for fifteen minutes and then another text came through.

I will phone you at 4pm.

'What are we going to say to her when she rings?' Amelia asked Marcus. They had really put their trust in him.

'Tell her you want to speak to Beth. Once you know that she is okay, ask Meredith what is going on and what exactly she is playing at,' Marcus replied.

'Do you not think she needs to tread a bit more carefully, Marcus?' Sam suggested.

'We need to know what Meredith wants. If we don't show confidence ourselves, we are not going to get anywhere,' Marcus spoke with an air of authority. 'Why don't we take a break and meet back here at 3.50pm.'

He stood up and left the room, leaving Paula to take over.

'Would any of you like to come for a coffee or a drink? Actually, you probably need to eat something,' she said warmly.

They all left the room and went to the Cave Wine Bar.

***

Beth's head still hurt; it felt like she had a bad hangover, but it was probably stress as well. She had no concept of time but felt like she had been there for hours. Suddenly the door opened and Meredith came in. She didn't turn the light on but she left the door slightly ajar so Beth could finally see her surroundings.

'I will be phoning your friends at 4pm and making an arrangement with them. You are to speak to them and tell them that you are fine and that they are not to worry. Do not engage with them or ask any questions.'

She left the room as soon as she finished speaking. Beth was confused, nothing was making any sense and she began to feel very scared.

***

They arrived back to the meeting room and sat around the table, waiting for the call. The atmosphere was tense when, suddenly, Amelia's phone rang. Jess answered it.

'Hello Meredith,' she said.

'Jess, it's Beth! How is Amelia?'

Before Jess had a chance to answer, she heard Meredith in the background aggressively telling Beth not to ask any questions. Meredith came back to the phone.

'As you have just heard, Jess, Beth is perfectly fine.'

'Where is she, Meredith? When are you going to let her go?'

'She is safe and will stay that way as long as you do not do anything stupid.'

'What do you mean? What are you involved in?'

'It is highly confidential and that is why Beth has to be isolated. She stuck her nose in and was in danger of blowing everything. You should try and enjoy the rest of the cruise and you will see her again in Rome.'

'You can't seriously expect us to abandon her and get on with the trip, Meredith? You know us better than that.'

Meredith's tone changed immediately.

'This is not a joke, Jess. You need to listen to me. Beth's life, and indeed yours and Amelia's, will be in danger if you discuss this with anyone. This confidential operation is much bigger than you could possibly imagine and I cannot protect you from the consequences if you cause it to fail.'

Meredith hung up.

Jess was visibly shaken. She had recorded the conversation as Marcus had instructed and played it back. They were all speechless; this was something that happened in movies, not to ordinary people like them. Totally overwhelmed, Amelia and Jess clung to each other and wept.

Rick spoke up. 'Marcus, I think we can all see now how serious this is. I don't think any of us has the expertise to deal with the situation. We can't leave Beth incarcerated until we get to Rome. Who knows what could happen to her between now and then? We have to consider contacting the police.'

'I agree, Rick, but I am concerned about compromising not only Beth, but also the safety of all the guests on the ship if we don't handle this properly. We are in quite a small place and I'm not sure how much use the local police would be. We also have a language barrier to deal with. I'm wondering if the Embassy might be a consideration? I have a trustworthy contact there.'

'The other thing we are up against is time. The ship is due to leave Taormina at 5.30pm which means we only have a little over an hour we depart,' Paula added.

'That answers the police issue. There is not enough time to liaise with them before our departure. There would be too much bureaucracy and it would be too dangerous. I think we have to make a decision now and I think it should be the Embassy,' Marcus said, looking directly at Amelia and Jess.

'I don't have the answer, Marcus, but I think you are able to see more clearly than us and that is probably the best thing to do as long as your contact is reliable,' Jess said. Amelia nodded in agreement.

'Leave it with me. I will make the call and phone you as soon as I have spoken to him. Why don't you take a break? Maybe go to the Panorama Lounge or wherever you feel comfortable.'

'Thank you, Marcus, we'll do that,' Amelia said.

***

Rick, Sam and the girls went to the Panorama Lounge because it was too hot to sit outside. They were conscious that there were people around them so they didn't discuss the situation, and it probably did them good to have a break from it. The time seemed to drag, however, as they waited for Marcus to call back.

By 6pm, there had been no call from Marcus and the *Santana* was still in port.

'Do you think the delayed departure has something to do with our situation?' Amelia asked.

'I was wondering the same thing,' Rick replied. 'But delays can happen for any reason.'

As he spoke, the *Santana* started to pull away.

'We never got to see Taormina,' Amelia said wearily; she wasn't feeling very well.

'To be honest, if I'd had to choose a place to miss on the itinerary I would have said Messina or Taormina. Don't worry; we have our next cruise to look forward to,' Jess said, in an effort to lighten the conversation.

'Are you sure you still want to come on another cruise with everything that has happened?' Amelia asked, shocked at how blasé Jess was being. 'Maybe Beth won't agree.'

'Of course! This is not exactly something that happens to people on cruises; it's an extreme situation. And besides, we won it – it's free,' Jess responded.

Amelia's phone rang. It was Marcus.

'I spoke to my contact and I think it was the right thing to do. Can you all come down to the meeting room now, please,' he asked.

***

A few minutes later, they were all gathered in the room.

'As you are probably aware,' Marcus said, 'there is no Irish Embassy in Taormina so there was no way they could have had someone on board at such short notice. However, having explained the situation to them, they feel that Beth should be alright until we get to Naples in the morning as long as we lie low and don't ruffle any feathers. The Embassy will send an official to Naples in advance of the ship's arrival tomorrow morning. In the meantime, they will liaise with the Department of Foreign Affairs to decide whether or not to involve the Italian police. They are well aware of the sensitivity of the situation and everything will be handled with the utmost discretion.'

'That's great, Marcus, thank you for all your help,' Jess said, with genuine gratitude. She looked at Amelia. 'Amelia!' she shouted. Her friend had fainted and fallen off the chair onto the floor.

'I'll call Dr Sakim,' Paula said as she dialled the medical centre.

***

The doctor arrived within minutes. He was very unhappy with the situation.

'Ms Brady, I need to take you to the medical centre and run a few tests,' he said to Amelia, who was sitting upright again though still feeling very unwell.

A short time later, she found herself hooked up to the blood pressure monitor as the nurse wheeled in the ultrasound machine.

'Ms Brady, your blood pressure is very high again and your baby is getting distressed. I am worried that you may have preeclampsia. I don't have the facilities to treat you on board, so we are going to have to get you to hospital in Naples,' Dr Sakim said.

He hooked her up to a drip and gave her something to ease her discomfort. Amelia was feeling so bad that she was almost relieved at what he said. It suddenly occurred to her that this development might help Beth as well.

The doctor rang the bridge and asked to speak to the captain. He was put through immediately and explained the situation to Jean Claude. He was surprised that the captain would not turn back, given that they had not travelled very far from Taormina, but it was not up to him to question the captain's orders. The *Santana* would continue onwards to Naples while Amelia would be airlifted from the ship to a hospital in Naples specialising in obstetrics.

The doctor spoke to Jess and Sam.

'Ms Brady has suspected preeclampsia and requires urgent hospital admission so we have arranged to have her airlifted to a hospital in Naples. She will require someone to accompany her so please organise that without delay. Please bring ship passes and passports for disembarkation purposes. Have you any questions?' Dr Sakim spoke in broken English.

'Oh God, Doctor! Is she going to be okay?' Jess asked, shocked by what she had just heard.

'I don't know, but I am sending her to the best obstetric hospital in Naples, so she will be very well looked after but time is of the essence and I need to go now.'

'I think you should go with her, Sam,' Jess said. 'They will only allow one person and I can't abandon Beth. Amelia will be safe with you and the hospital to look after her.'

She was trying to be practical. She was desperate to go with

Amelia but knew it was the right decision to send Sam as there was no way she could leave Beth alone on the ship.

***

The crew were hugely experienced at dealing with emergency situations and everything was handled with incredible efficiency. The helipad was located near the bow of the ship and Amelia was taken there by wheelchair, accompanied by Dr Sakim and his nurse who handed her over to the paramedics. The ship had stopped moving and crowds of guests gathered to see what was going on.

Once Amelia and Sam were safely on board and the paperwork had been signed off, the helicopter left for Naples. Within minutes, the *Santana* started moving again. The captain made an announcement explaining to the guests that a passenger had become seriously ill and had to be airlifted to hospital but that he would make up the time en route to Naples.

***

Meredith had seen the commotion; she couldn't believe it was Amelia. How much more trouble were these girls going to cause her? She tried to work out how this was going to affect the situation with Beth but her brain was too muddled; she was exhausted and stressed. She picked up her phone and dialled the captain.

'It is one of the bloody Irish bitches that is being airlifted, Jean Claude,' she said.

'I don't believe it! What have you done? If this deal succeeds, it will be a miracle.' Jean Claude was at the end of his tether. He couldn't believe the incompetence of Meredith and wished he had never brought her in on the deal. 'I don't think you have a clue how vulnerable you have left us,' he said viciously.

'It's not my fault that Amelia had to go to hospital. Look, it will all be fine, Jean Claude, trust me.'

She hung up, not believing a word of what she had just said. She needed to find Rick as soon as possible; she was sure that the girls would have confided in him.

***

Jess had been feeling very low. She went back to her room and when she walked in and looked around her, she felt sick with fear and sadness. The three of them had come on the holiday of a lifetime and now Amelia was fighting for her life in hospital and Beth's life was in serious danger.

Her phone rang; it was Stephen.

'Jess, what's going on? I have been trying to get through all afternoon.' He was a bit aggressive and Jess wasn't able for it. She started crying.

'Amelia is in hospital. She was airlifted half an hour ago and we still haven't found Beth.' She was trembling as she sobbed.

'Oh, Jess, I'm sorry if I sounded angry. I don't mean to take it out on you.'

'We have been in touch with the Irish Embassy and they have taken over now so I feel a bit more confident that they will help us find Beth. They told us to tread very carefully and lie low until we arrive in Naples in the morning.' She was doing her best to stop the tears but she was totally overwhelmed and felt very alone.

'Do you think I should fly out?' Stephen asked.

'I really don't know. Do what you think is best, but please don't contact the Embassy or the police. It is at a very delicate stage and you could mess it up.'

'What exactly happened that you know of?' Stephen was trying to be patient and gentle as he spoke.

'Beth is being held hostage by a woman we met on the ship because she discovered that the woman is involved in a massive trafficking operation. The ship's security has been breached and that is where the real difficulties are. We believe this is a huge operation that involves a large chain of people. There are two senior officers that we feel we can trust and they have been instrumental in getting the Embassy involved. The Embassy has said they will have someone in Naples tomorrow morning when we arrive. That's literally all I know at the moment, Stephen. You can't say anything to anyone.'

'Thanks, Jess, I'll let you go now but can you please keep in touch. I am really worried about Beth and all of you.'

Stephen felt slightly better but was still wondering if he should fly over.

***

Rick couldn't focus on what he was doing. His mind was on Jess and how scared and alone she must be feeling now that Amelia had gone. He knew that he needed to be with her and that she needed him.

Where are you, Jess? Would you like me to come to you? R

He didn't have to wait long for a reply.

Yes, Rick, I'm in my room, please do.

Minutes later he knocked gently and Jess opened the door.

'I'm so relieved you're here. I'm so scared, Rick,' she said as he held her in his arms.

He held her tightly and as he began to slowly release her, she kissed him longingly, desperate for his comfort. He was unsure how to react after everything that had happened. He felt nervous and uncomfortable and pulled away.

'What's wrong?' Jess was hurt at his sudden withdrawal.

'I'm not sure this is a good idea, Jess, you're very distressed and I don't want to confuse things.' He spoke gently and with genuine concern.

She went over to the bed and lay down, trying hard to hide her feelings.

'Please come and lie with me, Rick, I need you to hold me.'

They lay together silently for a while. Jess seemed to doze off and when she woke up, she kissed him with an urgency that overwhelmed her; this time he didn't refuse.

The phone rang; it was Marcus.

'Hi Jess, how are you doing?'

Marcus was aware that things had become particularly difficult for Jess now that Amelia had been taken to hospital, and he wanted to give her as much support as he could.

'Marcus, it's really great to hear from you. Rick is here with me. Do you have any news?'

'I do, yes. I was in touch with Eamonn in the Embassy and told him about Amelia. He thinks that the gravity of her situation might actually be hugely helpful to him in gaining access to the ship without causing suspicion. As an Irish citizen, Amelia is entitled to have a representative of the Irish Embassy make contact with the ship regarding her well-being. Because she became critically ill while on board, there are questions to be answered.' Marcus sounded quite upbeat, which lifted Jess's spirits somewhat.

'That sounds positive. Do we need to do anything at our end?' She had no idea what was needed.

'No, they know what to do and have all the experience so we'll leave it with them. They are well aware of the security issue. Have you heard from the hospital?'

'No, I was just about to pick up the phone when you rang. I'll call them in a few minutes. I feel so useless, Marcus, I am so worried about Beth and I can't help her,' Jess said, feeling a bit guilty about her earlier bedroom antics.

'I know, Jess, but the ship is too big, there is no way of finding her without putting her in danger. The best thing to do now is to have some food and get some rest. Tomorrow will probably be a long day. I'd appreciate if you would let me know how Amelia is when you've spoken to Sam.' He hung up.

Jess told Rick what Marcus had said and then she dialled Sam's number.

'Hi Sam, how is Amelia?'

'We're not long here. They whisked her off somewhere and I haven't seen her since. Everyone is speaking Italian and I don't understand a word so it's going to be tricky unless I find somebody who speaks English.'

'Was she conscious when you last saw her?'

'Yes, but she was quite distressed,' Sam replied. 'I'll call you as soon as I know anything. Any news on Beth?'

'No, but let's keep in touch.'

She hung up, she didn't have the energy or inclination to go into any more detail and she knew that Sam had enough on his mind.

The other problem was Paul.

'Rick, I don't know if you can help me with this, but I'm wondering what to do about Amelia's husband. Do you think I should call him?'

'I think that is a very tricky one. Why don't we order some food to the room and sit down and try and figure it out?' he replied.

***

Beth was exhausted. She had been trying to sleep but couldn't and this was making her more stressed. What if they killed her? What if she never saw Stephen and the kids again? Why hadn't Jess and Amelia sorted it all out? They were her best friends and best friends look out for each other. Where were they now when she needed them? She knew that they would be doing everything they could to find her; she was just upset.

Then her thoughts switched to Kale. Was he involved? Meredith hadn't mentioned him; maybe she would ask her if she saw her again. She swore to herself that if she got out alive, she would never take anything or anyone for granted again.

Suddenly the door opened; a tiny glimpse of light trickled into the room for a moment and then it was gone. Another tray, another blind tasting. How much longer could she bear it?

***

Meredith lay on her bed trying to read her book, but it was useless, there was no way she could concentrate. All she wanted to do was get to Rome and get off the ship and get her money. That's how it was all supposed to have worked out. What was she going to do next? She had no experience of this sort of thing; she was an amateur not an experienced criminal. She tried to work out a plan in her head about how she would deal with Beth when they got to Rome but she was totally exhausted and fell asleep.

***

Jess and Rick had finished eating and were sitting on the balcony with a glass of wine each, discussing the Paul situation.

'The problem I have is that I have known Paul for so long now that he is a good friend and I feel that he has a right to know that his wife is critically ill, but I don't feel it is up to me to tell him that Amelia is having an affair. But when he finds out about it, he is going to want to know why I didn't tell him.'

'It is not up to me, obviously, but if I was in your shoes, I would tell him. You don't have to say anything about Sam,' Rick said, hoping it would help.

'You're right. It's ludicrous keeping it from him, especially when she is so ill.'

She picked up her phone and dialled Paul. There was no answer. She tried once more, still no reply. She had tried her best; her conscience was eased.

BACK IN IRELAND

Amelia would be home in a few days and Paul still hadn't told Marla that he wanted to end things. He was enjoying the freedom of not having time constraints while she was away and didn't want to waste the opportunity. He knew he was being selfish and self-indulgent but he didn't care; he decided he would deal with it after Amelia had returned – what difference would another few days make? He had given Marla a week's paid holidays so that they could spend time together in her apartment and he had been enjoying every single moment with her.

He asked himself how he was going to give her up. When he was with her it felt right; it didn't feel like a sordid affair. She made him feel good and sex with her was quite erotic. He had been surprised by her confidence and the way she liked to take control. With Amelia it was different; they were used to each other, but he had never had reason to complain. While most of his friends were no longer getting any, he and Amelia shared very regular intimacy.

When he walked out the door of Marla's apartment it was 1am and he noticed two missed calls from Jess. Paul knew it was too late to phone back but he suddenly felt uneasy; why was Jess calling him? Had something happened to Amelia?

***

Stephen had been working on his surprise for Beth. It hadn't been easy because there had been a few problems and things were a little behind schedule but he was confident that it would be ready on time.

He got the shock of his life when Jess called. What the hell was going on? How could Beth have disappeared on a cruise ship? It didn't make any sense. Surely as three friends they were together all the time; there was something he wasn't being told. He didn't know what to do. He had tried to call Jess back, but there was no answer and the frustration was unbearable. Should he call the police? Jess had told him not to contact anyone, so maybe he should listen to her. He reluctantly decided to do nothing; he couldn't afford to interfere. For the moment.

He hadn't said anything to Bethany. He didn't know if this was the right thing to do or not, but he didn't want to upset her and he was having a hard enough time dealing with the situation without having to calm her down as well. He also thought that Ed might find out if he told Bethany and that would be a disaster. Any chance of keeping everything confidential would be out the window and Jess had told him to tread very carefully. No, he wouldn't tell Bethany; his mind was made up.

A bit later, he decided to call Jess again and this time he got through. It eased his mind a bit when she told him that the Embassy was now involved.

DAY TWELVE

NAPLES

'It's Paul.'

Jess saw his name come up on her phone. She was already awake; not surprisingly, she hadn't slept very well.

'Hi Jess, I'm sorry I missed your call last night, I tried Amelia also but her phone is switched off.'

'Paul, the reason I was trying to get you last night was to tell you that Amelia is in hospital. I don't know very much at the moment but she was taken ill on the ship last night and airlifted to a hospital in Naples.'

Jess blurted it all out but withheld the details about Sam and the pregnancy.

'What happened? What is wrong with her? Is she there on her own?' Paul was confused and had so many questions.

'I'm sorry, Paul, but I don't know what is wrong. She collapsed just after we left Taormina yesterday and they felt that they didn't have the facilities on board because her blood pressure was very high. That is why they took her to hospital. Beth and I couldn't go with her because we have another problem – Beth has been kidnapped and is being held hostage on board.

I know it sounds totally ridiculous, but I promise you, it is not a joke.'

'Ah, Jess, this is mad. It sounds like some sort of TV drama. Look, I don't mean to be flippant but at the moment I need to think about Amelia. Does Stephen know about Beth?'

Paul thought Jess was losing it. How could Beth have been kidnapped on a cruise ship? Maybe she was trying to make excuses for not going with Amelia to the hospital; he would call Stephen after he had called the hospital.

'What is the name of the hospital, Jess?'

'Ospedale Evangelico Villa Bretania,' she told him. She didn't have the phone number because she had been making contact through Sam. 'Stephen knows about Beth but he has been told not to tell anyone. It is all very delicate.'

'Thanks for trying to call me last night.' Paul said.

As soon as he hung up, Jess dialled Sam to get an update.

'Amelia is out of danger,' he said. 'She is conscious again but has lost a lot of blood. They had to operate late last night.'

'Thank God she's going to be okay, Sam. What about the baby?'

'She lost the baby. They had to do an emergency caesarean section'

'Oh God, I am so sorry. Are you okay?'

'Yes, Jess, thank you. The most important thing is that Amelia is okay.'

'Does she know about the baby?'

'Not yet, no.'

'Is it okay if I come in? Are visitors allowed?'

'Yes, it's a private hospital and they understand our situation with the ship.'

'Okay, I'll be there as soon as I can. Give her my love.'

***

Jess started to speak out loud as if she was talking to Beth, forgetting that it was Rick that was with her.

'I know it's a terrible thing to say, and maybe you won't agree with me but I think maybe it's for the best that she has lost the baby. She has three beautiful, healthy children and her life would have been turned upside down. The only thing now is that she is going to need a lot of TLC because it is still all far from sorted. Paul is going to have to know why she is in hospital and what's going to happen with Sam? It's all so bloody messy.'

'I agree with you, Jess,' Rick replied, not realising that she wasn't really talking to him. 'Clearly the pregnancy was endangering her life and would have continued to do so.'

His voice brought her back to reality and she suddenly realised that Beth wasn't with her.

'Rick, we are all fifty years old and, as far as I'm concerned, that is too old to have a baby. I was really freaked out about the whole thing. I would have had a breakdown had it been me. The thing is that Amelia had started to get used to the idea, and we don't know how the loss is going to affect her. She may be relieved or she may be devastated.'

Jess was feeling emotionally drained and totally exhausted. She was desperate to see Amelia so that she could see how she was, but she didn't want to be gone too long in case there were any developments with Beth.

'I'm going to call reception to see if they will allow me to disembark early and call me a taxi to take me to the hospital. It's going it be a long, tough day, Rick.'

She was quickly put through to the chief medical officer who gave her an update on the situation. He told her that Amelia was stable and that she had been taken to Ospedale Evangelico Villa Bretania, which Sam had already told her. She asked if it would be possible to be taken to the hospital as soon as possible. He said he would arrange it and call her back.

'I have to say, Rick, that guy couldn't have been more helpful. He is going to ring back with the arrangements shortly. I was just thinking that we are going to have to figure out what we're going to do if Amelia is too sick to leave hospital. It's highly unlikely they will allow her to leave given that she has just had major surgery.'

Jess was getting stressed again; she felt the burden of everything falling on her shoulders.

'Try not to worry about it for the moment. I think we should go and see her. There is so much to discuss with herself and Sam and she will want an update on Beth,' Rick said kindly.

'Are you saying you'll come with me?' Jess asked.

'Of course. You didn't think I'd leave you to do this on your own surely.'

Rick smiled and kissed her tenderly. He hadn't given any explanation to the sommelier for his absence but he really wasn't concerned; it was the last thing on his mind.

The phone rang.

'Hi Jess, it's Paula. I'd like to help you deal with the hospital here in Naples as well as with transportation and anything else you may need. I'm sure you would like to visit Amelia as soon as possible so I have arranged for a car to be here in thirty minutes. I will give you my direct phone number so that you call me when you want to come back.'

'Thank you for calling and for organising that, Paula. Have you any news on Beth? I don't suppose anything happened overnight?' Jess was trying to stay calm despite her anguish.

'No, unfortunately not. I imagine if Meredith makes contact it will be with you, but the Embassy representative will be here in an hour and will meet with Marcus and myself. I will call you immediately after the meeting.'

'Okay, and thank you again, Paula,' Jess said before hanging up.

***

Beth had slept for a few hours but she wasn't sure of the time. It was so dark in the room that she had no idea if it was night or day. She was trying to figure out how long she had been locked up. She estimated it was about three days but she knew she was probably wrong. Were Jess and Amelia still on board or was the cruise over? They wouldn't have left without her; they would never have abandoned her, of that she was sure. She knew Meredith and her gang were involved in something very serious, but what were they going to do with her? She would try asking her; she had nothing to lose.

***

Meredith had hardly slept. She knew she had made a mess of things and didn't know what to do. She was totally out of her depth and was going to have to make some decisions. Today.

***

Rick and Jess were downstairs on deck two, waiting for the car. When they arrived at the hospital, they were told to go to the waiting area. After what seemed like an eternity, Sam appeared. He gave Jess a hug.

'Have you told her about the baby yet?' Jess asked. She needed to know what she was dealing with before she went in.

'Yes, she knows now.'

Before she got a chance to ask any more questions, Sam opened the door to a large, bright room with one bed in it. Amelia was lying in a slightly raised position in the bed with a couple of monitors and lots of drips attached to her. She was asleep so Jess went back outside with Sam.

'What time did they operate?' she asked him.

'The helicopter got here very quickly and she was taken straight into theatre. It all happened so fast that I can barely remember.

I was told to wait and it seemed like she was gone for hours but then a doctor came out. He told me that they had operated but that they couldn't save the baby.'

Sam became very emotional and Jess put her arms around him. Then he continued, his voice shaking.

'It was made all the more difficult because they were asking me to give permission to operate and I didn't know what to do. I am not her husband, I am not her next of kin. I was so confused.'

'Sam, you had to allow them to do their job, and allowing them to operate was the right thing to do. You had no choice. It is exactly what anyone in your position would have done.'

Jess was trying to comfort him as best she could but the situation was very tricky.

'I rang Paul, Sam, I felt I had to.' She looked at him apologetically.

'That's fine, Jess, you had no choice really. What did you tell him?'

'I just said that she had collapsed and they couldn't treat her on the ship. I didn't mention the pregnancy.'

Jess was feeling uncomfortable having to explain herself to a man that she barely knew. As if he could read her mind, Sam got up and said he was going back in to sit with Amelia, leaving Jess and Rick on their own.

'I don't know what's going on with him, Rick, but Amelia is MY friend and I am going back in there.'

Jess felt a mounting rage rush through her. She needed to calm down; she couldn't blame Sam for everything that was going on. Just then, as she was about to go back into Amelia's room, Paul rang.

'Hi Jess, I rang the hospital earlier and they couldn't give me much information. Have you arrived there yet?'

'Yes, Paul, she was asleep when I went in but I am about to go in again. I don't know any more details at the moment. The doctors are Italian so we are waiting for an interpreter, but the nurse told us that she will be fine.'

Jessica hated lying to Paul but she felt it wasn't her secret to tell.

'Thank God she's okay. She is very lucky to have you. Do you think I should fly out, Jess?'

'No, Paul, I don't think it is necessary unless you want to. She is being very well looked after here. I will give you a call when she has woken up and you can have a word with her yourself then. In the meantime, please don't worry.' Jess felt she was handling Paul quite well.

'Thank you for everything, Jess.'

As she hung up, she felt a surge of anger flood through her.

'It's a long time since I had to lie like that and I hope it will be a long time before I have to do it again, Rick.'

***

Sam suddenly appeared.

'Amelia has woken up. She's asking for you.'

Jess ran to her friend and hugged her tightly. Not surprisingly, they were a lot of tears.

'How are you feeling, pet? What happened?' Jess wanted to know everything from the beginning.

'They have told me that it was pre-eclampsia. I should have been more careful once the high blood pressure was detected. It is more common in older women. The reason I lost the baby was because the placenta separated from my uterus. That's why I had the heavy bleeding – they couldn't save her.'

Sam interrupted. 'Darling, you nearly died. We are lucky to have you here.'

'How are you feeling now? Have they told you how long you need to stay?' Jess was concerned by the calmness in Amelia's voice.

'The doctor is fully aware that the ship leaves tonight and that we fly back from Rome tomorrow. He said that I won't be ready to leave hospital before Thursday. Sam has said he will stay on with me. I know you need to get back to try and find Beth.'

Amelia looked at Jess sadly; she would have loved her to stay but she knew Beth was in danger.

'You need to talk to Paul, Amelia. I told him you had been taken to hospital with abdominal bleeding but that's all he knows. I have a feeling he might fly out.'

Amelia looked at Sam and he squeezed her hand.

'Does he know that I was pregnant?' she asked anxiously.

Jess recounted her earlier conversation with Paul and Amelia breathed a sigh of relief.

'Thanks, Jess, I know that can't have been easy.' Amelia was very grateful.

'The problem is, you are going to have to make a decision about exactly how much you are going to tell him. If you decide not to tell him the truth, you need to make sure he never finds out,' Jess said.

'I know. I think I'll say nothing for the moment. He can't find out from so far away.'

Jess didn't agree with what Amelia was doing, but she said nothing. Instead she asked her friend how she was feeling.

'I'm very tired but, mostly, I'm upset about everything.' Amelia didn't know how to verbalise all the emotions she was feeling.

'I think you should sleep now. We will go for a walk and come back a bit later.'

Sam and Jess left the room and joined Rick in the waiting room.

***

Rick's phone rang, it was Marcus.

'I have just met the Embassy representative. I explained everything in detail and he would like to meet with you without delay. Can you meet us now?'

Rick told Jess what Marcus had said and she agreed that they would head straight there so he took the details and they rang Paula to send the car for them. Sam said he would stay with

Amelia and Jess assured him that they would ring as soon as the meeting had finished.

***

When Jess and Rick arrived at the café, the Embassy representative introduced himself as Eamonn Moran. Because he was from home, Jess immediately felt a bit better. After the initial introductions and enquiries about Amelia's well-being were over, they got down to business.

'The Embassy is not to be confused with the police and I am not here to get involved in resolving any crime that may be happening on the ship. My job is to look after Irish citizens in Italy and to give consular assistance. The Ambassador is being kept informed of everything as it happens, and my instructions are coming directly from him at the Embassy. Amelia is now in good hands so we can concentrate on Beth and her safety. The Embassy has many contacts that we will be using in order to help us. I have spoken to Marcus at length and he has given me a lot of information that will be very helpful in planning to secure Beth's safe release, but I have a few things I want to go through with you also.' Eamonn spoke with a quiet confidence that made Jess feel at ease.

'Will you be going on board yourself?' Jess asked.

'I can't discuss that with you at the moment because it is a very delicate operation. However, I want to assure you that we have immense expertise in diplomatic affairs. We don't normally get involved in kidnappings but, because there is no ransom involved, we feel confident that we can assist you. As I mentioned earlier, we are not concerned with the crime itself. That is not our responsibility and it would probably prevent us from helping Beth, so we will not be involving the police in our efforts. Once Beth is safe and off the ship, we will let the police take over,' he said.

'That sounds very positive, Eamonn. I feel comforted by what you've told me,' Jess said. 'I'm sure you'll agree that it is all surreal. I think I'll go back to the hospital for a little while and then return to the ship. Can you let me know when you have any news?'

Jess didn't know if that was the right thing to say, but she said it anyway.

'I will be in touch with Marcus, Jess. I know it is difficult but please try to be patient and hopefully we will have this resolved very soon.'

Eamonn got up and headed outside, signalling to Marcus to come with him.

***

Figuring that there was nothing more she could do for Beth for the moment, Jess headed back to the hospital with Rick. When they got there, they found that Amelia had woken up and was sitting up in bed.

'Are you feeling any better?' Jess asked.

Yes, I feel okay, a little bit sore now that the anaesthetic is wearing off, but I'll be fine. How is Beth? Any news?

Jess thought Amelia sounded quite upbeat for someone who had just lost her baby, but she put it down to the medication and hoped that she wouldn't suffer delayed shock or – worse still – post-natal depression.

She told her about the meeting with Eamonn and they chatted about what they thought the Embassy's strategy might be. After about an hour, the nurse came in and said that Amelia needed to rest, so Jess and Rick went back to the ship.

***

A few hours later, Jess's phone rang. It was Sam.

'Things are not good, Jess. Amelia's blood pressure is really high now and they are very concerned about her. I am waiting for the interpreter again but I understand from his mannerisms that things have deteriorated. I am not trying to alarm you, but maybe you should come back.'

Jess told Rick what Sam had said.

'What time is the ship leaving today?' she asked him.

'At 6pm tonight, I think it would be very risky to go back.'

'Sam, the boat is leaving at 6pm and the hospital is forty-five minutes away, not allowing for rush hour. I really don't think I can come as we would probably miss the departure and Beth would be left on her own.'

'Okay, I understand.' Sam sounded upset.

Jess was very confused. She was being pulled in every direction and it was overwhelming.

'Sam, I'm really sorry,' she said tearfully. 'Please keep in touch and let me know how she is.'

She put the phone down and cried in Rick's arms.

***

Meredith went to meet Jean Claude. She felt uneasy that she hadn't heard anything from the Irish bitches. Why had they not been harassing her for more information about Beth and her well-being? Their silence was making her nervous. Then she remembered Amelia had been taken to hospital; that was probably what was distracting Jess. Good, maybe she would leave everything alone until they arrived in Rome. But could she be sure?

'Well, Meredith, I hope you have things under control?' Jean Claude said. He totally irritated by this woman.

Meredith didn't know what to say to him.

'I don't know what to do next, Jean Claude. We leave shortly for Rome and we're so close to the finish line but I haven't worked out what I'm going to do with the girl,' she said wearily.

'I told you to sort it out, I have enough to do.' He spoke very aggressively and Meredith knew she was on her own with the Beth situation.

Just as she was about to leave, the phone rang. Jean Claude picked it up and quickly went pale.

***

Rick and Jess were sitting in the Sunset Bar at the top of the ship looking out at the Bay of Naples when Jess's phone rang.

'This is Monika from reception. The captain would like to see you. Is it convenient for you to come now, Ms Jennings?'

Jess said she would be there in five minutes and hung up.

'Rick, what do you think is going on?'

'I don't know. He could simply be enquiring about Amelia, or it could be about Beth. We'll have to wait and see but I think we should tell Marcus before we go.' Rick wasn't taking any chances.

They rang Marcus, told him the situation and headed down to meet Jean Claude.

***

The captain was looking very dapper and official in his uniform. He was a handsome man with typical Greek looks, come-to-bed eyes and a very naughty smile.

'Good afternoon, Jess, lovely to see you,' he said as he shook her hand.

'Hello Captain, I hope you don't mind, but Rick was with me when you requested to see me so I asked him to accompany me,' Jess replied nervously.

'Of course. I am sure you are wondering why I wanted to see you. Come with me, it would be better if we have a bit more privacy.'

He led them behind the reception area to a meeting room that was not unlike the one Marcus had used. When the three of them were seated he spoke.

'I received a call about twenty minutes ago from the Irish Ambassador enquiring about the well-being of your friend, Amelia Brady, and her whereabouts at this present time. The Ambassador also wanted to know what happened and said he will require a full medical report. Following on from this, he asked me for details about her travelling companions so I wanted to make you aware that we are obliged to provide the Embassy with the requested information. I realise that you may feel that this is a breach of data protection but I give you my assurance that it is a legal requirement in these circumstances. The Ambassador said that he would like you both to call him this evening. May I ask who is with Ms Brady in the hospital?'

Jess was totally thrown by what she had just heard. Did the captain know what was going on, or was this a cover-up? Whichever it was, he was certainly handling it superbly.

'Her partner is with her. I saw her earlier and she told us to stay on the ship and to enjoy the rest of the cruise,' Jess said.

She had decided to play along and see what happened.

'When I met you earlier in the week you had another girl with you; is she going to remain on the ship also?'

Jess looked at Rick, horrified. Clearly the captain either knew nothing about what was going on or was pretending he knew nothing.

'Beth is resting at the moment. She has been very stressed by what happened to Amelia,' Rick said, jumping in and saving Jess from thinking of a reply.

'I am very sorry to hear that. It has been a distressing time for you on the cruise since your friend became ill, but I would like to invite you all to join me tonight at the captain's table for the farewell dinner. Hopefully it will go some way towards reminding you of the good times you have had on board the *Santana*.'

Jean Claude smiled and stood up.

'I will send the details to your room. I hope to see you later.'

Jess was at a loss for words as they left the room.

***

The consultant arrived into the room. He spoke quite good English but with a very strong Italian accent that made it difficult to understand him.

'Amelia suffered pre-eclampsia and also placental abruption which means that the placenta separated from the uterus wall. This led to internal bleeding and her uterus has been severely damaged. As you know, we did an emergency caesarean section because both Amelia and the baby were in danger. We were going to remove her uterus at the time but we decided that it would be better to wait. We are going to need to give her a blood transfusion and, unfortunately, she will need to have a hysterectomy. Her uterus is too badly damaged to save. Her blood pressure is very high and this is a major concern so we are going to move her to ICU as a precaution. Please be aware that she is not a well woman and her situation is critical. We will need your consent to proceed with the surgery.'

'I have a slight problem,' Sam said. 'I am not Amelia's next of kin, I am not her husband.' He was embarrassed but realised that he had to tell the truth.

The interpreter translated for the consultant who then told Sam that he would need to get consent from her husband, sent by email or fax, as soon as possible. They left the room and within minutes the porters arrived and started moving Amelia down to ICU. Sam was very upset. He'd had no idea that Amelia was so sick and he suddenly felt very alone and vulnerable. He decided to ring Jess.

***

Jess had just arrived back to the room with Rick when she saw Sam's name come up on her phone.

'I have a problem, Jess, Amelia has deteriorated and they need to operate again but obviously I am not her next of kin and they need a signature of consent from Paul. They want to do a hysterectomy as soon as possible. Can you call him and tell him and get a fax or email from him?'

Sam felt a lot better getting Jess involved. He was really beginning to feel the strain and he wished she was in the hospital and not in the middle of the ocean.

'Oh God, Sam, poor Amelia! Yes, of course, I'll call him now and ring you back,' Jess said sadly.

She looked at Rick.

'It gets worse. We need to ring Paul to get consent for Amelia to have surgery,' she said. 'I think the decision has been made for her. Paul is going to have to know about the baby now.'

'What are you going to say to him?' Rick asked gently.

They talked about it for a few minutes, working out what to say, and then Jess picked up the phone.

Paul was still in the restaurant when he saw Jess's number. He went outside to talk.

'Paul, this is Jess. Is this a good time to talk?'

'Hi Jess, yes, I've just come outside. How is Amelia?' Paul felt that the news should be better because he hadn't heard from them since the morning.

'She's not good, Paul, her blood pressure has risen and she has lost a lot of blood. They need to do a hysterectomy and they need your consent as next of kin.'

Jess held back about the baby; she and Rick felt she didn't need to say it unless absolutely pushed.

'Why does she need it?'

'I don't know, Paul, we're having language difficulties so it's not easy to understand the doctors. The most important thing now is that she has this operation. She is quite ill, Paul, she is in ICU. Can you give me a fax number and email address so they can send the consent form to you?'

'Yes, of course. I really think I should come out now. I'm going to organise a flight as soon as possible.'

Paul was in shock; he couldn't believe this was happening to his beautiful wife who he loved more than anyone else in the world.

'I understand, Paul. She is critical so I think it's a good idea. In the meantime, I will call them with the fax number and email and you can expect to hear from them pretty quickly.'

Jess was quite stressed at this stage; she knew that things were getting messy with regard to Amelia, Paul and Sam.

'If Paul is coming out, we are going to have to get Sam to go home. Otherwise we are going to have chaos on our hands.'

She was very concerned about Amelia who wasn't out of danger yet; they'd had no further texts from Meredith so she was going to have to talk about Beth next. All of a sudden, she was overcome by sadness and became very emotional.

'Are you okay, Jess?' Rick asked, with concern in his voice.

'I don't know. I think it's all catching up with me. It's been a rollercoaster and I'm struggling to keep up. I was worried about the situation with Amelia and the pregnancy, and now I'm worried about her concealing it. I know that it is inevitable she is going to be found out and I wish she would tell Paul the truth. He doesn't need to know about Sam for the moment, but what's the harm in telling him that she was pregnant?'

Rick took her in his arms and held her tight; he hated to see her suffering like this.

***

Jean Claude smiled to himself as he went back up to the bridge. He was sure he had solved the problem with the Irish girls and he needed to talk to Meredith.

Meredith, meet me in my office in ten minutes. JC

Meredith didn't know what to expect. Was Jean Claude going to have a go at her again? She didn't really want to see him but knew she had no choice. Minutes later they were sitting in his office and she couldn't believe what she was hearing.

'So, you are telling me to release the girl so that she can join you for dinner as if nothing has happened? Are you insane?'

She thought he had lost his marbles.

'Don't you see, Meredith, because the other girl is now critically ill and could die, the Embassy is sniffing around looking to speak to your hostage. We have no choice,' he replied as if it was no problem at all.

'Okay, so I release her. What if she contacts the police?'

'We are at sea now and we arrive in Rome in the morning. Her friend is very sick in hospital – I think she can be persuaded to keep quiet in return for her freedom on the last night of the cruise. We had to get to this stage with the plan. Now nobody can interfere because there are no more stops on the cruise. Everything is set up and all we need to do now is release her on the understanding that she says nothing.'

Jean Claude spoke calmly in a firm, authoritative voice. He was well used to giving orders. He also knew that this would exonerate him from the kidnapping – not that he had been involved in the first place. Beth would never know that he'd had anything to do with it and he would deny all knowledge if it ever came out.

For the first time in her life, Meredith was speechless.

***

Beth heard the door open. The light was switched on and it took her eyes a while to adjust; she had been in the dark for quite a while now.

'We need to have a chat, Beth, I think we might be able to come to an agreement,' Meredith said in a mocking voice.

'What day is it, Meredith? How is Amelia?' Beth needed answers from this witch.

'It's Tuesday evening and we have just left Naples. I have no idea how Amelia is, but she is in a good hospital. Now, do you want to hear what I have to say or not?' Meredith was finding it hard to keep her cool.

'Yes, Meredith, I'm sorry,' Beth spluttered.

'The captain has invited Jess and Rick to join him for the gala dinner tonight. We will be in Rome tomorrow and he thought it would be a nice gesture after everything that has happened to Amelia. You have not been reported missing by your friends so, obviously, the captain has included you on the invitation. It seems that Jess has done what I asked and kept quiet.'

Meredith looked at Beth, trying to predict what she would say.

'Of course she has, Meredith, she wouldn't risk putting my life in danger. Are you saying you are going to let me go?' Beth was totally confused.

'Yes, but I am warning you, Beth, you must not say anything to anyone about what has happened or the safety of the entire ship and its passengers will be compromised. Do not underestimate the seriousness of what I am saying. I am sure you want to get off the ship safely to see your friends and family again. Nothing should be more important than that.'

Meredith felt she was taking a risk but she didn't have any other option.

'Yes, of course, I would have agreed to that from the beginning if you had given me the opportunity,' Beth said indignantly.

Meredith ignored this comment.

'Your friends need to keep quiet also; they have done well so far.'

'Yes, I will make sure of it.'

Beth couldn't believe Meredith was letting her go and she pinched herself several times to make sure she wasn't dreaming. She had so many questions but she knew it was too risky to aggravate the woman so she left them unasked.

She couldn't believe she was actually going to be free!

***

There was a knock on the door. When Jess opened it, she couldn't believe her eyes.

Beth looked exhausted; her face was marked with remnants of eyeliner and mascara streaks and her clothes were dishevelled. She looked a mess but she was safe. They held each other and cried until Jess eventually said that Beth should call Stephen. She reminded her to tell him to be careful not to do or say anything to anyone because they were still on the ship.

Rick knew the girls needed time alone so he gave Jess a hug and said he would ring in an hour, before slipping out the door.

When Beth picked up her phone she noticed there were eight missed calls and ten messages. Apart from one call from the girls, the other missed calls were from Kale and all the messages were from him.

'Have you seen Kale?' Beth looked at Jess questioningly.

'No, Beth, strangely enough, he has been nowhere to be seen, but my mind has been so preoccupied I never thought to look for him, to be honest,' Jess replied. 'We called him when you didn't come back yesterday morning. Sam went to his room but there was no reply. After that, we forgot about him.'

'It's just that he has been trying to call me, and there are several texts from him. I'll phone Stephen and then we can take a look at what they say.'

Beth had thought about him quite a lot during her incarceration.

'Stephen, it's Jess. I have some news,' Jess said before passing the phone to Beth.

'It's me, darling, I'm safe and well.'

Beth started to get emotional as she spoke. She was trembling and Jess held her hand.

'It's so good to hear your voice. I can't believe this happened; I felt so helpless. What happened to you? When will you be home?' Stephen said, overcome with relief.

Beth told him about what had happened to her and about how Amelia was in hospital. She said she still didn't really know what was going on and warned that he needed to maintain his silence until she was safely home.

'We are booked to fly home tomorrow, but we need to make sure Amelia is okay. I think Paul is flying out, which will be a big help. I have to go now, pet, but I'll send you a text before I go to bed to let you know I'm okay. I love you.'

Beth hung up, she needed to lie down for a little while.

The phone rang; it was Marcus.

'Hi Jess, how are things going? I just wanted to tell you that the Ambassador spoke to the captain earlier this evening. He was asking about Beth and yourself because of Amelia's illness and said he would be looking to speak with both of you in order to provide consular assistance. I am hopeful that this is the breakthrough we need.'

Before he could continue, Jess interrupted him.

'Beth is back! I'm sorry I didn't call you but she has literally just come through the door,' Jess lied. She couldn't help it – she had forgotten about Marcus and felt really guilty.

Marcus couldn't believe it. Getting the Embassy involved had clearly been the right thing to do even though he was worried at the time that he was taking a huge risk.

'That is fantastic news. I'll go now but we'll talk later.' He hung up.

Jess explained to Beth about Marcus and Paula and how they came to be involved. Beth, in turn, told Jess all about her time in the room. They both knew that Marcus had probably saved Beth's life.

'Let's look at the messages, Jess,' Beth suggested. As they were flicking through the texts, there was a knock at the door.

'Good evening, I have an invitation for you from the captain,' a member of the crew said as they handed Jess an envelope.

DEAR MS JENNINGS AND MS CARMODY, CAPTAIN JEAN CLAUDE VAKAS REQUESTS THE PLEASURE OF YOUR COMPANY AT THE FAREWELL DINNER OF THE SANTANA. COCKTAILS IN THE CAPTAIN'S LOUNGE AT 8PM FOLLOWED BY DINNER IN ORCHID AT 9PM DRESS: FORMAL

'With everything that has been going on, I forgot to tell you about this, Beth. The captain called us to a meeting earlier and invited us to this dinner. He told me that the Ambassador had phoned him about Amelia and was looking for our details so that the Embassy could provide us with consular assistance.'

Jess looked at Beth, searching her face for a reaction.

'That's all a bit odd,' Beth replied.

'No, it's not,' Jess said, and she went on to explain about Marcus contacting the Embassy and about the meeting with Eamonn.

'Do you think the captain is involved in the deal with Meredith and he is covering up, or is he genuinely oblivious to what is going on?' Beth asked.

'I can't imagine how he could not but be involved considering we saw him with Meredith and it was his daughter's wedding, but we'll have to wait and see,' Jess replied. 'It's getting late now, Beth, we need to get ready if we are going to go to this gala dinner. You are probably dying to have a shower.'

Jess was gently trying to get things moving, mindful of what her friend had been through.

'Yes, Jess, you go first,' Beth replied.

She was anxious to get time to read Kale's texts.

12th October 10am: Good morning, hope you slept well. Want to meet up today?

12th October 12.16pm: Are you in Taormina?

12th October 1.30pm: I don't know if you have forgotten your phone or you are ignoring me. Hope it's the former.

12th October 4.05pm: Are you okay, Beth?

12th October 5.20pm: This isn't like you. I'm worried. Please reply.

12th October 6.01pm: I know you would have seen the phone by now and I know we didn't fall out so I am worried now. Please get in touch.

12th October 6.30pm: Just called to your room and there is no answer. Where are you?

12th October 11.30pm: I have been looking for you all night. I don't know what's going on. Decided not to go dancing without you. I'm going to bed now.

13th October 9.09am: Are you there?

13th October 1pm: I've looked everywhere for you but you obviously don't want to be found. It was fun while it lasted. I hope I see you before we leave the ship to say goodbye.

Beth felt sick with sadness and a sense of loss. Jess came out of the bathroom and saw her face.

'What did he say?' she asked

'It's over, Jess,' Beth replied as she handed her the phone.

***

Jess and Beth agreed that they had to be very careful at the captain's party but they thought it would be a good chance for them to try and put everything out of their minds for a while. They both looked beautiful and turned heads when they walked into the room. Marcus, Rick and the captain were there to greet them; Jean Claude was oblivious to the fact that Marcus knew what was going on. Beth was relieved that Meredith was not there – Jean Claude had made sure that she would stay away.

They mingled for a while and then headed down to Orchid and the captain's table which was in the centre of the restaurant. It was beautifully set for the privileged guests who had been invited to dine there. Each place at the table had been allocated and had a name, so the girls found theirs and sat down. The menu was incredible and they were looking forward to a fantastic evening.

FAREWELL GALA DINNER – CAPTAIN'S TABLE

Veal Sweetbreads, Apple and Herbal Cream
J. Parent Les Clos Micault Pommard 1979
The Three Prawns
Picpoul de Pinet Prestige 2010 Domaine Cabrol, Languedoc
Candy-Shaped Stuffed Pasta with Provolone Cheese, Pumpkin and Bone Marrow
Ca' Salina Valdobbiadene Superiore D.O.C.G. Brut
Mullet With Zucchini White Cream, Edamame and Fermented Black Garlic
Pazo Señorans, Selección de Añada 2008
Wild Boar Capicola with Roasted Artichokes and Toasted Sunflower Seeds
2010 Fattoria di Petroio Chianti Classico Riserva
Chocolate Sphere with Banana Mousse and Tamarind
Klein Constantia Vin de Constance 2009
Selection of Cheese (Wine to be Paired with Cheese)

The evening was a resounding success and the girls managed to forget about their troubles for a while but they decided to have an early night. It had been a long couple of days and they had a very early start in the morning.

***

'There's a message on the phone, Beth,' Jess said.

She listened to it; it was Paul looking for them urgently so she rang him straight away. Jess had to think on her feet. She knew it wasn't up to her to tell Paul about the baby.

'Hi Paul, sorry we missed you earlier. We were at the captain's gala dinner. Did you get to speak to anyone about Amelia?'

'No, I spoke to someone with quite good English who was talking about her losing a baby.'

'I don't know, Paul. They didn't tell us very much because we're not her next of kin.'

Jess hated lying; if Amelia hadn't been so sick she would have strangled her!

'From what I understand, it seems that she was pregnant and lost the baby because she had pre-eclampsia. Amelia can tell me herself when she's up to it.'

Paul didn't believe that Jess knew nothing about the baby. She tried to change the subject.

'Have you checked flights, Paul? Have you any idea what time you'll be here?'

'Yes, there's a flight at 2pm so I will be here in the early evening. In the meantime, we can keep talking by phone. I'm sure you girls will want to get home and I know you don't want to leave her until I get there.'

Paul was well aware that Beth and Jess had families of their own and jobs to get home to. Amelia was very fortunate to have such amazing friends.

'Don't worry, Paul, we're not going anywhere until we're happy that she is in safe hands,' Jess reassured him before hanging up.

'Do you think Paul suspects anything?' Beth asked. 'Do you thing the doctors will let it slip that Sam has been here? There has been so much going on, Jess, it will be a miracle if Paul doesn't find out about it all tomorrow.'

BACK IN IRELAND

Paul got off the phone from Jess feeling very low. He couldn't believe that Amelia was in hospital. He felt helpless, but more than anything he felt guilty. What sort of a man had he turned into? He hardly recognised himself anymore. He thought back to when he had met Amelia and how they had planned their future. They had been through so much together and now, while his beautiful wife was fighting for her life in a foreign hospital, he was at home screwing the staff! Was it the male menopause? He had heard women talking about it in the gym. Maybe that's what he had; he decided he would look into it.

He had written down the name of the hospital but it was a nightmare trying to get through to the right department. He was frustrated because he couldn't get any information from the medics and because he felt that Jess wasn't telling him the full story. What the hell was going on? How did his perfectly healthy wife end up being airlifted to hospital while her best friend had been kidnapped? It was all too ridiculous; no one could believe it.

He decided that the only thing to do was to fly over so he began looking up flights. He also needed to organise staff cover and get Chantal to come down from Dublin to stay with Caroline. The latter was only seventeen and he didn't like leaving her alone at night. He reckoned he should be able to leave for Naples the following afternoon and be there by evening. In the meantime, he would keep making efforts to speak to the consultant directly so that he could find out what was really going on.

He was holding to speak to the consultant on the restaurant phone when Jess rang again, sounding quite upset. She told him that Amelia had deteriorated and that they needed to operate again but that the hospital required his written permission as soon as possible.

He put down the other phone and continued his conversation with her, getting all the details he needed in order to get things moving for Amelia. Although he was in shock, there was no time to dwell on things.

Once he had scanned the form back to the hospital and organised the flight, he rang Marla and told her what had happened. He explained that he would be leaving for Naples the next day, hoping for a bit of sympathy and understanding. How wrong he was. She told him that he had promised to spend the week with her and now here he was, putting Amelia first, as usual.

Paul was shocked. He hadn't time to deal with her selfish attitude and was annoyed that she was being so unsupportive. He put it out of his mind and got on with putting everything else in place so that he could leave the next day.

It was late evening by the time he had finished organising everything. He called the hospital again. This time he had better luck and got through to the consultant quite quickly. Once he had spoken to someone and established that Amelia was out of danger, he decided to phone Jess and give her an update but there was no answer so he left her a message:

Hi Jess, Stephen rang me and told me about Beth. I am so relieved for you all. I don't know if you've spoken to anyone about Amelia but I thought I'd give you an update just in case. She came through the operation well and is in the recovery area. She had to have a blood transfusion also and they mentioned something about a baby. Do you know what they are talking about?

As he hung up, he noticed a missed call from Marla. She was the last person he felt like seeing. He went home and didn't return her call. The way he was feeling, he didn't know if he ever wanted to speak to her again.

***

Stephen hadn't slept all night. He hadn't left the shop until after midnight, partly because there had been too much to do and partly because he had been avoiding Bethany. He had tried calling Jess again but there was no reply and he was out of his mind with worry. Just as he was dialling her number again, she rang through so he ended his own call and answered. She gave him an update, telling him about the Embassy and promising to call him as soon as she had further news. She said she knew how frustrated he must be feeling. She had no idea, he thought to himself; he was out of his mind with worry.

Later on that evening, as he was checking on the deliveries, he couldn't help but think about Beth and how excited she would be when she saw the shop. Then it suddenly dawned on him that he might never see her again. This was serious; he asked himself why he was not facing up to the gravity of the situation? He couldn't imagine his life without her. He left the shop, unable to focus on anything. He knew there was no point in staying on; the workmen had all left for the evening, and now that they were back on schedule the pressure was off. He got into his car and headed out towards the beach. He needed to clear his head.

As he was walking along in a daze, his phone rang. It was Jess. Within seconds, he was talking to Beth – she was safe; he couldn't believe it! She started to tell him what had happened, but he couldn't take it all in. And then she was gone.

He tried to recall what she had said. Did she say she was coming home or did she say something about Amelia? He couldn't remember. He found a bench and sat down and stared at the sea. After a few minutes, he decided to phone Paul. He still couldn't remember what Beth had said, but maybe Paul would know something.

DAY THIRTEEN

ROME

Amelia had slept badly. The doctors had come in and woken her just as she had finally nodded off. She felt awful and strangely melancholic. What the hell had happened? How had she ended up in ICU? She tried to piece together the bits that she remembered, but apart from the helicopter and arriving into the hospital, she couldn't remember much else. Where were her friends? Was Sam still here? Was anyone still here?

She rang the bell and a nurse came over. She didn't speak English so Amelia used sign language to tell her that she wanted a phone. The nurse disappeared and returned with her mobile phone. At last Amelia began to feel a bit more at ease. She started dialling.

'Jess, it's me. Are you still in Italy?'

Jess sat bolt upright in the bed and looked over at Beth.

'Yes, love, how are you feeling?' Amelia had no idea that it was 6am.

'Oh, thank God you are here. I had a terrible night. I am very confused because no one is telling me anything and I can't remember much. Can you come in soon? I need you to fill in all the gaps and tell me what's going on. What surgery did they do to me? Is the baby okay?'

Jess was taken aback that Amelia had forgotten about the baby, and that she had forgotten that Jess was still on the ship because of Beth.

'You had a hysterectomy and a blood transfusion, sweetheart. You have been very sick. Paul is on his way over from Ireland.'

'Oh my God! What about Sam? Is he still here?' She sounded panicky.

'Yes, he is, but he knows that he will have to leave because Paul will be here this afternoon.'

'Can you come in and see me?'

'Of course, love, but it's only 6am.'

Jess realised that Amelia had no idea of the time and had also forgotten that she and Beth were on the ship on their way to Rome.

'Oh God, I am sorry for waking you, Jess, I'll see you later and thanks for everything.'

She hung up and dialled Sam's number; there was no answer so she dialled again.

'Amelia, is that you?' Sam sounded very sleepy.

'Yes, who else would it be?' Amelia was irritated by his comment.

Sam looked at this watch. He had gone to a nearby hotel for the night to try and get some rest.

'It's 6.10am, darling, I thought it might have been one of the medical staff ringing from your phone. How are you feeling?'

'I am confused. I don't remember much but I'm okay. I need you to tell me what's been going on. Jess told me Paul is coming over later today.'

Any sense of well-being that she had felt up to now started to go out the window once she realised what she had just said to Sam.

'I know. He told her last night that he would be arriving this afternoon so I will have to be gone by then. In the meantime, I will come in and spend some time with you.'

'Oh Sam, I don't think they will let you in before 9am so go back to sleep for a while.'

***

Amelia hung up and thought about her conversation with Sam. She was tired and weak and it was all a terrible mess. At least he knew he had to go home before Paul arrived, but what about the baby? Nobody had told her about the baby. She rang the bell again.

A nurse came over.

'I want to know about my baby. Is my baby okay?'

She was using sign language again to explain what she meant. The nurse understood what she was asking. She took Amelia's hand and looked at her kindly as she shook her head.

'Mi dispiace, ma il bambino non è sopravvissuto all'operazione (I am sorry but your baby did not survive the operation).'

Amelia started to get upset; she had no memory of the day before, so this was the first time she had heard about her baby and she was devastated. The nurse was very gentle and understanding. She put her arms around her and let her cry. After a while, she left and Amelia fell asleep.

***

'It's weird, Jess, but I'm not looking forward to the day and I don't know why. Have you heard from Rick?' Beth's exhaustion was obvious in her voice.

'I know what you mean. It's probably because we don't know what lies ahead and we have so much to organise. I got a text from him last night. He said he would meet us for breakfast before we disembark.'

They had packed their bags the night before and put them outside the door so they only had a small carry-on bag to worry about.

'How do you feel about him? Are you in love with him, Jess?'

'I haven't had time to dwell on it with everything that's been going on, but I would be lying if I said that I don't have strong feelings for him. He has been amazing throughout this whole ordeal.'

***

Rick was sitting at a nicely laid table in the dining room when the girls arrived.

'Good morning ladies. How are you both today?'

'Tired. I never thought I'd say it, but I'm looking forward to getting home,' Beth replied, smiling.

'That's not surprising. Have you heard from the hospital?' Rick asked with genuine concern.

'Yes, Amelia phoned me at 6.10am! What's worrying me is that she has very little recollection of anything that has happened over the past thirty-six hours and didn't remember that she had lost the baby,' Beth said solemnly.

'I think she will have a lot of questions. She is very confused,' Jess added.

'What are you planning on doing once you disembark? Are you going home today or are you going to stay on for a bit?' Rick was curious to know what Jess was doing. He had left her alone since Beth had come back and hadn't seen her apart from at the gala dinner.

'We don't really know yet, Rick. I called the airline to tell them about the situation so they are fine. It's really about Amelia. Paul arrives later today so there is no need for us to stay but we don't know whether we should take a train to Naples and see her before we go home. There is a flight this evening from Rome and, ideally, we would like to get that but if we go to Naples we will have to stay over and get a flight tomorrow morning,' Jess replied.

'On a different note, were there any noticeable happenings this morning on the ship? You know – the Meredith problem?' Beth asked.

'I saw some police at the docks but there was no major fracas, so either they weren't caught or else it was kept very quiet,' Rick answered.

'It certainly looks like they've gotten away with whatever it is they are up to. What are your plans, Rick?' Jess looked at him, sad to be saying goodbye.

'I fly home today and I am going to France next week on a buying trip. I need to recover from the drama of meeting these wonderful Irish girls and all that went with it! I also hope I will be seeing them again.' Rick was laughing as he spoke and winked over at Jess. 'Are you going to report the kidnapping once you get home, Beth?' he asked.

'I don't know. I haven't really thought about it, but I feel that it shouldn't be ignored so I will think about it and talk it through with the Jess and Amelia. I'm sure Stephen will have his thoughts on it too. What do you feel I should do?' Beth was pleased he was concerned.

'I definitely don't think you should ignore it. You've had an extremely traumatic experience that could have had a very different outcome, and you also missed out on part of your holiday. Let me know if I can be of any help,' Rick replied kindly.

Jess and Rick said their goodbyes. They tried to make it quick, neither of them wanting to leave the other.

***

The two girls collected their luggage, jumped in a taxi and headed for the train station to catch the train to Naples. They knew they couldn't leave Italy without seeing Amelia. When they arrived Sam was in the waiting room. He said that he had been asked to wait outside while they were changing Amelia's dressings. He was thrilled to see Beth and Jess and filled them in on what had been happening.

After a while, when nobody had come out to them, they decided to ring the bell. They checked in with the nurse who directed them to Amelia. She was in a small room with glass-fronted sliding doors, one of about six that surrounded a central nurses' station. The entire environment was sterile, quiet and a bit intimidating. It was acutely evident that everyone there was seriously ill.

Amelia had a complicated looking monitor beside her showing lots of different graphs and numbers. She also had a number of tubes attached to the cannula in her arm. She was propped up by lots of pillows and although her face was pale, she was awake and smiled at them. They gave her a huge hug before sitting down.

'Tell me everything. I don't know why, but my memory has blanked out most of the past thirty-six hours and I want to know exactly what happened, from the beginning,' Amelia said, a gentle sadness etched on her face. 'I especially want to know what happened to my baby.'

They recounted events as they had happened, beginning with when she had collapsed on the ship. Gradually, Amelia started to remember, though she still had questions.

'What about the medical stuff? Why am I now in ICU and how did I lose my baby? I'm sorry to be asking you all this, but I don't understand when they tell me anything.'

Beth took over.

'It's okay, love, it's just that it's not easy for us to tell you this. They did an emergency caesarean to try and save the baby when you first came in, but the placenta had been damaged and it was too late. I'm so sorry, pet.'

Beth held Amelia, tears rolling down her own face. She had been through a terrible trauma herself and it was only just starting to hit her. After a few moments, Amelia pulled away gently.

'Why am I here in ICU if I only had a caesarean section? That's not a big deal, surely?' she asked.

'Your blood pressure started to rocket yesterday afternoon, and after doing a scan they realised that your uterus had ruptured and needed to be removed. You also lost a lot of blood and needed a transfusion. You gave us all a terrible fright.' Jess was also very emotional; the whole ordeal had caught up on herself and Beth.

The three girls huddled together for a few moments and cried. It had been a rollercoaster couple of days and they were all totally overwhelmed.

'What happens now? How long am I going to be here?' Amelia asked, looked at each of her friends in turn.

'I honestly don't know but you won't be going anywhere for a few days. You've had two major surgeries in the past twelve hours. Paul is due here this afternoon so he will find out everything. He speaks a bit of Italian from his hotel management days, doesn't he?'

'Yes, I do,' he replied.

***

Sam was sitting in the waiting room outside the ICU when he saw Paul go past. He was in shock: why was Amelia's husband here so early? He wasn't supposed to be arriving until the evening. Paul didn't seem to have noticed him; he had looked at him briefly but didn't recognise him out of context. Sam didn't know what he should do.

***

'Paul!' all three girls said in unison.

Paul went over to his wife and held her in his arms for a few moments before turning to Jess and Beth and giving them a friendly kiss.

'How come you are here so early?' Jess asked, looking totally horrified. She couldn't help thinking about Sam and what was going to happen next.

'Chantal found an earlier flight from Dublin so I drove up very early this morning.'

Paul sensed there was something a bit odd going on, but he couldn't work it out. He put it out of his mind; he just wanted to look after Amelia.

'I am so glad you are here, darling, maybe you can find out how long I will be here. I just want to go home.' Amelia had become very emotional.

'We'll give you a bit of time together and go and get a coffee,' Beth said. 'Is there anything we can get you, Paul?' She was anxious to get out and see where Sam was.

'No, thanks, Beth, see you in a little while and thanks for everything you have done for Amelia.'

***

The girls left the ICU but there was no sign of Sam so Jess rang him.

'Sam, where are you?'

'I am back at the hotel. Paul passed me earlier and I was afraid he would see me again. I didn't know where else to go really. Can you come over?' Sam didn't sound like himself.

'Yes, we'll get a taxi now.'

***

Sam was sitting in the bar of the hotel with a large gin and tonic in front of him. He looked quite shook.

'Are you okay, Sam?' Beth asked him, suddenly concerned that they had a problem on their hands.

'No, not really, Beth,' he answered. 'Over the past couple of days, it has been me and not Paul that has been here for Amelia and now it's as if I don't exist. Paul went past earlier and saw me, but I don't think it registered with him who I was, but I found myself wanting to go up to him and tell him everything. I have to leave now and go back to my own life. I don't know whether Amelia and I have a future together; it's all in her hands and I can't bear it. I honestly don't know how I am going to cope. This time together has been amazing and I just want to be with her.'

Sam was really emotional as he spoke so Beth went over and put her arms around his shoulders.

'I know, Sam, but Amelia is in hospital and you need to wait until she gets home before you do anything rash. Any decisions about the future need to be made by the two of you together. Paul coming early has thrown you and left you without the chance to say goodbye to Amelia properly, but you will see her when she gets home. Then you can sort everything out together. At the moment, there is probably quite a high risk of Paul finding out what has been going on, so we will have to deal with that, if and when it happens. In the meantime, my suggestion would be that we try and get you home.'

Sam looked at Beth; there was nothing more to be said.

'I can arrange for you to take a train to Rome this afternoon and a late flight back to Dublin tonight if you want?' Jess offered.

'Yes, thanks, Jess, I am happy to go to Rome. I want to get our luggage sorted out. Paula has kept it for us. Getting that organised will keep me occupied.'

***

When the girls left, Paul and Amelia talked for a while about what had happened to her. He had already spoken to the consultant so he knew the full medical details.

'Did you know you were pregnant when you went on the cruise, love?'

'No, of course not, darling, otherwise I would have told you. I thought I had missed my periods because of the menopause. I didn't think I could be pregnant at fifty. You can imagine how shocked I was when I found out. I was completely horrified.'

Amelia was getting very upset talking about it and just wanted to go to sleep.

'Why didn't you call me and tell me?'

'Because I was trying to come to terms with it myself. I was not exactly thrilled, Paul.'

He looked at her sadly, squeezed her hand and went to look for a doctor. About five minutes later, he returned.

'The nurse said the consultant is on his way. She told me that your friends have been very good to you and a man called Sam wouldn't leave your side. Who is he?'

Amelia was shocked: she was going to have to think very fast to get away with this.

'He was a guy we met on the ship. He lives in Naples. Jess couldn't come with me because of Beth so he came instead.'

The words came out of her mouth before she knew it and she realised it sounded stupid.

'I'm really tired, Paul, I can't talk anymore at the moment. I need to get some sleep,' she said.

Paul had brought a newspaper with him so he sat by her bed and waited for the consultant while she slept.

***

After Sam left for Rome, the girls sat talking for a while; they needed to work out their own plans.

'We need to get home ourselves, Jess. Are we going back to Rome for the flight this evening or waiting until tomorrow morning for the Naples flight?' Beth wasn't in the humour to make decisions.

'I think we should stay one last night. It would be a terrible rush to get to Rome and, besides, it will give us a chance to make sure Amelia is okay and the dust has settled. I can't help feeling that there are going to be fireworks today,' Jess replied. 'I can organise flights for tomorrow morning. There's one at 11am and we already have the hotel provisionally booked for tonight.'

'Good, another decision made. What do you think we should say if Paul asks us about Sam?' Beth was trying to pre-empt the inevitable.

'I have absolutely no idea. I think we are going to have to rely on Amelia to do most of the talking and play it by ear.'

***

The girls arrived at the hospital and rang the ICU bell. They were told that the doctor was with Amelia and they would have to wait. Jess went out to phone Rick.

'Hello Jess. How are you and how is Amelia?'

'I am fine, but a bit weary. Amelia is out of danger now but is still in ICU and her husband has arrived from Ireland. Where are you?'

'I am on a train on my way to Naples.' He sounded a little apprehensive.

Jess was taken aback.

'Are you coming to see me?' she asked.

'Yes, of course, Jess. Why else would I be coming to Naples? When we parted this morning I realised that I should have gone with you. I want to be with you.'

'I don't know what to say, Rick. I have to go to the hospital now. The best thing to do is to call me when you get here.'

She was a bit short with him but he had caught her off-guard.

***

Jess went back into the waiting room. She couldn't believe Rick was already missing her.

'Rick is on a train, Beth, he is on his way to Naples!'

'That's fantastic, Jess, I'm so happy for you.' Beth was truly delighted for her friend.

A nurse told them they could go into Amelia's room. When they entered, they saw that Paul looked very angry and that Amelia was crying.

'What's wrong, Amelia?' Beth went over and gave her friend a hug.

'It seems that we have a problem here, but then, you two are well aware of that,' Paul snapped.

'Don't have a go at them, Paul, it's not their fault,' Amelia pleaded with her husband.

Jess and Beth looked at each other in shock: Paul must have found out about Sam.

'The consultant came in to talk to me about Amelia. He was a bit confused as to who I was. He told me that it was great to be able to speak to someone in Italian because Amelia's partner hadn't understood him very well,' Paul said in a mocking tone.

'Paul, I never meant to hurt you, please believe me,' Amelia said.

She was getting very stressed and her blood pressure was starting to rise. A bell went off on the monitor and a nurse came running in and told them that they would have to leave the ICU for a while.

***

Paul and the girls went out to the waiting room. Beth and Jess were feeling very uncomfortable. They knew he was going to question them about Sam and they really didn't want to talk to him about it.

'What is going on with Amelia? Why was this guy on your cruise? I thought you were on a girls' holiday?' he challenged them.

'Paul, it isn't fair to question us. This is between yourself and Amelia,' Jess replied, terrified that she would say the wrong thing.

Her phone rang; it was Rick.

'Excuse me. I have to take this call.'

She went outside, leaving Beth with Paul.

'I am just at the hospital entrance now. Can you come down?' Rick sounded jovial.

'Yes, give me five minutes. I will have Beth with me. There has been chaos and she needs to get away too.'

Jess went back in to the waiting room where she found Paul interrogating Beth; she had never seen him like this before. It was true what they said – no one knows what goes on behind closed doors. One thing they discovered was that Paul was not the gentle soul they'd thought him to be.

'Beth, I need you to come downstairs with me. Rick is here and he needs to talk to us about our stuff from the ship,' Jess lied, but there was no way she was leaving Beth with Paul.

Paul looked at her curiously.

'We'll be back shortly, Paul. Can you text me when there is news on Amelia?'

Paul was taken aback with this sudden departure of the two girls, but everything was such an unbelievable mess and web of lies that he didn't know whether he was coming or going. But he was determined to get to the truth, one way or another.

***

Jess felt her heart skip a beat when she saw Rick; there was no doubt that she had fallen for this man. Beth said hello, gave him a hug and left them alone for a few minutes while she went to the bathroom.

'I missed you the moment you walked away. I thought that it would be lovely to do something nice for you while you are still in

Naples. You have been through a lot over the past couple of days,' Rick said, hoping that Jess wouldn't find him too keen or suffocating.

'Well, I am very happy to see you, especially now that there has been such drama. When Beth comes back we'll go and find a little bar and I'll tell you all about it. We really need a break from this place.' She kissed him tenderly.

Beth arrived back and the three of them took a walk down the road until they found a small tavern. They didn't want to be too far from the hospital in case they needed to get back to Amelia quickly.

They filled Rick in on everything that had happened to Amelia and how Paul had arrived unexpectedly and had spoken to the consultant in Italian, resulting in Sam's exposure.

'What's going to happen now?' Rick asked.

'I have no idea,' Jess answered. 'Amelia's blood pressure started to soar in the middle of the row and they sent us all out so she's obviously not out of the woods yet and can't afford this kind of stress. To be fair, though, Paul has had an awful shock and is entitled to be annoyed. It really is a total disaster. I knew she would probably be found out at some stage, but not so soon.'

'Did he know about the baby?' Rick asked again.

'Yes, I think he knows everything now, but, thankfully, he hasn't questioned us about it. We're in a very difficult situation because we don't know how much he knows and how much we should be saying. I feel very uncomfortable with the whole thing and a bit cross, to be honest,' Jess said, looking at Beth.

'Me too. I'm fed up, tired and frustrated but once Amelia is okay I don't really care whether she chooses Paul or Sam,' Beth said, meaning every word. 'At this stage, I don't think it is up to us to worry about making a mistake in what we say either.'

As if his ears were burning, Paul rang.

'Amelia has deteriorated again. Her kidneys are failing and they are putting her on dialysis. I really don't know how she became so ill from a pregnancy.' Paul sounded strange.

'Pre-eclampsia is a very serious condition and unfortunately she got it severely. She could have died, Paul,' Beth said.

'She is sleeping and I am going to stay with her. But I want to know about this guy – Sam –one way or another. I will find out the truth.' Paul couldn't stop himself from lashing out.

'Paul, I really think you need to calm down. You're not helping Amelia by going on about this. You need to focus your attention on helping her get well. Everything else can wait.' Jess spoke firmly. 'Do you want us to come back and sit with her?'

'No, it's fine. You have done so much already. Have some dinner or something and I will keep in touch. Thank you, Jess, and sorry for snapping at you.'

'That's okay, Paul. I know you're going through a difficult time. We'll see you later,' Jess responded.

***

'What are your plans? How long more are you staying?' Rick asked.

'We are booked on a flight leaving for Dublin at 11am tomorrow. At this stage, we have to go even though I feel bad leaving Amelia behind when she is still critical, but our families need us too,' Jess replied. 'We have a hotel booked that is very near the hospital, Sam has been staying there and he said it was fine. He went to Rome earlier to try and sort out the luggage that Amelia and he had left on the ship. I can't imagine that he will manage to bring it home but at least he can organise for it to be sent on.'

'Alright then, why don't we do something nice this evening? I think you both deserve a treat.' Rick felt happy.

He was glad he had made the journey to Naples; Jess was the best thing that had happened to him in a very long time. He went back to the hotel with the girls and waited in the bar while they got ready.

Jess sent Paul a text to check on Amelia.

How is Amelia?

No change, Jess, I will text you if I have any news.

We are going for some dinner now but I will have the phone with me and we can come back at any time if you need us. Jess xx

They felt much better now that they had showered, washed their hair and were freshly made-up. Rick knew they didn't want to be too far from the hospital and had found a lovely restaurant just ten minutes away. Jess and Beth settled down to order and started to relax knowing that there was nothing more they could for Amelia.

Sam rang Jess.

'Hi, how is Amelia?'

'Hi Sam. Her blood pressure has risen again so she is now on dialysis because there is something wrong with her kidneys but she is stable so don't worry. How are you getting on?'

'I have been over to the ship's office in Civitavecchia and arranged for the luggage to be sent home. Unfortunately there was too much for me to take by myself, what with all the glamorous outfits and handbags that were involved! They were very helpful and asked about Amelia on several occasions.'

'You're very good to do all that, Sam, you've saved us a lot of hassle, and we appreciate it. I know you are very worried about Amelia but we will keep you updated. I'll call you when I have any news.'

'I didn't get a chance to say goodbye to her before I left so can you tell her that I love her and I'll be in touch?' Sam asked, somewhat nervously.

'Yes, I will.'

Jess hung up. She told Beth what Sam had said.

'I am worried about him, Jess, we don't know him very well and he is totally in love with Amelia. I don't think he is going to give her up without a fight.' Beth was deeply concerned.

'I think Paul needs to be very careful in how he handles things while he is here because it could influence things with Amelia. She is very vulnerable and very pro-Sam at the moment so he could very easily lose her. I didn't like the way he spoke to us today and if that is the way he behaves at home, then he has had us all fooled,' Jess said, still cross at the way Paul had treated them earlier.

The waiter arrived with a delicious amuse-bouche of ravioli of black truffle with parmesan foam, putting an end to the conversation.

***

Paul had been sitting by Amelia's bedside for hours. He couldn't take his eyes off her or the monitors. What if she didn't recover? What would he do then? He suddenly realised that he needed to get some perspective on things; any row he was going to have with Amelia would have to wait until she was stronger.

'Paul?' Amelia had woken up.

Paul got up from his chair and went over to the bed.

'Yes, my darling, how do you feel?'

'I don't know. I feel weird and totally exhausted. I'm sorry Paul, I...'

'Sssh, love, we don't need to talk about it now. You need to get yourself better and we can talk then.'

Amelia closed her eyes. She pretended to go back to sleep but tormenting thoughts were tearing through her head and the monitor started beeping again, bringing the nurses running.

They gave her an injection to sedate her and then spoke to Paul, telling him that he should go home as Amelia would sleep now for the rest of the night.

Paul left the ICU wondering what he would do next. Should he call Jess and Beth? He hadn't been very nice to them earlier and maybe they wouldn't want to talk to him? He decided to call Beth as she had been a bit nicer to him than Jess.

***

Rick and the girls had just finished their main course when the phone rang.

'Hi Paul,' Beth said.

'Beth, hi, how are you getting on? I just wanted to fill you in on things. Amelia has been given an injection to sedate her. They said it will take her through the night so they have sent me home.' He paused, giving her a chance to reply.

'Oh, that's good. The sleep will do her good, I'm sure. Where are you? Do you want to join us?' Beth looked at Jess as she spoke, shrugging her shoulders and making a face.

'I'm still in the hospital and at a bit of a loose end. I'd love to join you. I also need to find somewhere to stay. Do you think there are any rooms in your hotel?'

'I'll give them a ring for you. In the meantime, why don't you take a taxi over here.'

Beth gave him the name of the restaurant and then called the hotel to book a room.

'You are always so kind, Beth, and you do the right thing. What are we going to do with him?' Jess asked her friend.

'Look, he's Amelia's husband and we've known him for years, let's wipe the slate clean and start again. If he gets difficult with us, we'll deal with it,' Beth answered.

***

Paul arrived and Jess introduced him to Rick. He sat down and the wine was poured.

'I've booked a room for you in our hotel for the next two nights and you can liaise with them directly after that. I know you have no idea how long you will need it,' Beth said softly.

'Thanks, Beth, I appreciate it. I want to thank both of you for everything you've done for Amelia; she is very lucky to have such wonderful friends. On a lighter note, did you enjoy yourselves on the cruise before all the drama happened?' Paul asked in a kind voice.

'Yes, we've had a fantastic trip. I met Rick at a wine tasting a few days after we arrived. He has a wine company that supplies the ship,' Jess said, smiling over at Rick.

'Are you a friend of this Sam fellow that was with Amelia when she was brought into the hospital?' Paul asked Rick.

'I met him on board. It's very sociable and you tend to meet a lot of people,' Rick replied warily.

Beth and Jess looked at each other worriedly, wondering where the conversation would go next.

'I think we should go back to the hotel. We have to be in the airport at 9am tomorrow morning.' Jess was trying to prevent Paul from fishing for more information; what happened on the cruise, stayed on the cruise.

***

Back at the hotel, Paul went to check in and Beth went to her room; she wanted to give Jess some time with Rick.

'I have booked a room here also as I needed somewhere to stay, darling. Will you have a drink with me in the bar before you go to bed?' Rick looked into her eyes with his irresistible charm.

'Just one and then I'm off.' Jess grinned as she gave him a quick kiss.

Paul looked over to the bar and saw them deep in conversation so he decided not to disturb them. He went straight up to bed knowing that whatever had happened on the ship was not going to be revealed tonight.

***

'What about us, Jess? Can I come and see you in Dublin before

I go to France next week? I don't think I can wait the two weeks until I get back,' Rick said.

'Yes, I would like that.'

'I have a very good feeling about the future,' he said joyfully.

He kissed her longingly and, after a couple of minutes, took her by the hand and led her upstairs. Jess had no hesitation in following. He opened the door and led her inside, both of them hungry with desire and pulling at each other's clothes frantically.

'You are taking over my every thought. All I want is you.' His tongue moved inside her mouth as he started to undress her.

She undid his belt and could feel him hard against her. They were standing naked, enveloped in each other's embrace. She moved backwards slowly, taking him with her until she reached the bed. She lay back as he found her and took her gently. They made love with an intensity that was different this time; they had found each other and they were not going to let go.

When Jess looked at her watch, it was half past midnight. She really needed to get to back to her own room. She felt bad leaving Beth on her own.

'Rick, I need to go back to my room. Beth and I have an early start and we have a lot to do before we leave,' she said as she lay, still naked, in his arms.

'Yes, darling, I understand. Will you come and say goodbye in the morning?'

'Yes, of course!'

She kissed him again, hardly able to believe how strongly she felt about him.

***

Back in the room, Beth was still awake and reading a book on her kindle.

'No prizes for guessing where you were!' she said as she winked at Jess. 'Goodnight, my dearest friend.'

DAY FOURTEEN

NAPLES: HEADING FOR HOME

BETH WOKE UP. SHE felt a sadness suddenly overwhelm her; part of her was dying to go home but the other part of her was afraid of facing up to her feelings about her marriage, and her mind still hadn't processed the kidnapping. She lay in bed, alone with her thoughts until Jess whispered in her ear that it was time to get up.

'Well, it's over now until next year. Let's hope we have a less dramatic trip on the next cruise,' Jess said to Beth, not daring to suggest that her dear friend might be put off ever going on one again.

'It's comforting to know we have it to look forward to, Jess. To be honest, I'm not sure how I feel about going home. I haven't spoken to Stephen more than once since we left, apart from the call to tell him that I was safe. I know that there is a lot of work to be done if I am to save my marriage.'

'Oh Beth, I'm sorry. I never realised you were so unhappy. What are you going to do?'

'We have a lot of talking to do and maybe we need some more counselling. The kidnapping put a lot of things into perspective and made me realise that I do love him and I want our marriage to work. I think we have lost our way, so maybe some good has come out of the trauma by helping me realise what is important. I know I will never love him the way I loved Sonny. When he broke my heart, it never really healed, but it's time to move on and learn to love again.'

The two friends hugged. Beth wiped the tears from her eyes and they got on with showering and getting ready to leave. Jess wanted to say goodbye to Rick but she didn't want to offend Beth by slipping away.

Don't come to my room, darling, it will be harder that way and anyway I have no intention of saying goodbye. I will see you in a few days in Dublin. xxxxx

Jess blushed as she felt a shiver of happiness rush through her body.

'Show me that phone!' Beth demanded. She looked at it and smiled; her adored friend had found love again.

***

When they went down to breakfast, Paul was already there.

'Good morning ladies, how did you sleep?' He seemed strangely cheerful.

'We slept fine, Paul. Did you get a chance to check with the hospital yet?' Beth asked.

'Yes, Amelia had a good night and her blood pressure has come down. The consultant wants to see me at 10.30am to discuss things. I'm hoping he will let me take her home soon. Are you two heading to the airport now?'

'Yes, we'll just have a quick coffee and then go. Can you keep us updated? Our flight leaves at 11am so we will have the phone on until then,' Jess said.

'That goes without saying,' Paul replied. He had calmed down a lot and was sorry that he had given the girls a hard time. 'By the way, I want to apologise for the way I spoke to you yesterday. It was completely out of order.'

'That's okay, Paul, we understand that you were upset. We'll go now and see you when you get home. Give our love to Amelia in case we can't get her on the phone.' Beth was being her usual forgiving self.

***

When Paul arrived at the hospital, Amelia was sitting up, waiting for him. She looked a lot better but was still very pale and unwell. He had decided that he would not talk about the guy from the ship until they got home because Amelia wasn't well enough even though it was driving him mad.

'Can you find out what's going on, Paul? I don't understand a word they're saying?' Amelia was unusually snappy but Paul let it go. He knew she was frustrated.

'I'm meeting the consultant shortly and I'll find out when we can go home, darling.'

The consultant arrived on time and spoke to Paul in Italian while Amelia looked on, fed up that she couldn't understand and that they were discussing her without her participation.

When he had gone, Paul looked pleased.

'He says that everything is going well and that you are going to be moved out of ICU today,' Paul explained; he was delighted as all he wanted to do was to go home.

Amelia had mixed emotions. Part of her wanted to stay in Naples and avoid facing her problems, but she knew she had to go home at some point, and she also missed the children.

Paul remembered that he had promised Beth and Jess that he would let them know the outcome of the meeting with the consultant so he rang them their phones were both switched off so he sent a text instead.

Amelia is out of ICU and will be allowed home in a few days. Have a safe journey. Thanks again for everything. I will keep in touch. Paul.

Amelia looked at him and tears ran down her face.

'I can't do this, Paul. I can't keep this from you any longer.'

He waited for her to continue.

'That guy they told you about from the ship, the one that brought me in.' She was stuttering.

'What about him?'

'I've been having an affair with him, Paul. He has a restaurant at home and I met him at a dinner for the Prema Foundation. I didn't plan for it to happen. I tried to stop it because I love you and I am happy with you, but I couldn't. He booked himself on the cruise without telling me; that's why he was with me when I came to the hospital.'

Paul looked at his wife; he was speechless and thought he was hearing things.

'Say something, Paul,' Amelia pleaded in desperation.

'I thought I knew you,' he said very calmly. 'You are the love of my life. I can't believe this is the Amelia that I married. What has happened to you?'

'I don't know. All I know is that I never meant to hurt you.'

'And do you love him?' Paul wasn't sure he wanted to know the answer.

Amelia hesitated; she didn't want to lie but she didn't want to hurt Paul any more than she had already. 'I don't know. I'm sorry; I know that's not what you want to hear.'

'Well, I'll make it simple, then. Who do you want to be with – him or me?'

Thoughts of Marla flashed into his head as he spoke; he knew he had no right to condemn Amelia when he was doing the same thing himself.

Amelia was silent.

'I take it from your silence that either you don't know or you want to be with him.'

'No, Paul, I don't know what I want, but I do know that I love you.'

'Can you give him up?'

'I don't know.' Amelia didn't know what else to say. 'Are you saying you could forgive me if I did?'

'I'm not saying that. I don't know the answer to that. I am very confused at the moment but I need to know where I stand. Then I can work out what I am going to do. I need to know how serious things are with this Sam guy and how realistic it is to think that you can give him up.' Paul was devastated as the reality of the situation began to sink in. 'Have you forgotten that we have three beautiful children to think about, Amelia?'

'No, of course not, but they are practically grown up now. This is about you and me and our future together. I am truly sorry.' Amelia didn't know what she was saying; the words just kept coming out of her mouth. 'Maybe we need to take a break to think about things.'

'You want a break so you can go off and practise living with your fancy man – is that it? I don't think so. If you want a chance to fix things with me, you need to say so now. I'm not going to hang around while you have a little trial run with your lover.' Paul had gone from being upset to being furious. 'Jesus, Amelia, have you no respect for me or for yourself?'

Amelia started to get very stressed.

'Paul, I don't know what to say to you. This is all my fault, I know.'

'I want my wife to get well and come home and for things to be the way they were, and I want that bastard out of our lives.' Paul's voice was getting louder and more aggressive.

'Paul, I need to come to terms with losing the baby. I had gotten used to the idea of being pregnant once I got over the shock, and it has been devastating to lose our little girl. I am not talking about living with him; I just need some time to myself and I am simply suggesting that one of us moves out for a few months to see if we miss each other and to find out if we have a future together.' Amelia was totally exhausted at this stage.

'That is ridiculous. I don't need a break. I have figured it out now. I told you what I want – I want you. Surely you should be happy that I am willing to stay with you after everything that you have done?'

Paul had become very sanctimonious all of a sudden; he totally ignored what had she said about the baby and all thoughts of Marla had gone completely.

Amelia looked at him. She knew he would never be able to forgive her and she didn't want a future like that for them, or for their children. She didn't like the way he was being so aggressive. She wasn't used to seeing him like that and she wasn't sure that he was the same man she had fallen in love with.

'We're going around in circles, Paul. I'm tired now and need to sleep. I think you should go back to the hotel. We can figure out the details later.'

***

Beth and Jess had no luggage to collect so they went straight through to the arrivals hall. As the doors opened, they saw Stephen, Bethany and Ed waiting for them.

'Welcome home, darling. We've missed you,' Stephen whispered in Beth's ear before she went over to hug her two children.

While she was in conversation with Bethany, Stephen took the opportunity to tell Jess about the surprise he had planned. He asked her if she would be free to come to the opening of the new art gallery at 4pm.

***

Paul had been back at the hotel since 12pm and he had done a lot of thinking. He'd thought about everything Amelia had said. He couldn't believe that his life had been turned upside down overnight. He needed to make some decisions. Amelia had decided she wanted a break so if he wanted to try and save their marriage, he would have to agree to it. The question was, did he want to save his marriage?

This was his opportunity to be with Marla if he wanted, with the added bonus that he wouldn't look like the bad boy. His head was tormented from it all; he had spent ages trying to figure out the logistics, such as who would tell the children and who would move out. Technically, it should be Amelia that should go but, given that her health was so bad, it seemed cruel and, besides, there was a flat above the restaurant and he would have more privacy there.

What was he going to do about Marla? Did they have a future?

***

He went back into the hospital and sat down beside Amelia.

'I've been thinking about things and I think that it would be best if I moved out. I will wait until you are well and take you home and then we can organise things. I also thought that we should tell the kids together. I don't think there is any need to tell them about your lover unless you want to.'

'You are being very reasonable, Paul, thank you.'

Paul departed, leaving Amelia in a very emotional state. She lay back on her pillow and cried until she had no more tears left.

***

Sometime later the phone rang. It was Sam.

'Hi darling. Am I disturbing you? I hope I didn't wake you.'

'No, Sam, I was just going to call you. I have a bit of news.'

'What? Are you okay?" Sam said, worriedly.

'Yes, it's a long story but, in a nutshell, Paul found out that you had brought me in here and was asking me who you were, so, in the end, I confessed everything.' Amelia didn't have the energy to go into details.

'And how did he react?' Sam was excited, but he didn't know what to say.

'He was gutted. It has been agony telling my husband that I have been having an affair and that I want a break from our marriage.' Amelia was getting irritable now; it had been a long day.

'A break?'

'Yes, one of us is going to move out for a while.'

'Are you going to move in with me?'

'No, not for the moment, darling. I need some time to get over the baby and think about things. Paul is going to stay and bring me home. Then he is going to move out of the house and into the apartment above the restaurant. I'm exhausted now, so do you mind if I call you back later?'

She didn't wait for Sam's response; she just hung up and went straight to sleep.

***

Sam was over the moon with happiness, he couldn't believe that Amelia and Paul were splitting up and that she would finally be his. What a good decision it had been to book the cruise, he thought.

VENICE

SIX MONTHS LATER

JESS AND RICK HAD been hardly apart since the cruise. They were on a short break in Venice when Rick had suggested an early morning ride on a gondola. In true Rick style, he had arranged a very ornate private gondola and it was a beautiful sunny day as they weaved their way through the narrow canals and under the bridges, cuddling as they enjoyed the views.

As they were passing under Rialto Bridge, another gondola went by and, as it did, the gondolier passed them a beautifully wrapped box with Jess's name on it. She unwrapped the box to revel a beautiful emerald ring inside. Rick looked at her, took her hand and proposed. Jess was so shocked she nearly fell into the canal. Then the gondolier opened the champagne and toasted their future together.

They decided to extend their stay for a few days to celebrate privately together before telling their friends the news. Over breakfast, they spotted an article in the newspaper accompanied by a picture of Jean Claude and Meredith. It was in Italian so Rick used his phone to translate it.

Police in Rome have uncovered a major drug operation on the Santana cruise ship. Drugs worth $2 million were seized this morning at

Port of Civitavecchia and the ship's captain, Jean Claude Vakas, and an American woman, Meredith Taylor, were arrested at the scene. It is believed that it was a sophisticated operation that had been going on for some time and there were a number of people involved.

Police have spent months keeping the ship under surveillance but it has been a particularly difficult case and they believe that some passengers that travelled on cruises with the ship over the past eight months may be able to help them with their investigation.

Police would like to hear from anyone who has any information. Please contact them confidentially on 0800-58787.

'I don't believe it, Rick, they have finally caught up with them! I need to ring the girls!' Jess smiled at Rick, delighted with what he had read to her.

***

Beth was in the gallery with Stephen when Jess rang. She had been overwhelmed by what Stephen had done for her. The opening had been amazing and not only were they already making a profit, they were gaining an international reputation. Things had really improved between Stephen and herself; they were making an effort to spend time together and go on date nights and she felt happier with him than she had been in a very long time.

'Beth, Rick and I are in Venice and there is an article in the newspaper about the *Santana*. You are not going to believe it, but they have caught Meredith and Jean Claude!' Jess said excitedly.

Beth was quiet as she read out Rick's translation.

'Say something, Beth,' Jess said.

'I'm just a bit shocked and overwhelmed, Jess, and don't know how I feel. I suppose I need a bit of time to let it all sink in. I've been trying to forget about it and move on. I've been seeing a counsellor and now I am going to have to talk to the police and face it all again.'

'I'll be home in a few days and we can talk about it. I have a feeling it might be the closure that you need. If you think about it, you never really did get to see them punished for what they did to you,' Jess said gently.

'Maybe you're right, Jess. I'll wait to talk to you before I contact the police. The Embassy will probably be in touch with them too. By the way, how is Venice?'

'Well, I thought I was on a short break but Rick has just proposed so we are staying for a few more days. We haven't told anyone our news yet,' Jess said excitedly.

'That's fantastic. I am so happy for you both. It was certainly a very memorable cruise!' Beth replied.

***

When she had finished talking to Beth, Jess rang Amelia and told her about the article.

'Well, thank goodness they've been finally caught,' Amelia said. 'I always felt Beth should have said something when she got home, but I know she just wanted to try and forget about it.'

'Yes, I agree. Hopefully now this will help her to move on because she had a terrifying experience. How are things between yourself and the kids, Amelia? Are they okay with Sam yet?' Jess asked kindly.

'They're coming around slowly. They can see that he loves me and that there is no way back for myself and their dad. I have so much to tell you, Jess – you won't believe what Paul was up to while I was away,' Amelia said as she thought about much her life had changed since she'd gone on the cruise.

THE END

About the author

RÓISÍN CURRAN IS A Travel Counsellor and lives in Dun Laoghaire, Co. Dublin with her partner Ciaran and her son Nick, *Mediterranean Menopause* is her first novel.

If you fancy taking a cruise like Amelia, Jess and Beth why not contact roisin.curran@travelcounsellors.com

www.travelcounsellors.ie/roisin.curran

36055482R00176

Printed in Poland
by Amazon Fulfillment
Poland Sp. z o.o., Wrocław